KITE

KITE
A Novel

Ed Minus

VIKING

VIKING
Viking Penguin Inc., 40 West 23rd Street,
New York, New York 10010, U.S.A.
Penguin Books Ltd, Harmondsworth,
Middlesex, England
Penguin Books Australia Ltd, Ringwood,
Victoria, Australia
Penguin Books Canada Limited, 2801 John Street,
Markham, Ontario, Canada L3R 1B4
Penguin Books (N.Z.) Ltd, 182–190 Wairau Road,
Auckland 10, New Zealand

First published in 1985 by Viking Penguin Inc.
Published simultaneously in Canada

LIBRARY OF CONGRESS CATALOGING IN PUBLICATION DATA
Minus, Ed.
  Kite.
  I. Title.
PS3563.I56K5 1985   813'.54   84-20910
ISBN 0-670-80427-4

The opening chapter of this novel appeared originally, in different form, in
Red Clay Reader 6, under the title "The Greyhound Minstrel."

Grateful acknowledgment is made to Acuff-Rose Publications, Inc., and
House of Bryant Publications for permission to reprint portions of lyrics
from "Wake Up, Little Susie," written by Boudleaux Bryant and Felice
Bryant. Copyright © 1957 by House of Bryant Publications, Gatlinburg,
Tennessee 37738. All rights outside the U.S.A. controlled by Acuff-Rose
Publications, Inc., and by House of Bryant Publications for the U.S.A. All
rights reserved.

The author gratefully acknowledges a grant from the South Carolina Arts
Commission.

Printed in the United States of America
by The Book Press, Brattleboro, Vermont
Set in Janson

For John Stevenson
   John Lane
   and
   Dan Columbo

KITE

All our righteousnesses are as filthy rags;
and we all do fade as a leaf.

Isaiah 64:6

Part One

He brought me up also out of an horrible pit,
out of the miry clay.

Psalms 40:2

His host was Wm. Tiny. There was a restroom in the rear for his convenience. He could have smoked a cigarette if he had had one, and if he smoked; but pipes and cigars were not allowed. Something else that was not allowed was talking to the driver while the coach was in motion. Coach, he supposed, was just a fancy word for bus. The coach was in motion.

It was after nine o'clock on a night in late May, and the bus was traveling through a desolate and tranquil countryside. A high full moon made it possible for Kite to distinguish fields of corn from fields of grain, and fields of grain from fallow fields of broomstraw and milkweed. There were very few houses in sight and most of them were dark. On the horizon, massive light-colored clouds were waiting.

Two rows in front of him and across the aisle sat a boy about nine or ten with a face like a hamster's. Kite had noticed him, and the colored man beside him, when he first got on. Kite had never ridden on a bus by himself before, and he was comforted when he saw that there was someone on board who was younger and probably no more experienced than he was. The boy wore a blue uniform with an emblem on one sleeve and with yellow cord trim around the collar and at the pockets and on the cap, which he was now wearing on his knee. That knee and one elbow were all Kite could see of him now, but he could hear every word he said, and so could everybody else in the front half of the bus.

"Let me see now. Okay. I got another one. What's orange and goes click-click?"

On the boy's right, next to the window, slouched a young black-skinned man with sunken cheeks and temples. He had on a snug black sport coat, a pink shirt, and a narrow black tie with a white stripe down the middle of it.

"I don't believe I know," the man said very softly.

"A ballpoint carrot." The boy paused for a response that didn't come. "Okay. I got another one for you. What's yellow and weighs a thousand pounds and sings and has four legs?"

Out of respect for the difficulty of this one, or perhaps just marking time, the young man waited a moment before he said again, in the same tone, "I don't believe I know."

"Are you sure?" the boy said. "Make a guess."

"I can't guess it," the colored man told him very quietly.

"Do you give up?"

The man didn't answer.

"I said, 'Do you give up?'"

"All right," the man said.

"Two five-hundred-pound canaries."

The man said nothing. Instead, he turned his whole body toward the window, resting the side of his face against the seat.

"What's the difference between the North Pole and the South Pole?"

Kite turned toward the window on his side of the bus; toward the dark. The moonlight on a freshly plowed field made it look like a lake. He glanced toward the glowing green hands and numbers on the small clock above the windshield. He had been on the bus for less than two hours, but already the Baptist Home seemed a thousand miles away. This time two nights ago he was sitting in the stifling parlor suffering through study hours. He had felt a tap on his shoulder, but when he turned nobody was there. Then a hand pressed down hard on each shoulder and Greg Bridwell whispered in his ear. "Mizriz Massingale wants to see you. Upstairs in her office."

Kite knew at once that they had found out about him and Jarlene. Somebody must have seen them. Or Jarlene—she was so proud of herself—had told one of her loudmouth girl-friends.

"Right now?" he said.

"Right now."

He stood up. What would they do to him? Nobody else had ever been caught at anything as bad as this. Not in the five years he had been there.

Eleven desks and study tables lined the four walls of the parlor, all of them facing the walls and at each one a boy who was taking special classes in a course he was failing. Kite could feel all of them watching him as he sauntered across the room. As far as he knew, no one had ever been kicked out of Baptist—but he might be the first. Miss Terrell and the others rolled out the word "reformatory" now and then, but he knew those were only threats.

He started up the stairs but stopped on the second step. Maybe he should leave right now . . . make a run for it. Brid-well, who had come up behind him as quietly as before, goosed him sharply in the ass.

"You gonna get it this time, little stud."

Ordinarily, he would have chased Bridwell down and sat on his face until he cried or begged. This time, leaning across the banister, he swung at him only once, and wildly. Brid-well's cowardice and cruelty, his eagerness to kick anybody who was down, seemed insignificant compared to what was in store upstairs. Even if they let him stay, they would make it hard on him for a long time to come.

"What's wrong, Kite?"

Mrs. Massingale had appeared at the top of the stairs and

was gazing down at him. As he climbed slowly toward her he felt tiny spiders crawling all over his balls. . . .

The man in the seat beside him, whose upper arm pressed against his and whose hip was hard against *his* hip, suddenly whimpered in his sleep. He shifted his body toward the window for an instant and then leaned back against Kite again, more heavily than before. He had been asleep ever since Kite got on the bus. His breathing was harsh and uneven, he made constant small sucking noises in his mouth, and sometimes he moaned as if he was hurting.

Kite turned toward the couple across the aisle from him, but they didn't seem to have heard the man's whimpering. They were reading a comic book to each other. Kite felt sure that they were husband and wife; but both were very young, not yet twenty. The young man sat with his back to the window, his feet (in white socks) on the seat, his legs drawn up against his body so that his knees were just under his chin. The girl was curled up facing him, halfway sitting on her legs. Kite's view was of her back, her calves and ankles, and the soles of her feet. She was also wearing white socks; her shoes were on the floor beside her husband's. Where her heel was, where the ball of her foot came, and under the toes the socks were grimy, almost black; but the fine high arch of her foot was still clean and white. Her legs were brown, the calves full and hard. She had on a thin white blouse that buttoned down the back, and when she moved a certain way the cloth gaped open between the buttons all the way down, showing a chainlike pattern of smooth brown skin.

The young man held the comic book between them; he read a page and then she read a page. They had turned on both little spotlights, and he had to tilt the book back and forth so that each in turn could see. The husband's voice was nasal and he read haltingly; sometimes he spelled a word and the girl pronounced it for him. She had a beautiful voice, clear and tender. They were reading a story about a savage African tribe and a priceless ruby. Kite heard phrases like "the goddess of Bethlana," "the Blood Ruby," and "mystic spell." The girl's light brown hair was pinned up in back, exposing the

nape of her neck; and as she read, her husband laid his arm
across her shoulder and with the tips of his fingers gently
stroked the slight furrow at the base of her skull, where her
hair was especially soft and shiny.

Kite turned toward the window again. He remembered the
lines and the creases on the back of Mrs. Massingale's neck—
like a hairnet. And he remembered Mrs. Massingale's smile, a
smile that was pleasant but never a fraction or a wrinkle more
than pleasant. He had learned long ago that it meant nothing.
Almost anything. That night, two nights ago, she had closed
the door behind him and told him to sit down. She took a
stance behind her desk, and when she didn't sit down he
looked up at her and saw that she was smiling pleasantly.
Then she stopped. And sat down.

"You remember your aunt and uncle, don't you, Kite? Mr.
and Mrs. Lacey? Who send us that nice box of clothes every
Christmas? They stopped by to see you a yea. or so ago?"

"Yes, ma'am."

"Well, they have had a terrible thing to happen. Your little
four-year-old cousin Hampton was playing at a friend's
house, and somehow—I don't believe they know yet just how
it happened—but somehow he got locked up in the corncrib.
And it caught afire somehow."

Mrs. Massingale pressed the tips of her bony fingers hard
against her mouth and frowned at him, and he frowned back.

"Well, your Aunt Ruth and Uncle Hampton have decided
that they want to have you come live with them now. They
wrote us a letter to that effect several weeks ago. We chatted
with them on the telephone a number of times. And last week
Reverend Sills and Mr. James and Miss Terrell drove all the
way up to Lenfield for a visit. And so, to make a long story
short, we have given our approval."

She paused expectantly, but Kite said nothing. He could
not get it out of his head that this was some kind of punishment; that he was being sent up to Lenfield to be burned alive
in a corncrib because he and Jarlene had been fucking.

"I hope you realize," Mrs. Massingale went on, "what an
extremely fortunate boy you are. A boy your age. The chance

to live in a good Christian home with people who can care for you and do for you just like your own mother and father."

He could not remember his own mother and father, and his memory of the Laceys was uncertain and shadowy. What he did remember, what was not uncertain, was that almost every day for the past five years he had been told that Baptist was a good Christian home.

"Yes, ma'am," he said.

Something else he remembered was the shellacked peach stone he had found in the pocket of a seersucker coat that the Laceys had sent him one Christmas. Like most of what they sent, the coat had been much too large for him, and Cromer Hughes had gotten it.

The next thing that came into his mind was that when Jarlene heard he was leaving she would want to do it again, one last time. But, as it turned out, he had been wrong about that. And if he had thought about it for a minute, if he had remembered how she took on when Loper got run over, he would have known better. After all, it had occurred to him more than once that the motherly way she treated him sometimes was not all that different from the way she treated the animals. He had felt all along that if the dogs or the cats or the chickens or the cows had wanted to fuck her and had been able to, she would have let them. That was part of what had gotten him excited right from the start, part of what had kept him excited for such a long time (at least it seemed a long time now) before they had ever done anything at all. Seeing the way she stroked and cuddled and cooed over one or another of the animals all the time, he couldn't keep from thinking that if he were Brownie or Loper, *he* would be able to get away with nuzzling her neck and boobs, licking her knees and ankles. After she talked about what sad and souful eyes Brownie had, he practiced in the mirror to make his own eyes as appealing as the dog's. But when he tried it out, all she did was give him a funny look and ask him if he felt all right.

Then he got lucky. He and Jimmy were skateboarding in the culvert behind the school when a wheel jammed just as he got to the top of the curve. He tried to break his fall with his hands and scraped most of the flesh off both of them. For a

couple of weeks his hands were so bandaged up he looked like
he had on white boxing gloves. And it was Jarlene who in-
sisted on feeding him at every meal. Most of his friends had
ragged him about that, but he had loved it.

One evening at supper, in between spoonfuls of Brunswick
stew, Jarlene said, "How are your hands feeling now? Do
they still hurt?"

"Not so much anymore. Most of the time they just itch.
Not as bad as my head does, though. Trouble is, when I get in
the shower all I can do is get wet, I can't really scrub down."

"I'll wash your hair for you," she said. "I wash Nessa's and
Peggy's. We could go down to the river."

There were still a couple of hours of daylight left, and bed
check was not until nine thirty. They had sauntered off in different directions and met half an hour later at a spot where
the pasture sloped off into the water, behind a stand of willows. She helped him take his shirt off, and he lay down on
his back across a big smooth rock and let his head dip back in
the water. His neck stretched until his Adam's apple stood
out like an egg, and he felt her cup her hand over it for a second. Then he sat up again and turned around, looking out
across the river at the worn-out pasture on the other side. Jarlene stood behind him and poured some bright green sham-
poo into the palm of her hand, then rubbed her palms
together, and then put her hands in his dark hair. Her fingertips and fingernails felt wonderful against his scalp, and soon
the white lather was dripping down on his shoulders.
"Harder," he kept saying. "Harder, harder."   And then he
suddenly realized he might as well have been talking to his
cock. Jarlene had on shorts, and he could feel her cool knees
against his back.

When it was time to rinse his hair, when Jarlene's fingers
got tired, he lay down on his stomach, but that didn't work. It
hurt his cock and he couldn't get his head all the way under
the water.

"Turn over," Jarlene said. She was kneeling beside him.

He turned onto his back again, scraping his shoulders on
the rock, and lowered his head into the water. He closed his
eyes and felt Jarlene's fingers moving through his hair as

gently as the river. He thought that he was floating downstream. Floating and floating. Then Jarlene put her hand between his shoulder blades. He raised his head and slid forward a little. Jarlene used both her hands to smooth some of the water out of his hair. Then she got to her feet and looked down at him, glancing back and forth from his face to the ridge of his cock straining against the faded blue of his cut-offs. Kite propped himself up on his elbows and raised his hips a little.

"That's something else I haven't been able to do too good lately."

He thought she looked down at his hard-on the same way she might have looked at a small animal caught in a trap. Then she knelt down again, unfastened the button at the top of his jeans, and eased the zipper down. When she lifted the elastic band of his underpants away from his stomach, he lifted his ass again and she pulled both pairs of pants halfway down to his knees. In contrast to his cock, his spine and shoulders and neck felt like they were melting. He was lying flat again, his head turned to one side. He thought he had closed his eyes for no more than a second, but when he opened them Jarlene had taken all her clothes off and was spreading them out on the rock beside him. Kite had always thought that Jarlene's face was not so much pretty as kind. Hopeful. And now it seemed to him that her body looked kind too, in just the same way, and he didn't even think about whether it was pretty or not. When she lay down next to him, on her side, he saw that her breasts were almost exactly the same size and whiteness as his bandaged hands.

"Oh, Jesus," he said. "Oh, Jesus."

"What's wrong?"

"I just wish I could touch you. I feel like my hands are gonna go crazy."

"You can touch me," she said. "With your mouth. With your face."

That was when he felt that he really had turned into one of her pets. That he didn't have hands, but paws. That he couldn't speak but could only whimper and lick and suck and nuzzle. And the way she helped him and fondled him and crooned over him made him feel not only like an animal but like a baby. And yet, at the same time, he felt like a grown man. He felt famous.

With what seemed a terrible effort, the man next to him leaned his body away from Kite's; he straightened his back and pressed his shoulders and the back of his head against the seat. Kite glanced toward him and saw that he was awake. He was rubbing his hand over his jaw and across his mouth. His breathing was heavy, and he seemed almost to be moaning under his breath. A moment later he bent forward until his head nearly touched the seat in front of him. He dangled one arm between his legs, located a small paper cup on the floor at his feet, and leaned back again. He put the cup to his mouth.

"Now listen," the hamster-faced boy was saying. "This is a funny one. Now listen. What's the difference between an elephant and a grape?"

The colored man looked out the window; the boy leaned forward.

"What's the difference between an elephant and a grape?" he said again.

The young man shook his head.

"You don't know *any* difference between an *el*ephant and a *grape?*"

"They's lots of differences," the man said.

"A grape's purple," the boy told him bluntly. "Now: You know what Tarzan said when he saw the elephants coming?"

The young man shook his head.

"You know who Tarzan is?"

"Sure. Yeah."

"You know what he said when he saw the elephants coming?"

"I said no."

"He said, 'Here come the grapes.' He was color-blind." For the first time the boy laughed out loud. Two middle-aged women who were sitting across from him began to laugh too. The colored man gave the boy a quick angry look. Kite wished the man would tell the boy to shut up.

Nearer the front of the bus a baby started crying. A few minutes later a soldier stood up and headed down the aisle, holding on to the seats with both hands to keep his balance. There was something bearlike about the set of his shoulders and the sleepy way he moved, but his sunburned face looked kind and intelligent. Kite heard the restroom door open and then close. When Kite boarded the bus, this soldier and another one were sleeping soundly in the seats just behind the driver. One slept with his cheek pressed against the window, and the other one slept with his head on his companion's shoulder. Their mouths were slightly open and their knees spread apart; their large hands lay limp against their thighs.

The man next to Kite was speaking to him, but Kite could not understand what he was saying. He leaned toward him and the man repeated his question, but the words were blurred and garbled. At first Kite thought that he was speaking a foreign language, then that maybe he was drunk. "I'm sorry," Kite said, leaning still closer. When he repeated the question a third time, Kite understood. "Lenfield," he told him. "I'm on my way to Lenfield." He wanted to keep talking in order to put off more questions, but he could not think what to say; the reason he was going to Lenfield seemed too complicated to try to explain.

The man put the small cup to his mouth. At first Kite had thought that he was drinking from it, but he was spitting into it. He continued to make small sucking noises in his mouth. Now he was speaking again, but Kite could not understand him. He turned so that he could watch the man's lips. The words came again, but despite the effort they cost him they were not words—only noises, ugly and senseless. He made them again, and again, while Kite nodded at him stupidly. But at last, miraculously, the sounds became more than a hopeless babbling. "I been on this dog all day long," he was saying. "I been on this dog all day long."

"I just got on in Thornton," Kite told him.

The man's breath was sour. His face looked bloated, the sallow, unshaven flesh like a thick rubber mask, behind which his eyes were dry and vacant. The backs of his hands were dotted with chocolate-colored spots. He was wearing a stiff black suit and a white shirt that was badly wrinkled. Now that he had finally gotten through to Kite, he leaned back with a sigh that was almost a whimper and closed his eyes.

Across the aisle the husband was reading. He had moved his hand from the girl's neck to her thigh. Kite wanted very badly to reach out and touch that shallow spot at her hairline where the husband's blunt fingers had been stroking. He felt an aching desire to grasp her foot and hold it tight, digging his thumb into the high firm arch. If only her husband would go to sleep. But he turned the page and the girl began to read.

Kite looked out the window again and saw a large open field bordered by black woods. He leaned back and closed his eyes and wondered if Uncle Hampton would be like the man beside him who couldn't talk, and if Aunt Ruth would be like the girl across the aisle. She would probably be more like Mrs. Massingale or Miss Terrell. But she couldn't be *that* old if Little Hampton was only four. On the other hand, she could not be as young as the girl with the comic book either. She might still be young though. Young enough to wear tight shorts and go barefooted. Young enough to still have full high pointy boobs. Young enough . . .

He felt himself getting hard. Don't get your hopes up, he told himself.

He wondered if Uncle Hampton would take him hunting. He had never been hunting. He had never even owned a real gun. He saw himself and the sunburned soldier heading out across a field of broomstraw on a rose-colored autumn afternoon, their shotguns balanced easily on their shoulders. He saw them huddled in the icy early-morning darkness, deep in the thickets beside a lake, waiting for the ducks to come in. He saw them in a boat on a river. He saw. . . .

Don't get your hopes up, he told himself. He opened his eyes and stared at the taillights of a car several hundred feet in front of the bus. The priceless blood rubies of Bethlana.

A tantalizing scrap of a popular song snagged in his mind. At the last stop two old women in flowered dresses had gotten on the bus. One of them was blind and carried a shopping bag in one hand and in the other a transistor radio made to look like a book. The woman who was not blind led her friend slowly down the aisle and seated her two rows behind Kite. She told her good-by and said she would pray for her. Then she moved back up the aisle and off the bus. Even before the good-bys were over the blind woman had turned on the radio, and she had had it on ever since. She did not like news programs, weather reports, talk shows, or commercials—only music; and she seemed to be searching, sometimes almost frantically, for one particular station, maybe one particular song. She stayed at one spot on the dial no more than five or ten minutes at a time; and in the process of changing from one station to another she went up and down the dial from end to end. About half an hour earlier she had happened on a station that promised uninterrupted music, but halfway through a song called "Rain of Love" the needle stuck at the word "turning," which was then repeated over and over: *turning, turning, turning.* . . . Now, each time she scanned the dial, she stopped at that spot, sometimes for half a minute or more: *turning, turning, turning, turning.* . . . "Call the station," she kept saying. "Somebody call the station."

"In a rabbit gum, I reckon," the colored man said.

"There's an even better way," the boy told him.

The man said nothing.

"Do you know what it is?"

"Ahn-uh."

"You're supposed to say, 'I give up.' "

"All right," the man said.

"Do you give up?"

"All right."

"Hide behind a tree and make a noise like a carrot." The boy started laughing again but stopped abruptly. "Okay. I'll give you a real easy one this time. . . ."

The man on Kite's left put the small white cup to his mouth again, and Kite, almost involuntarily, turned toward him. There was something stupid-looking about the slackness of the lower part of his face. His lips and his chin were trembling and his mouth stayed open as if his tongue was badly swollen. He lowered the cup and began to talk again. The tone and the cadence of his voice, and the dark lines that crossed his forehead, conveyed a troubled urgency. But the sounds that came out of his mouth conveyed nothing. Like his face, they were slack and stupid, as empty of meaning as his eyes and so distorted they sounded less than human. And yet, the more he talked the less difficult it became for Kite to guess at what he was saying. More often, and more readily, the ugly noises resembled words and the words fitted together. He watched Kite closely, and when Kite frowned he repeated what he had said.

Kite understood that his home was in Taylors, a small town some fifty miles north of Lenfield. He had caught a bus there that morning at four thirty and had arrived in Atlanta around ten. He said there was a dental clinic there where teeth were extracted at the rate of a dollar a tooth and where false teeth could be purchased for not much more than that. Between eleven and four Mr. Harnes (Harves? Hartz?) had had all his teeth pulled and impressions made for upper and lower plates, which would be mailed to him next week. The important thing was—Mr. Harnes seemed especially proud of the fact and kept coming back to it—he had had to miss only one day of work.

His gums were still bleeding, of course—he apologized for

the spitting—and he said that he still felt "doped up." Except
for a bowl of soup, he had not had anything to eat since early
morning. He tried to tell Kite something about his wife: she,
too, it seemed, was planning to undergo this ordeal as soon as
they could afford it. There was something else, about a telephone call, but Kite could not grasp what that was all about
or why Mr. Harnes was so troubled about it. At last, the effort of talking tired him into silence again. Even as he talked
he had continued to spit into the cup after every sentence or
so. Kite had begun to wonder how much blood he must have
swallowed while he was asleep, and how much more the cup
would hold, how often he had to empty it.

The soldier, Kite suddenly realized, had not yet come out
of the restroom. He leaned into the aisle and looked up front
to make sure he had not gone by while he had his eyes closed.
His seat was empty. It seemed a long time since he had gone
back, and it occurred to Kite that he might be sick and that
perhaps somebody should see about him. But then again,
maybe he had just fallen asleep in there. Or maybe he was in
there jacking off. Or drawing dirty pictures on the walls.

Kite thought of Jimmy Skelton, his best friend at Baptist.
He remembered what Jimmy liked to write on the walls—and
on the desks, and in the library books, and on the blackboards.
Always the same thing: "I love pussy." Only Jimmy always
put a lot of o's in "love": "I loooooove pussy." Wherever you
saw that, you knew Jimmy had been there. Kite realized
again, and even more acutely than before, how much he was
going to miss Jimmy. They were the only two who were not
afraid of the teachers or of Mr. James. They could always
count on each other to sneak off with—to the movies or
King's poolroom or down to the river. Once they had even
sneaked off and hitchhiked to the fair in Cannonsburg. And
without getting caught. Kite wondered who Jimmy would
find for a best friend now that he was gone. And he wondered
who *he* would find for a best friend in Lenfield. When they
had moved him from Brightwood to Baptist—he was going
on ten—he had missed Brightwood for a long time. It was the
only home he could remember, it was where he had grown
up, and he had cried every night for a week without ever

really knowing exactly what it was he missed. He did not think there was much chance he would miss Baptist that way. But he *would* miss Jimmy. And Jarlene. And he would miss the feeling of being one of the older boys and of knowing his way around, knowing how much he could get away with. He would miss the feeling of knowing that most of the others there liked him—even, in a way, most of the teachers. He wondered if the Laceys would like him. He felt pretty sure he could make them like him if he tried hard enough, and if it seemed worthwhile to try that hard. There was, of course, no way of knowing what his life would be like from now on, and it seemed a waste of time to guess. He knew that the Laceys were not poor—if they were, they would not have sent those clothes every year. But he hoped that they were not very rich either. He hoped that their house would not be too fancy and that he wouldn't have to be careful all the time about doing and saying exactly what was proper. If the Laceys were rich, they would probably think they had done him a tremendous favor and would expect him to kiss ass all day long. If that's what they expected, they were in for a disappointment. On the other hand, if they really were rich, maybe he could talk them into taking Jimmy too.

He looked at the clock. The bus was due to get to Lenfield in less than half an hour. His stomach felt uneasy. The baby started crying again, but this time the mother quieted it very quickly.

"You still can't think of any?"

"I don't believe so," the colored man said. He was gazing out the window again. He had turned his whole body, so that only his right arm and shoulder were against the back of the seat.

"It's not as much fun when I have to do all the asking," the boy complained. "Do you know any jokes?"

The man shook his head.

"Not any you can tell me, huh?"

"Tha's right."

The boy said, "You wanta hear the dirtiest joke I know?"

The young man said nothing.

"Okay. There was this beautiful snow-white horse galloping down the road, and it slipped and fell in a mudhole. That's the dirtiest joke I know."

This time the two women laughed, but the boy did not. Why didn't the colored man just move? Kite wondered. He had decided long ago that if the boy ever left *his* seat he would take it.

"What has wheels and cuts grass and lives in a tree?"

The young man said nothing.

"Do you give up?"

He nodded.

"You have to guess," the boy said. "I'm not gonna tell you till you guess."

The couple on Kite's right had finished one comic book and were about to start another. They had half a dozen or more tucked into the pockets of the seats in front of them. On the cover of one of the books was a picture of a doctor and a nurse embracing passionately. The girl chose one called "Monsters of Tomorrow." She had not yet opened it; she was reading every word on the cover, front and back; the back was an ad for greeting cards. Out of the corner of his eye Kite watched the husband's hand move from the girl's calf to her thigh and then disappear. Kite's own hands were tingling, throbbing. He imagined undoing the buttons of her blouse and slowly folding back the pieces of cloth and then unfastening the brassiere. He pressed the palms of his hands against her shoulder blades and then smoothed his hands down to the small of her back. His fingertips snagged the top of her underpants and slowly peeled them down the swell of her buttocks. . . .

He turned away, toward the window. An island of light slid past. Then another.

turning, turning, turning, turning. . . .

Mr. Harnes whimpered in his sleep.

Kite decided to go see if the soldier was all right. He got up carefully and headed down the aisle toward the restroom— just as the soldier came out. When they squeezed past each other, Kite could smell whiskey very strong. He went on toward the back of the bus and into the restroom. It was even smaller than he had imagined, about the size of a telephone booth. He closed the door and turned the lock. There was a small metal toilet with a black seat, a small metal lavatory, and a mirror. He had to straddle the john and brace one hand against the wall to keep his balance. And to keep from pissing on the floor. It would have been pretty hard to jack off in there. He wished he had a pen, so that he could write Jimmy's motto on the wall. He turned to the lavatory, where a sign said, "This water is not for drinking." On the opposite wall was a small red button below a sign that said, "In case of emergency." Kite looked at himself in the mirror. Unlike most of the boys in his class at Baptist, his skin was smooth and clear; but in this bluish light his face seemed pale and his eyes and hair looked very dark. His hair was thick and curly. Mrs. Massingale had tried to make him get it cut before he left, but he had talked her out of that. He remembered how Jarlene had held onto his hair with both hands last night. And afterward, how she kissed his face and stroked it with her face. The only trouble was that she was crying all the time. He should have waited until this morning to tell her. He had not realized she would act that way. He continued to gaze at himself in the mirror. He was almost certain that Aunt Ruth would like him, but he was not so sure about Uncle Hampton. He watched himself whistle the first part of a song that he liked; when he got to the last part he sang it:

> Well, what're we gonna tell your MA-MA?
> What're we gonna tell your PA?
> What're we gonna tell our friends
> When they say—OO-la-la?

> Wake up, little SU-zy!
> Wake up, little SU-zy!
> We gotta go home
> We gotta go home.

Kite recognized the Laceys as soon as he saw them. The bus stop in Lenfield was a Gulf gas station, and his aunt and uncle were standing in front of a little tin manger that housed a family of vending machines. Both of the Laceys were short and plump—but hard plump. Kite could tell right off that they were not rich. For one thing, his uncle had on overalls and heavy mud-crusted work shoes. As the bus came to a stop, the Laceys moved toward it, and Kite, seeing them out of the high windows—he was standing now—thought they looked almost like midgets. Once on the ground, though, he saw that all three of them were very nearly the same height.

His Aunt Ruth hugged him and kissed him on the cheek. She was much younger than Mrs. Massingale, but she was wearing the same kind of old-fashioned dress Mrs. Massingale always wore: dark blue with tiny white and yellow flowers on it.

"We're so glad to *see* you, Kite. And this is Uncle Hampton."

As they shook hands, Uncle Hampton, with his left hand, clutched the biceps of Kite's right arm and sort of gouged his fingers into the muscle, as if searching, it seemed to Kite, for a button or a catch that would release the arm at the shoulder socket and allow him to lift it off.

"You've growed some since the last time we saw you."

"Yessir."

They waited for the driver to open up the underside of the bus and drag out Kite's suitcase and the two cardboard boxes that his winter clothes were packed in. Aunt Ruth took the suitcase, and Kite and Uncle Hampton carried the boxes. As they crossed the street toward the car (a dark green Chevrolet, not very new) Kite saw that a boy about his own age was leaning against the front fender. He came forward to meet them and took the suitcase from Aunt Ruth.

"This here's Andrew Crowley," Hampton said. "He lives down the road from us." Kite shifted the box under one arm, so that he could shake hands with Andrew. They put the suitcase and the boxes in the trunk, Kite and Andrew climbed into the back seat, and the Laceys got in up front. Aunt Ruth sat with her back to the door, so that she could look at Kite.

"What time did you leave Thornton?"

" 'Round six thirty."

"So you've had supper."

"Yes, ma'am."

"Well, Kite," Hampton said, "we can't begin to tell you how glad we are you decided to come. We feel bad we didn't get down to see you more."

"That's all right," Kite said. It had not occurred to him that he had made a decision; that he had had a choice.

Aunt Ruth said, "I guess Mrs. Massingale told you about ... everything."

"Yes, ma'am."

"Well, we think everything's gonna work out just fine," Hampton said.

"Yessir," Kite said. "I think so too."

"The ways of the Lord passeth all our understanding," Hampton said.

"Yessir."

Andrew tapped Kite's arm with his knuckles. "You like to ride motorcycles?"

"I never have ridden one, but—"

"And no need to start," Aunt Ruth said sharply.

"Aw, Miz Lacey, c'mon."

"Pos'tively not."

Andrew looked at Kite and shrugged his shoulders and his eyebrows.

"And this is Lenfield." Aunt Ruth ducked her head a little to look out at a row of storefronts. "What there is of it."

Kite saw that railroad tracks ran parallel to what he guessed to be the main street. Except for that, Lenfield looked pretty much like Thornton, maybe a little smaller.

"The picture show's only open on Fridays and Saturdays now," Andrew told him. "The Clock's where everybody hangs out at. It's down the other end of town."

"Kite ain't gonna wanta waste his time hanging out around the Clock," Hampton said.

"You ought to drive by the high school, Hampton."

"Kite ain't in any hurry to see the high school, are you, Kite?"

"No, sir. I don't guess so."

Aunt Ruth said, "You two boys will be in the same grade, come September, even though Andrew's already fifteen."

They accepted that news in silence.

"That's a long way off, idn't it, boys?"

"Yessir."

"You going out for football?" Andrew said.

Before Kite could answer, his aunt said, "I expeck Kite'll need to concentrate on his books to begin with. School here may not be as easy as what he's been used to down in Thornton."

Kite wondered how much Mrs. Massingale had told them about his bad grades.

"Well, if he don't go out this year," Hampton said decisively, "he'll go out next."

"How big is the school here?" Kite said.

"It's about four hundred in the senior high," Andrew said, "nine through twelve."

"If you like to play softball," Hampton said, "the church has got a softball team you could get on. Andrew's on it. I would be myself if I had the time."

Aunt Ruth winked at them.

"Are you going out for football?" Kite asked Andrew.

"I sure am. I was second string last year, and my older brother, Tommy, was co-captain, few years back."

"Andrew's gonna be helping me out at the shed, when packing starts," Hampton said. "I expeck we could find some work for you too, if you'd like to make some pocket money."

"I sure would," Kite said. "That'd be fine."

"But that won't be for a few weeks yet," Ruth told him. "We aren't gonna put you to work soon as you get here."

"I don't imagine Kite's afraid of working. They don't coddle you boys down at Baptist Home, do they, Kite?"

"No, sir," Kite said. Then: "What kind of packing is it?"

"Peaches, boy! Didn't you know this is peach-growing country you're in now? We ship more peaches from this one county than the whole upper state put together. 'Course, not much of that's mine. I just got three small orchards. But I do some packing for some other folks."

"I hope you like peaches," Aunt Ruth said, " 'cause you'll be seeing and eating and hearing an awful lot about 'em for the next month or so."

"Yes, ma'am," Kite said. "I like 'em fine."

Andrew spoke up again. "Do you like to go swiming?"

"Sure," Kite said.

"We got this great place to swim at down on the river. Deep enough to dive in."

"And just fulla snakes," Aunt Ruth said.

"No, *ma'am*," Andrew said. "We hadn't seen a single one, till yesterday we saw a little ringneck."

"Well, we'll see," Ruth said.

"You can't keep the boy in a bottle," Hampton said.

She turned back toward the front of the car, giving him a

sharp look as she did, which he didn't acknowledge, but just kept looking straight ahead.

They rode for a while without talking.

A pale flash of lightning in the distance caught Kite's eye. He suddenly realized that they were out in the country. He had assumed all along—without knowing why—that the Laceys lived in town, in a neighborhood like those around Baptist, with sidewalks and streetlamps and only side yards between the houses. For a moment or two the darkness and emptiness of the countryside made him a little uneasy, but then the full sweet smell of honeysuckle flowed into the car like a soothing promise.

Before long, they turned off the main road and onto a much narrower one. They drove less than half a mile before stopping to let Andrew out in front of a dark two-story frame house with pastureland on both sides of it.

"I'll prob'ly see you at church tomorrow," Andrew told Kite. "Good night, Miz Lacey; Mr. Lacey. Thanks for asking me to go with you."

"I'll see you," Kite said.

The Laceys' house was about two miles farther on and sat back some distance from the road. As they neared the end of the long driveway, a full-grown Irish setter cantered into the beam of the headlights.

"That's Clown," Ruth said. "He's gonna be glad to see you."

While Hampton was opening the trunk, Kite knelt down to make friends with the dog, scratching the top of his head with one hand and patting him on the neck with the other, while the dog sniffed at him and made quick nervous jerks with his whole body. The house was in the middle of a dozen large shade trees, which made the yard very dark. Kite could see that there was an open porch all the way across the front of the house and a smaller screened-in porch at the back. An apricot-colored light was burning on one of the posts that flanked the front steps. Kite saw a shadow move against the steps and then stand up. Hampton and Ruth were headed toward the back part of the house and Kite was following.

"Who's that over yonder?" he said, coming to a stop.

Hampton turned and looked where Kite was looking in time to see the shadowy figure move off across the front yard and blend into the other shadows.

"Oh, that's just Boydy," Hampton said. "He thinks he has to look after the place for us anytime we go off. Specially at night. You'll be seein' him around."

"He's not right in the head," Aunt Ruth told him. "You can tell it when you get close enough to look at his eyes. Some people won't even tolerate him around their place. He's one of God's creatures, though, just like all of us. Hampton lets him help out."

They went in through the kitchen, a good-sized L-shaped room, pine-paneled and with rugs on the floor. Next was a small and very crowded den: an overstuffed couch, a large easy chair, a television set, a sewing machine, and a card table covered with papers (Hampton's office). From there Kite followed Hampton down a hallway and up a narrow flight of stairs that led to a single large room, like an attic with windows.

"This is gonna be your room, Kite. As you can see, it's not quite finished yet, and it may be hot up here in the daytime, but it usely cools off pretty good at night, with all these winders open. And you got this little bathroom here. And there's a tub and a shower downstairs."

"This is a real nice room," Kite said.

Aunt Ruth had followed them up the stairs. "Are you hungry, Kite? I'll be glad to get you some cake and milk."

"Yes, ma'am, that'd be great."

When she had gone, Hampton leaned against the foot of the bed and spoke in a quieter voice. "You know, Kite, me and your Aunt Ruth have had a real hard time since Little Hampton died. Your Aunt Ruth just hadn't got back to her old self yet—and I don't know if she ever will be—so you'll have to be understanding sometimes. But having you here is gonna be a big help to the both of us, and we want you to feel right at home. It'll take a little time for us to get to know each other, but that'll come."

"Yessir," Kite said. Then: "I really do appreciate you all

wanting me to live here, and I'll cert'ly try to help out any way I can."

"I know you will." Hampton stared at the floor and rubbed the knuckle of his thumb back and forth across his forehead. Then he stood away from the bed. "Well, me and your Aunt Ruth are already up past our usual bedtime, and we have to get up for church and Sunday school in the morning, so we'll be going on to bed pretty soon. If you think of anything you need, just holler."

"All right," Kite said. "Good night."

Kite looked around the room, which was lighted only by a lamp on the bedside table and by the light from the stairwell. Then he went into the bathroom and turned on the brighter overhead light. The bathroom was not much more than twice the size of the one on the bus, but it was very clean and white, and there were pale green curtains at the window and a yellow towel and washrag and a new cake of soap. Kite looked at himself in the mirror. Then he heard Aunt Ruth coming up the stairs.

He met her at the door and took the cake and milk. "I could've come down for it," he said.

"No, that's all right." She glanced around the room. "Do you need anything else?"

"No, ma'am. Not that I know of." He set the plate and glass on the bedside table and sat down on the edge of the bed. "This sure does look good."

"Are your Sunday clothes in here?" She tapped the side of her shoe against his suitcase.

"Yes, ma'am."

"I guess maybe we better take 'em out and hang 'em up so they won't be wrinkled for in the morning. You want me to see about 'em?"

"No, ma'am. Thank you anyway. I can do it."

"Well, I know you're prob'ly tired out after that long trip. And we'll have plenty of time to talk tomorrow." She leaned over and kissed him on the cheek.

"Yes, ma'am."

"You certainly do have your mama's beautiful eyes," she said, and before he could say anything to that (and he was not at all sure what to say) she had turned away and moved back toward the door. He had seen, not for the first time, that her own eyes were glistening.

When she was halfway down the stairs she stopped and said, "Don't forget to say your prayers."

"No, ma'am. I won't."

It was banana layer cake. He could see the tiny specks of banana seeds in the cake part, and there were slices of banana, pecans, and whipped cream between the layers and on the top and side. She had given him a thick wedge of it, and the milk was ice cold. While he ate and drank, his eyes continued to wander around the room. There was a fireplace in one end and that whole wall was brick, painted white; the other walls were plasterboard. The ceiling was beveled on two sides; the floor was just sanded subflooring painted gray, and there was a small rug with roses on it beside the bed. There were seven windows. Seven! Three across the back, two dormer windows in front, a small one beside the chimney, and the bathroom window. Besides the bed and the bedside table, there was a very old and lumpy-looking easy chair, a chest of drawers with an oval mirror mounted on top, and a large wardrobe. There were two pictures, Bible scenes, on one wall.

Halfway through the cake, Kite stopped eating long

enough to take his shoes and socks off. Then he sat with his back against the headboard and rubbed his feet up and down on the tufted bedspread. He could not remember ever sleeping in a room by himself, and it felt strange and unreal—as if he was another person, somebody he had known a long time ago but had not been with for many years and did not know how to talk to. He wished that Jimmy was there. Or Jarlene. He wished that Jarlene was there, just to talk to; he would not even want to do it to her right now—though that would be nice, sometime, in this big bed. They never had done it in a bed. But he mainly just wanted somebody to talk to. Somebody to tell about the old guy on the bus. Somebody to tell about Andrew's motorcycle. Somebody who would say, "Man, look at all these windows! You got your own fuckin' room—with seven windows in it. Man, oh, man!"

Some noises came from downstairs for a while; then the house got very quiet. The only sounds were the cicadas. And dogs barking far off in the distance. And those sounds somehow made the silence even louder. He took the plate, glass, and fork into the bathroom and rinsed them off. He tried to be as quiet as possible, but every sound seemd to echo. He opened his suitcase and hung his Sunday coat and pants, his white shirt, and two other pairs of pants in the wardrobe. His other shirts and his underwear and socks he put in the chest.

In the bottom of the suitcase was a spiral notebook, and in the notebook were a dozen or more pictures of naked or nearly naked women, pictures he had torn out of magazines or dirty books. He had thought about leaving those pictures behind. Had even wanted to—in a way. He had told himself that he was going to be starting a clean new life where he would no longer have any need or use for pictures like that. But he had not convinced himself. I can always get rid of 'em when I get up there, he had decided. Without opening the notebook, he slid it under his socks and underwear. Then he took it out again and put it under the tissue paper that lined the drawer. He took his toothbrush, toothpaste, hairbrush, and comb into the bathroom and brushed his teeth, watching himself in the mirror.

He pulled the spread back to the bottom of the bed and folded back the sheet. Then he turned out the lamp. He felt his way over to the back windows and looked out, but all he could see were masses of shadows, very still and quiet; the moon was gone.

He moved back to the bed and knelt beside it and said one of the children's prayers he had been taught at Brightwood, and added, "Please bless my friends and teachers and Dr. Sills down at Baptist Home. Especially Jimmy and Jarlene. Please help Jarlene not to miss me too much. Please bless Aunt Ruth and Uncle Hampton. And please help me to be the kind of boy they want me to be. Amen."

He stood up and undressed down to his underpants and got into bed. He lay awake for a long time, listening to the sounds that chipped away at the silence and thinking about Baptist and Thornton—not the people so much, mainly just the place: the streets, the sidewalks, the buildings, the trees. He felt close to crying. Then he thought about the girl on the bus, the girl with those dirty white socks on and the blouse that gaped open all the way down the back. And then he thought about Jarlene. He lifted his legs and ass and slipped off his underpants. He turned onto his stomach and slid closer to the edge of the bed, gliding his hard cock against the cool powder-smooth sheet, feeling his whole body jerk with pleasure, the same way Clown's had when he was petting him. He reached down and picked up one of his white socks off the floor. Then he twisted onto his back again, turned the sock halfway inside out, so that it made a long pocket, and slipped it onto his cock, squeezing and rubbing, squirming his shoulders against the sheet and tightening his ass. He thought about how hard and smooth Jarlene was all over, her breasts like firm round muscles. He thought about how good it felt when she put her mouth on him. All over. Everywhere. How good it felt when he was inside her and she locked her legs around him and clenched her cunt. He clenched his fist. The bed was squeaking, so he tried to keep his body still and move only his hand. And then, even the sound he was making sucking in his breath—and, a few seconds later, gasping it out—sounded loud to him.

Afterward, he stuffed the sock under the mattress and lay very still.
Satisfied again.
Sorry again.

He had been working at the edge of the melon field for hours, down on his hands and knees. The sun felt like a steam iron against the top of his head and on his back and shoulders. He had on tennis shoes, jeans, a T-shirt, and a headband. All along the barbed-wire fence lay a strip of earth that the tractor had skirted. It was his job to clear off the honeysuckle vines before they spread into the melons. The ground was dry and hard and the roots of the honeysuckle had gone deeper than usual. Even at the surface the vines crisscrossed and tangled and wrapped around the fenceposts, so that pulling them free was like working a Chinese puzzle made out of copper wires. The sides of his hands and fingers were almost raw.

The watermelons were planted on a terraced hillside and he had started at the bottom; he was not yet even a quarter of the way to where the fence ended, at the edge of the woods. Bridwell was supposed to have come back to help him. He should have been back long before now; all he had to do was drive the wagon down to the lower pasture and set out the new salt licks. Kite felt sure he was sitting in the river up to his nose, cool as a goddamned cucumber. That pizza-faced son of a bitch. Meanwhile *he* was sweating his ass off. He kept wishing that the melons were ripe, so he could smash one open against the top of a fencepost and bury his face in the sweet red wetness. But they were not yet even as big as softballs— still small enough, most of them, to be hidden by the gray-green leaves. It was hard to believe that in a matter of weeks they would be bigger than cannonballs. Hard to believe that plants no bigger than gourd or squash vines could produce fruit five or six times that size. There was something sort of magical—and comical—about the way watermelons grew. Like a snake blowing up a balloon. Like seeing Mrs. Wessup and her son walk down the aisle at church, Mrs. Wessup tiny and shriveled and her son as big as a bear.

He kept thinking that he heard the rumble and creak of the wagon on the dirt road, but the wagon didn't come. Then he realized that the sound must be thunder, even though the only clouds he could see were white and feathery. It occurred to him that the sun might have shifted enough by now to cast at least a narrow strip of shade at the edge of the woods. He decided to move to the top of the hill and work from that end for a while. The vines would be thicker and more tangled there, but the ground might be softer.

He was not even halfway up the hill, still several hundred feet from the far end of the fence, when he saw his mama and daddy standing side by side in the shadow of the woods. His mama had on a white dress and his daddy had on a tan uniform. At almost exactly that same instant he heard the sound of the wagon and turned and looked back down the road and saw Bridwell and the mule. Bridwell's hair was slicked-down wet, and he held a bottle of Coca-Cola between his thighs. Kite raised his hand, but Bridwell didn't wave back. It would be just like him to drive right on past and make him walk home. When he turned toward the woods again, his mama and daddy had disappeared. Why didn't they wait for him? They must not have seen him. When he tried to run he kept tripping over the vines, and the air all around him seemed to be turning to Jell-O. He tried to call out to them, but his throat was dry and his tongue felt swollen. Even his teeth felt soft and rubbery, like the false teeth you make out of watermelon rind. . . .

He woke to the sound of rain on a tin roof. Then thunder. At first he didn't know where he was. When he remembered, he groped for the lamp and turned it on. He knew where he was, but he still felt confused. He got up and put down all the windows. The rain had already come in at the back, and he wiped off the windowsills with toilet paper. The room seemed, in the middle of the night, even more like something he was dreaming, except that he was not even part of it—he was watching himself in a movie. He went into the bathroom and looked at himself in the mirror again.

Once he was back in bed and had turned off the light, the muffled sound of the rain on the leaves and the roof drowned out the uneasy silence, and those sounds, and the darkness and the warmth, made him feel like an animal in a burrow.

He heard a tiny baby crying somewhere in the distance. He thought it was Little Hampton. He had not been killed in the fire after all. It was just a mistake. Somebody had found him and brought him back home. That meant that *he* would be sent right back to Baptist—and he hadn't even ridden on Andrew's motorcycle yet. He felt so cheated that his hands made tight fists.

He opened his eyes. The room was bright. And warm. He had had his own room for only one night. Little Hampton kept crying. . . .

But Little Hampton was too old to sound like that. And now he wasn't even sure it was a baby. But he couldn't turn it into what it was. He sat up. The sun was shining straight through the front windows, and last night's rain sparkled in the screens; the green leaves just beyond were wet and shiny. That was where the crying was coming from. From the leaves. It was a mockingbird. A mockingbird yelling at a cat or a snake. Or just for the hell of it. Not Little Hampton crying, just a mockingbird. Little Hampton was dead. And gone. But *he* was here.

He lay back against the pillow, smiling, then stretched and

kicked off the sheet. He lay still and listened. The house was quiet; it must be very early. He got out of bed, put his underpants on, and started raising the windows. The morning air washed in cool and clean. The dormer windows opened above the sharply sloping roof and looked down into the front yard, where half a dozen large wooden lawn chairs made a circle and long shadows. From the small window by the chimney he could see the car parked in the driveway, and beyond the driveway a strip of grass at the edge of a wall of pinewoods.

Then he moved to the windows at the back of the house and saw the mountains for the first time. The back lawn was deep, with flowers at the far end, in front of a ragged hedgerow. Beyond the fence: orchards, fields, and woods, tumbling toward the horizon. And all along the horizon lay the mountains, low and gentle and pale violet to the west; higher, clearer, darker blue-purple as they moved northward. Here and there, with the morning sunlight on them, Kite could see outcroppings of rock and the shapes of trees, but the whole range was mostly a soft smooth silhouette against the sky— like a long blue train rolling out of the tunnel of the woods. He could not even take it all in without turning his head. How many miles was that, from end to end? And how far away were the nearest ones? The farthest ones? How could he not have known they were there last night? How could he not have felt them there even in the dark? Waiting. Like another surprise. Like Ruth and Hampton living in the country. Like Andrew. Like Clown. What would it be like to stand on the highest of those mountains and look back down at where he was now? This house would just be a white speck against the green. You couldn't even tell it was a house. But he was *in* that speck. That banana seed. Living in it. He wanted to signal, to shout to whoever was up on those mountaintops right now. But what could he say? How could he tell them?

He gazed at the mountains for a long time. The mockingbird had flown, but other birds were making their own racket now in every tree. The house, though, was still quiet. He went back to the bed and lay down again, yawning, and closed his eyes. He wished he had somebody to talk to. Somebody to talk about the mountains with. And the yard. And the room. He wondered what it would feel like to sleep beside a girl all night long and wake up beside her in the morning.

Downstairs, in the den, Hampton turned the television set on full blast, and the sound of the Gambrell Brothers Gospel Quartet came gushing up the stairs. Kite's eyes snapped open.

We are *lost* and lone-ly chil-drun,
Drown-ding *in* the Devil's flood.
Walk a-*cross* the rag-ing war-ters,
Come and *bathe* us in Thy blood.

He sat up on the edge of the bed and stared around the room, remembering how he had felt when he waked up in the middle of the night.

We are *suff*'ring in Sin's bon-dage.
Come, sweet *Jee*-sus, set us free.
We shall *fol*-low in Thy footsteps.
Lead us *on* to Cal-va-ry.

He knelt beside the bed, his hands clenched in front of him, but he could not think what to say. The Gambrell Brothers were still puling away, but Hampton had lowered the volume. Kite thought of the Caro syrup Nurse Maybry made him gargle when he had a sore throat. He stood up and went to the back windows and looked out at the beautiful blue mountains again.

"Dear Heavenly Father, I know that I don't much deserve to be in this nice place. And I know that I am not much of a replacement for Little Hampton, who was a pure and innocent little child. But I am truly thankful that You have brought me up here, and I pray that You will help me to give up the bad practices and thoughts that I have got used to in the past. So I won't disappoint Aunt Ruth and Uncle Hampton. And so I won't make You sorry You gave me this new life."

And all the time, dancing in the back of his mind like the whine of the Gambrell Brothers, was a fearsome and shameful suspicion:

It's a trick. It's a trick.

In warm weather the Laceys ate most of their meals on the back porch, which was screened on the two open sides and shaded by a massive broadleaf oak. When Kite, his hair still damp from the shower, came out through the kitchen door, his aunt and uncle were already sitting down, but they had not started eating. Aunt Ruth was pouring coffee. She sat at one end of the small porcelain-topped table and Uncle Hampton sat at the other end. Kite took his place at the side. In the middle of the table was a jelly glass full of cornflowers.

The three of them bowed their heads.

"Our Lord and Savior, our Provider and Redeemer," Hampton said. "Please bless this food, prepared in Christian love, to the nourishment of our physical bodies, and bless this day and Thy Holy Word to the nourishment of our souls. We are deeply grateful that we can assemble here together as a Christian family, and we pray that Thou willst guide us in our individual lives and in our relationships one to another. As we go about each day. Help us to accept Thy will in its infinite wisdom and forgive us of our many sins and failings. In Jesus' name and for His sake, we pray. Amen."

There was a dish of brains and eggs, a bowl of hominy, and biscuits the size of Kite's fist. He helped himself.

"I didn't know the mountains were so close."

"Sure are," Hampton said. "You got one of the finest views anywhere around here from your room."

"Yessir, it sure is pretty. How far away are they?"

"Oh, we can be up in the mountains in less than an hour. Up around Glassy."

"We'll have to go up there on a picnic sometime," Aunt Ruth said.

"Boy! That'd be great!"

"We'll have to try to do that, then, sometime before packing starts."

"Your Aunt Ruth's grandaddy used to have a real nice summer house up at Caesars Head, but it burnt down in a forest fire a good many years ago."

There was a quick cold silence, and Kite saw that his aunt was staring hard at her plate.

"Does every one of those humps have a name?" Kite's open hand traced a series of ridges in the air.

"Every one that I know of," Hampton said. "I can tell you most of 'em we can see from here."

"Have some jelly, Kite." Aunt Ruth passed him a plate shaped like a leaf and divided into three sections.

"Your Aunt Ruth's got all fancied up for you," Hampton said. "She usely just gives me one kind, and in the jar. This morning we got us a choice of peach preserves, pear preserves, or muscadine jelly."

Kite laughed and took a spoonful of jelly. "Everything sure is good."

"Well, it's a pleasure to see somebody eat like they enjoy it."

"Now, honey," Hampton said, "you know you get to see me eat like that three times a day."

"And anybody can tell it to look at you too. Now Kite here can use a little more meat on his bones. I'm gonna start giving him his share and a half of yours too."

"He'll prob'ly need it once we start working." Winking at him.

Kite smiled. He was sitting with his back to the yard, facing the window that looked into the dining room. The room itself was dim and shadowy, but in the opposite wall he could see another window framing the bright green yard on the other side of the house. He watched a scarlet tanager moving back and forth between the trees and the hedge.

"Can I ask you something?" he said to his aunt.

"Why, certainly, what is it?" She was frowning in a way that made him think perhaps he shouldn't ask after all. But he went ahead.

"You said last night I had my mama's eyes. But I never have even seen a picture of her. I don't know what she looked like. I was just wondering—"

"Oh, I wish to goodness I *did* have a picture." She looked relieved. "But I don't. Just the ones in my mind. Your mama was a good many years older than me. I can remember when I was a little girl, following Jessie around, trying to copy everything she did. I thought she was the prettiest thing. It just about broke my heart—all of us's heart—when she left home. Left to run off with your daddy, as a matter of fact. Who was every bit as handsome as she was pretty. It's no wonder you're such a nice-looking boy."

"Now don't give him the big head," Hampton said. "Here, have some more eggs."

Kite took the dish and spooned out another helping. There were other things he wanted to ask about, but he decided to wait.

After breakfast he went back upstairs, brushed his teeth, combed his hair, and put on his Sunday clothes. When he took his coat off the wire hanger, he felt the weight of the Prince Albert tobacco tin in the inside pocket. He took it out, thumbed open the lid, and pulled out the white cloth sack with the yellow drawstring. He dumped the change into his palm, put three quarters in his pants pocket, and returned the rest to the pouch and the pouch to the tin. He opened the second drawer of the chest and slid the tin under his socks and underwear. He resisted the urge to take out the notebook that he had hidden under the tissue paper, but he stood there for a moment and let some of the pictures come to mind, one by one. . . .

The sleeves of his coat were much too short. He tried lifting his shoulders and bending his wrists. Maybe it would be all right to take the coat off when he got there. He would see what the other boys did. He looked at himself in the mirror. The white shirt, open at the neck, and the powder-blue coat made him look less pale. His dark hair was soft against his forehead. He wondered how long it would be before Hampton or Ruth began to nag at him to get a haircut, and he wondered now long he could resist.

When he got back downstairs they were still in their bedroom. He went out the back door and strolled up the driveway in the shade of the pinewoods. The yard was bright and bristling. There was not much grass at the front or sides of the house because of the sandy soil and the dense shade, but in the deep, open, sunlit back yard there was a fine natural lawn. Between the lawn and the side yard stood several flowering shrubs the size of small trees: quince, lilac, service, sweet olive. They formed a sort of passageway onto the lawn, which looked from this angle like a brightly lit stage seen from the wings. At that hour of the morning, just after nine, the grass was still brimming with dew. Kite wished that he was barefooted. Walking across the lawn early in the morning would be almost like wading, except that you would leave a trail: the grass would be brighter and greener where you had walked.

He heard the screen door slam and looked back to see Aunt Ruth coming down the walk. She was wearing a yellow and white dress and a little white hat. It looked as if she had put the hat on and had then stuck little twists of hair up under the edge of it.

"Your Uncle Hampton is as slow as molasses," she told him. "Specially on Sunday morning." She was carrying a heart-shaped cardboard fan with a flat wooden handle. "His garden's back there beside the barn, but I'll let him show that to you. Be sure to brag on it, he's so proud of it."

"Yes, ma'am, I will."

"Let's walk back down this way. He'll prob'ly have you working out there if I know him. He'd have me out there weeding and chopping if I gave him half a chance."

"I used to work in the garden some down at Baptist," Kite said.

"Well, I *will* say this for Hampton, he's a good provider. He keeps us in fresh vegetables all summer long. And I put up a lot too. See that little shallow place there?"

Kite looked where she was pointing with the fan: a saucer-shaped spot, about the size of a large birdbath, at the edge of the front yard.

"Yes, ma'am."

"I'll tell you a little story about that. When me and Hampton first moved out here, right after we got married—that was about nine years ago—there was a big old unpainted barn of a house that sat just beyond that little dip. And that was where the well was, except it had gone dry. The folks who were living there then, the Thompsons, had to haul water from all the way down at the branch. I don't know how long it was since they had used the well, but it was covered over with a sort of round wood platform, too big and heavy for any of their children to be able to budge it.

"Well, I wanted Hampton to build our house back yonder, right where it is, so we could have a better view. But all this—" she waved her outstretched arm in the direction of the house—"all this was just a jungle of blackberry briars and scrub pines and sumac and honeysuckle. So in the spring, when we started cleaning all that out, we decided to dump it down the old well, so it wouldn't just take root again. It took Hampton and Boydy both to drag the lid off. And there was this pitch-black hole about a yard or so across. We were afraid the earth around it might give way, so Hampton crawled up to it real slow, on his hands and knees. And then I did the same thing. So we ended up stretched out on our stomachs, our heads hanging over the edge, looking down at this little circle of light. It was like looking through the wrong end of a telescope. We dropped some rocks down it, and it seemed like it took five minutes for 'em to splash. Then Hampton dropped lighted matches, and then set little bundles of broomstraw on fire and dropped those down, and we could see the clay sides all the way down, and the reflection of the fire in the water before it went out."

"How deep was it?" Kite asked.

"I don't have much idea about that," she said. "Hampton can prob'ly tell you. Anyway, it turned out the only practical thing for us to do was to drill a new well. Which meant the safest thing to do was go ahead and fill up the old one.

"Well, at first it seemed hopeless. We must have dumped in a hundred wheelbarrowfuls of rocks and cinders and vines and underbrush. Boulders too big to pick up Hampton would roll to the edge, and they would go rumbling down like thunder. The same with uprooted stumps. It didn't take too long for the water to go, but then there was nothing—just blackness. So the job got slower, we couldn't tell we were making any progress at all.

"Once our own house got underway, they started tearing down the old Thompson place, most of which was rotten and worthless. Some of it we saved back for firewood, and the old bricks went into our walkway, but most of it went down the well: whole beams and timbers. And later on a lot of scraps and waste from our building. Then one day, it must have been close to Thanksgiving, I came out here late in the afternoon—Hampton had been working all day—and he called me over to the well, and you could see the bottom. It was still a long way down, but the end was in sight. And, as it so happened, our own house was almost finished too: we got to celebrate that Christmas in it. By that time the well was just about full. But then there at the last—early that spring, I guess—we got impatient and had a truckload of dirt hauled in. Then emptied several barrowfuls of woods earth on top of that, which brought it up to the top.

"So to mark that sizable accomplishment, I planted some iris bulbs in it, some I had brought from my family's place in town. Hampton, of course, said they never would live, it was the wrong time—but he was mistaken for once. They came up healthy as could be and were in full bloom by the middle of that May. Iris are hardy. Up until then I hadn't even known for sure what color they were gonna be. They were

white, most of 'em, with a few pale violet ones mixed in, and
fine heavy blossoms, just beautiful. That very same month,
though, we had an awful lot of rain; came later than usual. We
didn't have much of a stand of grass yet, and we found ourselves living in a swamp. And the branch came up to twice its
normal size. Then, what we should've known would happen,
happened. All that stuff we had thrown down the well settled
and sank. Hampton said it might have been that one of the
stumps had lodged part way down and finely come loose.
Anyway, we woke up one morning to find that only the heads
of the iris were in sight above the ground. We thought we
were seeing things. It looked almost like the water was bub-
bling up out of the well.

"We talked about trying to transplant 'em, but that *was* the
wrong time, and we didn't get around to it. By the next day
they had sunk out of sight—unless you went up to the edge
and looked down in the hole. So I just let 'em go. Hampton
brought another load of dirt and dumped it in on top of 'em. I
didn't even watch, I just thought of all the other stuff that had
gone down that well. Parts of the old Thompson house, parts
of our new one, the rocks, the briars. . . .

"You can tell that it keeps on sinking. But it's very gradual
now. It's looked just like this for a good many years."

They had walked down the driveway, almost to the road,
and had then turned around and ambled back. Now they
were standing beside the shallow circle again, gazing down at
it as if, Kite thought, they half expected the irises to pop right
back up any minute now. Then they both looked up at the
same time, and Kite saw that Aunt Ruth's eyes were full and
glistening. He looked off past her hat toward the pinewoods at
the far end of the driveway.

"How old is whoever that was on the front steps last
night?"

"What?" She looked at him as if he were a stranger.

"When we were going inside. Somebody Hampton said
watched the place for you."

"Must've been Boydy."

"Yeah. How old is he?"

"Oh, he's not a boy, if that's what you mean. He's older

than me and Hampton. In fact, he used to work for Hampton's daddy. But I don't know exackly how old he is. I doubt if he knows himself."

"Is he a colored man?"

"Oh, yes, he's colored. No doubt about that."

"He was standing off in the woods down yonder when we walked past. Just watching us."

"That sounds like Boydy. He's like a woods animal. Or a child. Leery of strangers. You'll prob'ly see him sniffin' around the edges for a while before he comes out in the open. Before he decides you belong here after all."

They heard the screen door slam and turned toward the house.

"Well, here comes Christmas," she said. "It's about time."

Kite had thought that they would go to church in town, but his uncle turned left out of the driveway and headed in the opposite direction. There were fine-looking orchards on both sides of the road.

"I wish you could've been here when the trees were in bloom," Ruth said. "They just take your breath away."

"He can see 'em next year," Hampton said. "Important thing is, he got here in time to see the peaches."

"I always think it's so remarkable the way the colors go." She had twisted herself around until she was sitting sidesaddle again. "You know, late in the winter—sometimes we still got snow on the ground—the trees take on a kind of reddish color. Like redbuds do later on. Sometimes you can't even tell it up close, but off at a distance they have this reddish haze. Then early in April the pink blossoms come. Pure pink, not pink and white like apple blossoms. And then the green leaves. But with the peaches it's just the opposite. First they're dark green. Then lighter green. Then yellowish pink.

Then golden red." She looked back at him as if (he thought) she expected him to recite the sequence of colors after her. He just nodded. "I don't know how anybody can live out in the country the way we do, and observe the wonders of nature, without realizing that it's all God's handiwork. I just think it's a sin anybody has to live in a city."

Hampton said, "Do you have any money for the collection plate, Kite?"

"No, sir, I sure don't. I forgot to bring any."

"Well, I don't think I got any change either. We'll have to stop at Grunyan's."

His aunt make a clicking sound with her tongue.

Grunyan's, half a mile farther on, turned out to be a combination barbecue joint, grocery store, and gas station. Hampton pulled up in front and handed Kite a dollar bill.

"You wanta run in and get some silver?"

"Get yourself some chewing gum too if you want to," Ruth hollered after him.

There was a single checkout counter just inside the door. Two customers stood in front of it and a man in a butcher's apron behind it. Kite went to the right, toward the produce bins, and around a bright tin garbage can full of brooms and mops. He came up in front of a magazine rack that was just behind the checkout. He looked back and forth across the shelves, until he got to the bottom shelf, where he stopped. The cover of *Male* magazine showed a beautiful blond girl whose hands were tied above her head. Her armpits were very smooth and white. Her blouse was badly torn and seeemed to be held together by a single button. A big brown hand held a silver dagger poised right at that button. The girl had turned her head to one side; she was holding her breath. Kite bent forward to get a better look. Then he straightened up and hurried back outside to the car.

"Is it okay if I buy a *Saturday Evening Post* magazine? I'll pay you back soon as we get home."

"Sure," Hampton said. "Sure. Just hurry up, though. Aunt Ruth's about to have a conniption fit."

Back inside the store, Kite stooped down at the magazine rack, carefully hitching up his pants legs so the cuffs wouldn't brush the dark oily floor. He leafed idly through a copy of the *Post*, as if looking at the cartoons, and then casually laid a copy of *Male* inside it. Holding the *Post* halfway rolled up in one hand and the dollar bill in the other, he stood up and headed for the checkout.

"Just this magazine," he said to the man at the counter, showing him the picture of a chimpanzee in rompers. The man took the dollar bill, rang up the sale, and gave him his change.

Before Kite got to the door, the man said, "You must be the Laceys' new boy."

"Yessir," Kite said.

"Well, I hope you're gonna like it up here." He waved at Ruth and Hampton through the window.

"Oh, yessir," Kite said. "I do."

When he had climbed into the back seat again, he handed Hampton the change.

"You keep that for the collection plate."

"I'll pay you back when we get home," Kite said.

"You don't have to do that," his aunt told him.

Hampton said, "I'll let you help me out a dollar's worth in the garden tomorrow."

"Yessir."

Kite sat with one ankle cocked across the other knee and the magazine propped against his leg.

"There's an article in here on the War Between the States."

"So that's what you were after," Hampton said.

"Mrs. Massingale told us history was your favorite subject."

"Yes, ma'am. Did you know there was a Confederate general named Cummings?"

"Must've been a great-grandaddy of yours, eh?"

"Could have been," Kite said. "Couldn't he?" And he wondered again how much Mrs. Massingale had told them about his grades in the subjects that were not his favorite.

He continued to pretend to study the first few pages of the *Post*, keeping a firm grip on the part that sandwiched the girl in the torn blouse. He had begun to wonder where he should leave the magazines when they got to the church. There didn't seem to be any good place to stick them out of sight. But suppose Ruth or Hampton got back to the car first and picked up the *Post* and the copy of *Male* fell out. What could he say if they found out he had swiped a trashy book like that? He should have thought about that before he took it. But there was no way they could know that he had stolen it. He'd just say it must have got stuck in there by accident, he didn't even realize it was in there. Would they believe that? Maybe so. Probably not. He should have waited. It was crazy to do something like that the first day he was here. And why had he lied about having any money? That was stupid too. Stop acting like a dumb kid, he told himself.

When they slowed up at a crossroads, Kite glanced out the window and saw a sign nailed to a tree: CALVARY BAPTIST CHURCH 1 MILE.

"Is that where we're going?"

"That's it."

"But we're gonna be late for Sunday school," his aunt said. "I know it good as I know my name."

Even though he knew what Calvary was in the Bible, Kite saw in his mind a little church way out on the prairie, with wild Indians circling it on ponies and whooping and hollering for blood, some of them sliding off the pony's back and holding on with just their legs while they shot flaming arrows from under the pony's head. And when the cavalry came to the rescue it would be General Cummings in the lead.

As they pulled into the church parking lot, Kite spotted two boys his age or older in their shirt sleeves.

"Would it be all right if I just left my coat in the car?"

"Perfeckly all right," Aunt Ruth said.

"I'd do exackly the same thing," Hampton said, "if Miss Ruth would let me."

"Well, now, you're a grown man, Hampton, there's a difference. So try and act it."

Hampton winked at Kite, who had put the *Post* magazine down on the back seat and then put his coat on top of it.

The Calvary Baptist Church was yellow brick across the front and cement block painted white on the sides and back. It had a fine white steeple that looked too big and tall for the rest of the building. On the side where they had parked, near the back, a little white metal awning jutted out over half a dozen cement steps that led down into the basement. Kite followed Ruth and Hampton down the steps and along a bare corridor where the walls and the floor were cool gray cement. At a door with the numbers 5–10 on it, Aunt Ruth whispered, "This is the young people's department. We'll meet you back out in front when Sunday school's over." And she eased the door open for him.

He had stepped inside and she had closed the door behind him before he realized that except for two women at the front of the room it was almost all small children. He didn't see any boys his own age, and only a couple of girls that came even close. He started to turn around and go back out, but one of the women smiled at him and nodded toward an empty chair near the far wall. The trouble was that that chair, like all the others, was a little tiny one, made for a small child. The top of the back didn't come much above his knees. He thought about just standing, but that made him feel even more conspicuous and he was also afraid it might obligate him to take some special part in the program. So he moved across the room, aware of all the little children bending their necks back and staring up at him as if he was some sort of giant or monster. It was not until after he had sat down in the chair that he realized he had interrupted a prayer.

"Let's bow our heads again now, children," one of the women said.

When Kite bowed his head his face came close to his knees, which were sticking up at an angle that cramped his stomach and ribs and made his pants feel too tight.

After the prayer, the other woman—they looked almost exactly alike, Kite thought—showed pictures of Bible scenes that the members of the class had painted in Vacation Bible School and told the stories that went along with the pictures. They were the stories Kite had heard a thousand times: Noah and the ark, Jonah and the whale, Joseph and the coat of many colors, Moses in the bulrushes. Kite tried to pay attention, but the two oldest girls, who were sitting in the row in front of him, kept glancing back at him and whispering to each other.

Neither one of them was even halfway cute. Finally, the other woman sat down at a yellow upright piano, looked over her shoulder at them, and said, "Let's stand and sing 'Jesus Loves Me, This I Know.' " Even though it was a children's song and even though he felt awkwardly tall again, Kite was glad to get to unbend. Once he was standing, his eyes were level with the bottom of the window in the wall right beside him. And the bottom of the window was even with the ground. So he looked out at blades of grass and up through the lowest branches of the shrubbery. It was the same view a small animal or insect would have had. After that song they took up the collection. Then they prayed another prayer. And then sang another song.

Before the class was dismissed, one of the women said, "We're real glad to have a visitor with us today. Are you Benny's big brother?"

"No, ma'am," Kite said, "I'm Kite Cummings. The Laceys' nephew."

The woman looked puzzled and seemed to be waiting for a better explanation, but Kite didn't know what else to say.

"Well, we cert'ly hope you'll come back again," she said.

Only one small patch of half a dozen pines had been left standing in the middle of the church parking lot, and that was where Kite spotted his uncle when he came up out of the basement.

"I think I went to the wrong place," he said. "There was only little children in there. Nobody near my age."

"Uh-oh," Hampton said. "We better ask Andrew when he comes along. Though I don't think the Crowleys get here in time for Sunday school ordinarily."

Hampton took a small pocketknife out of his pants pocket and began to scrape at his thumbnail.

"Speaking of the Crowleys," he said. "Something else I should tell you. Andrew has a little brother, 'bout six years old, thinks the sun rises and sets on Andrew. Follers him everywhere. Little Hampton was a good bit younger, of course, but him and Chaplin were getting to be pretty good buddies. Sometimes it upsets Ruth when she sees little Chaplin. She'll prob'ly make over him a good bit—but if she starts crying, you'll know why it is. She'll be all right. I just wanted to tell you."

"I understand," Kite said. "Does Andrew's little brother know what happened to Little Hampton?"

"All he knows is he's gone. We didn't tell him about the accident. But I think his mama and daddy might have told him not to ask me or Ruth about him. He never has, anyway."

A red Pontiac, even older than Hampton's Chevrolet, was pulling into a parking space just to the left of where they were standing. A large red-faced man with a straw hat on was driving, but it was the girl on the other side of him that caught Kite's eye. She had silky blond hair and pale skin that made him think of the girl on the cover of the *Male* magazine. When she got out of the car, he saw that she might be as old as twenty or twenty-one and that even though her lavender dress was crisp and new and securely buttoned, what was underneath it was even rounder and fuller and more exciting than in the picture. Something else that excited him (though he wasn't sure why) was the black velvet ribbon she wore around her neck. It fit almost tight enough to be uncomfortable, he thought, but it made her skin look even softer and paler, and there was a little silver pin clipped onto it at the front.

"Who is that?" Kite said.

"That's Joe Dundean and his daughter."

Kite could tell from the tone of Hampton's voice and from the set of his mouth that he did not think much of one or the other or both of them and that more questions might not be welcome. He watched them walk toward the church. Mr. Dundean was in his shirt sleeves and wore suspenders, and his daughter had on high-heel shoes that left her feet mostly bare and made the calves of her legs swell and harden with each step. Kite wanted badly to follow her and took a couple of nonchalant steps in that direction, hoping his uncle might follow suit and that the two of them could trail the Dundeans into the church. But Hampton didn't budge. Kite brought himself up short and then shifted idly from one foot to the other, looking up at the steeple as if that were the reason he had moved out from under the trees. There was a cross at the top.

"Can you go up in the steeple?" he said, turning back to his uncle.

"You can go up as high as those little round winders. You get a real good view of the mountains from up there."

"That's what I was wondering about," Kite said.

"When we first took Little Hampton up in the mountains, he was real disappointed. He had thought all the trees were gonna have blue leaves."

Kite smiled. "They sure are pretty," he said.

"Here come the Crowleys." Hampton waved to a group of half a dozen folks headed toward them across the parking lot. Kite was glad to see a familiar face.

Hampton introduced him to Andrew's mother and father, Mr. Crowley's mother, Andrew's older sister, Connie, his ten-year-old brother, Bass—"And this young feller here, this is Chaplin Crowley. This is Andrew's shadder. You keeping big brother in line these days?"

"Yes, sir," Chaplin said.

Kite shook hands with all of them, wondering, in particular, how he would have felt about Connie Crowley if she was somebody other than who she was. He guessed her to be a year or so older than him and Andrew. She was pretty in a wholesome rosy-cheeked way, and she had given him a very friendly smile and hello—but the fact that she was Andrew's sister made her look and feel more like a sister to him, too. Maybe it was just that his mind was still on Mr. Dundean's daughter.

Andrew said, "They won't let me ride my bike on Sundays. Not to church, anyway. If they did I could give you a ride home."

"That's okay," Kite said.

"You boys are gonna have to do some fast talking to get Miss Ruth's approval on this motorcycle business," Hampton said.

"We're just gonna ride on the back roads," Andrew said. "We don't get out on the highway."

"Well, you'll have to talk to the boss."

"You let me do the talking," Andrew's mother said. "I don't want you all worrying Ruth."

"Here she comes," Andrew said.

"And I didn't say right this minute, either. We'll talk about it sometime next week. You boys got all summer."

Aunt Ruth had been joined by a young man with sandy hair and a sandy-red mustache and a young woman with the same coloring in a bright blue dress. As soon as she spotted Hampton and Kite and the Crowleys, Aunt Ruth waved at them, pointed the young couple in their direction, and then headed off at an angle toward a station wagon several rows of cars toward the highway, where two men were lifting a woman into a wheelchair.

"That's Agnes Wydman," Hampton told him. "I reckon she must be a third or fourth cousin of yours. Now here's somebody I specially wanted you to meet." It was the young man with the mustache. "This is Dr. Tom Estelle. And his wife, Louise. Dr. Estelle's our newest dentist in town. But that's not the main reason I wanted you to meet him."

"You and me got something in common," the dentist said, as Kite was shaking hands with him and his wife. "I grew up down at Baptist Home too. Matter of fact, I spent about eight years down there. It's not such a bad place, is it?"

"No, sir," Kite said. "I liked it there okay. Most of the time."

"I expect you're gonna like it up here a lot better, though."

"Yessir. I like it a lot already."

"And old Andrew here can show you the ropes." He punched at Andrew's shoulder. "Introduce you to the good-looking girls."

Kite and Andrew both grinned.

"These two can worry about the girls after they get all my peaches packed and shipped," Hampton said.

Everybody laughed.

"And they'll be rich enough by then to court 'em in style," Mr. Crowley said.

Everybody laughed even louder. Then the whole crowd began to move toward the church. Aunt Ruth joined them at the bottom of the steps that led up to the front doors and bent

down to kiss Chaplin on the cheek. As they were going up the
steps she said to Kite, "I think you're gonna like our preacher,
he's a real young fella."

But that comment did not fully prepare Kite for the youth-
fulness of the man—he looked more like a boy, not much
older than Kite himself—who was sitting on the platform, to
the left of the pulpit. His face was round and smooth, his
brown hair neatly parted and brushed; he had big brown eyes
and a sweet smile, with which he seemed to be blessing the
congregation as they drifted in. He was wearing a plain white
robe that resembled a nightshirt and that made him seem
both younger and shorter than he really was—so short, in
fact, that Kite thought he might not be able to see over the top
of the pulpit and would have to stand to the side of it. On the
program, opposite SERMON: *Too Late for the Lord* was his
name: ......REV. BOBBY FAIRFOREST. It suited him.

The church itself was smaller and narrower inside than it
looked from outside. And it was bright and warm. Kite and
the Laceys sat about halfway down, Kite in the middle. The
Crowleys were in the pew just in front of them, and the Dundeans—he had spotted her bright blond hair as they came
down the aisle—were several rows behind.

As soon as they were seated his aunt and uncle bowed their
heads, so Kite did too. He had been taught down at Baptist
that the best way to pray was first to let his mind become as
calm and clear and quiet as a pool of water deep in a forest—
so that God could get through to *him*, just as he was trying
and hoping to get through to God. ("Praying," Rev. Sills was
fond of saying, "is just like making a telephone call. You have
to give God time to answer, and you have to let Him do some
of the talking.") It was only in church, as a rule, that Kite
consciously took the time to try that. It was easy enough to let
his mind go blank (a little harder today than usual because he
kept thinking of all the new people he had met, the new
names and faces—Mr. Dundean's daughter and Connie
Crowley, in particular), but he had never felt really certain
that God had gotten through to him. And there had not been
many times when he felt for sure that he had gotten through
to God. He knew that that was where faith came in, but most

of the time, when he let his mind go blank, he began to get sleepy. And that was what was happening now. He was glad when it was time to stand and sing the first hymn, "In This House of Glory, We."

When Rev. Fairforest finally came forward to preach (after two more hymns, two prayers, the offering, and announcements), he had no trouble at all seeing over the top of the pulpit, but he did not stay behind it very much of the time, and when he *was* behind it he seemed to be grappling with it, as if trying to turn it over or maybe climb up on top of it. Most of the rest of the time he was striding from one end of the platform to the other, sometimes gazing up at the ceiling or out the window, but often coming right down to the front edge of the platform and looking out at the congregation. His arms were often in motion too: stretched out like Christ's on the cross or up above his head, his elbows bent and his hands open, as if he were feeling the sides of an invisible stovepipe hat, and at other times he held both fists hard against his chest, just under his chin, as if he were playing the game where you had to guess which hand held something. His voice was constantly changing too: from loud to soft, from low to high, from sweet to harsh.

Kite was fascinated. He was accustomed to the slow and somber sermons of Rev. Sills, who hardly moved at all and who rarely changed expression or tone of voice. Kite had thought that because Rev. Fairforest looked so young he might be nervous or self-conscious. But he was just the opposite. Kite had never seen anybody who seemed so sure of himself, so sure of exactly what to say at every second, and exactly how to say it, and exactly what motion or gesture to put with it. And yet, there was something almost funny about the contrast between the way Rev. Fairforest looked and the way he talked and acted. It was like seeing a little baby with a mustache. Or a hard-on. Kite felt himself grinning, and then he realized that he was so amazed by Rev. Fairforest himself that he could not keep track of what he was saying.

The sermon had begun with a story about a lumberjack somewhere out West who had gone to a prayer meeting and who had seemed "much convicted." But when one of the

Lord's workers at the meeting asked the lumberjack to confess
his sins and take Jesus as his Savior, he had said, "No. I will
attend to that matter when I am through hauling logs; I have
one more month to work yet." Four weeks from that day the
lumberjack went swimming with a friend at a lake in the
mountains. He had used profane language while he was un-
dressing. And when he plunged into the lake, he swam into
deep cold water, was taken with a cramp, screamed wildly for
help, then sank to the bottom.

"He was one month too late," Rev. Fairforest said, holding
up one finger at them.

When he thought about that story later on, Kite was not al-
together sure he believed it, and he wondered what had happened to the lumberjack's friend and if he had tried to save
him. But when Rev. Fairforest told the story, he told it so dra-
matically and it seemed so real that a woman somewhere near
the back of the church had cried out when the lumberjack
sank to the bottom.

Kite could not remember just what came next in the sermon, but he knew that one way or another Rev. Fairforest
had worked up from the drowned lumberjack to the end of
the world. He had talked about the time when sinners would
become "like the chaff of a summer thrashing floor" or like
stubble to be burned till "neither root nor branch" was left.
But Jesus would come down "with healing in his wings" and
would make the righteous like "calves of the stall."

Then, at the end of the sermon, Rev. Fairforest had talked
about "the approaching last days of the earth" and about the
inevitable war between the United States and godless Russia,
when hydrogen bombs would rain down by the hundreds and
the planet would be enveloped by a massive storm of fire, and
everyone who was not killed outright would have his eyeballs
melted right out of his head and his tongue melted to the roof
of his mouth and would spend the rest of his days in agony,
blind and burnt and starving.

"And our beautiful earth," Rev. Fairforest said, "this beautiful green and golden earth that God gave to us for our home,
our beautiful home itself will have become a raging hell of
pain and torment.

"Let us pray."

When Kite first bowed his head and closed his eyes, he felt that he would like to become a preacher like Rev. Fairforest, and he decided that when he got home he would throw away all the pictures he had of naked women, including the copy of *Male* he had stolen. He would find an old abandoned well and drop them into it. Then he asked God to forgive him for stealing that trashy magazine in the first place and for lying about not having any money. But he could not decide whether or not to ask forgiveness for the way he had thought about Mr. Dundean's daughter. He wondered if he would have a chance to see her again on the way out. He might even have a chance to speak to her, or at least to smile at her. He wondered what Ruth and Hampton would say if he went right up and introduced himself to her and told her how much he liked that black ribbon around her neck. Then he thought again about the girl holding her breath on the back seat of the car, under his powder-blue sport coat. And he thought how nice it would be to take her up to his room when he got home and flick that last little button off and see what was underneath. And he realized that if the end of the world was really just around the corner he was not going to have time to get to be a preacher anyway.

As Rev. Fairforest continued to pray, his voice rising and falling, rising and falling, Kite began to feel sleepy again. He felt like he was back on the bus, and Rev. Fairforest's voice was the hum of the motor, and Rev. Fairforest himself was the driver. What would happen, Kite wondered, if he suddenly shouted out, "Hey! Open your eyes! Look out where you're going!" He knew what would happen: he would be back down at Baptist before sundown. He would not have been away even twenty-four hours. It was just before sundown yesterday that Mrs. Massingale and Rev. Sills had driven him down to the bus station. And now that long bus ride and Rev. Fairforest's long prayer and his first night in his own room all seemed parts of the same dark tunnel. But when he came out of that tunnel he would be looking at the beautiful blue mountains again.

When they got back home after church, Hampton said, "Let's get out of these fancy clothes, Kite. Then we can walk out back and take a look at the garden while Aunt Ruth finishes up dinner."

"I don't suppose it would occur to you that I might need a little help," Ruth said.

"Well, just holler, honey," Hampton said. "We'll both come a-running."

Upstairs, Kite closed the door to his room, tossed the *Saturday Evening Post* onto the bed, and shucked off all his clothes. He hung his coat and pants and white shirt in the wardrobe. Then he brought the roll of toilet paper from the bathroom and put it down beside the magazine, folded the pillow against the footboard, and lay down very gingerly. He picked up the *Post* and let the copy of *Male* slide out of it face down. He quickly leafed through it, starting from the back, but except for some ads for other dirty books and magazines there was nothing as exciting as the girl on the cover. She had not budged an inch, she had not gotten away from him the way Mr. Dundean's daughter had—but the knife seemed a fraction closer to the crucial button. He held the magazine up in front of his face with one hand and held onto his cock with the other. He could not decide whether he wanted to be the guy with the knife or the guy who saved her from the guy with the knife. And if he was the guy with the knife, he could not decide whether he wanted to tease her with it or whether he wanted to cut her down—so that she would be so grateful to him she would do whatever he asked. It was very hot in his room now, and he imagined the girl sweating while she hung there waiting for him to have his way with her.

"Are you coming, Kite?"

Jesus. That was . . . He couldn't remember his name.

"Kite? Are you coming to look at the garden?"

"Yessir." He could hardly hear his own voice.

"*Kite?*"

"Yes, *sir*. I'll be down in just a minute."

When he got downstairs, Hampton had already gone out the back door. He caught up with him halfway up the driveway.

"That Bobby Fairforest is somethin' else, idn't he?" Hampton said. He had said that several times on the way home.

"He sure is," Kite said. "I never have heard that young a preacher before to be as good as he was."

"All the ladies cert'ly do like him. But I guess you know all about how that feels."

"A little bit," Kite said.

"Well, there's nothing wrong with pleasing the ladies," Hampton said. "Long as you don't make that your main business."

Kite felt tempted to ask him what Mr. Dundean's daughter's name was, but he decided he could wait until he saw Andrew again.

"That little Connie Crowley's a pretty little girl," Hampton said.

"Yessir, she sure is."

They came around the corner of the barn and there was Hampton's garden. It was not as large as the garden at Baptist, but it was much more beautiful. The soil was far richer, almost chocolate brown, and clean as a pin. At Baptist they had only grown a few things—mostly corn and potatoes and beans—but a winter's supply of those. Hampton's garden had a much bigger variety. And the variety made it seem almost exotic in a way. But the long rows were plumb-line straight and evenly spaced, like the plants themselves, and in each set of rows the leaves had their own distinctive shape and texture and shade of green, all still and tender in the sun. Kite felt sure that from up on top of the barn the garden would look like an enormous green and brown striped flag or awning.

"Boy!" Kite said. "This is beautiful!" He would have bragged on it even if Aunt Ruth had not told him to. "I never have seen a garden this pretty. How many different things you got planted?"

"Oh, I guess maybe a dozen or so in all."

"What's that just this side of the beans?" Kite said.

"Peppers. Sweet peppers."

"What are these three rows right here?"

"Peanuts. You like peanuts, don't you?"

"Yessir. Specially boiled peanuts."

"Well, your Aunt Ruth'll boil 'em long as you'll pick 'em."

"How soon will they be ready?"

"Oh, not before mid-August at the earliest."

Kite walked on down beside the fence, midway the width of the garden. In addition to corn, tomatoes, and potatoes, he could identify okra, squash, cabbage, cucumbers, beets.

"What's that down at the very end?"

"Artichokes. I bet you never have tasted artichoke pickle."

"No, sir, I don't think so."

"You got a treat coming. By the end of the summer I bet you won't eat beans without it."

"Do you grow any watermelons?"

"No, melons don't do too good 'less you can plant a whole lot of 'em, and I don't have the room for it. Andrew's daddy usely has a melon field. We'll get some from him when they begin to come in."

"You must spend an awful lot of time out here," Kite said.

"*Too* much if you ask Aunt Ruth. I usely get up just after

daylight and work for an hour or two while it's still fairly cool. Then sometimes again in the evening. But when the peaches start coming in, I won't have as much time. Or energy. That's why I'm so glad to have you to help out."

"Yessir," Kite said. "I think it'll be a pleasure to work in a garden this pretty. I did some farm work down at Baptist."

"Well, I hope you'll still feel that way after you've put in some time out here."

When they got back to the house, Kite set the table while Hampton fixed the iced tea. Then they helped Ruth put the dinner on the table: fried chicken, potato salad, green beans, hot biscuits, sliced tomatoes and cucumbers, cantaloupe, and for dessert, strawberry shortcake.

Halfway through the meal, Clown appeared at the back door, his legs and flanks wet and muddy.

"Been down to the branch, boy?"

Kite remembered that Ruth had mentioned the branch when she was telling him about the well.

"You didn't go anywhere else, did you, Clown?" She paused as if she expected him to answer. "He takes an interest in the neighbors' chickens now and then," she said. "We've had complaints about him."

"May just have to get rid of him if he don't learn to behave hisself."

"Where *is* the branch?" Kite said.

"It's down in the woods apiece. Not far. When the weather's warm Clown likes to go down there for a dip. He'll be makin' several trips a day come August."

After dinner Kite helped clear the table. Then Hampton showed him where they kept Clown's dog food and how much they gave him. Feeding Clown would be one of his jobs from now on.

When he came back inside, Hampton said to him, "Kite, me and your Aunt Ruth usely take some flowers out to Little Hampton's grave after dinner on Sundays. We thought you might want to ride over there with us and see where your mama and daddy's buried at."

"All right." He had known that his parents were buried at Lenfield, but it hadn't occurred to him to ask to see their graves. He wondered if the Laceys had expected him to. "I guess I better go put my other clothes back on."

"I wouldn't bother 'bout that," Hampton said. "There won't be nobody over there. It's just a little fam'ly plot."

Kite thought Aunt Ruth gave them both a funny look, but he didn't say anything else.

"I tell you what, Kite," she said, "why don't you go in there in the living room and bring me that vase of roses off of the organ, and we'll take them too."

It was the first time he had set foot in the living room, and it looked to him as if it could have been the first time anybody had set foot in there. It didn't even seem to be part of the same house. Everything was placed just so, as if an alarm might go off if you even just nudged a little doodad to one side. The furniture looked so uncomfortable it made him think he was back in church. Or in a museum. Or a hospital. It was the kind of room that looked like somebody had died. If I was these roses, he thought, I believe I'd rather be out in the graveyard than in here.

Hampton held the vase while Kite climbed into the back seat and then handed them back to him, to hold between his knees. Aunt Ruth had an armful of gladiolas.

The cemetery was on the other side of town, and on the way they passed the high school that he would go to in the fall. It was a two-story brick building with cement facing painted white around the doors and windows. It looked bigger and more impressive than Kite had expected in such a small town. It made him feel a little uneasy.

"Have you thought about what you want to do after high school, Kite? You want to go on to college, don't you?"

"Yes, ma'am, I guess so. I haven't really thought about it very much yet."

"You still got plenty of time," Hampton said. "But we cert'ly want to help you go if you want to. There's the Bible Institute over in Willisburg. And a technical college in High View. 'Course I always say somebody who works his own way through it gets a whole lot more out of it than somebody who has it give to him on a platter."

"Yessir." That seemed a long way off, and even more unreal than what had already happened to him. And after all, if the world was likely to come to an end any time now, what was the point of planning for after high school?

As they drove along, Kite kept thinking about the sermon Rev. Fairforest had preached that morning. Especially about the last part of it. He had heard Rev. Sills preach about the end of the world more than once, and even though the two preachers were not at all alike they did have one thing in common. As you listened to them get more and more involved in what they were saying, it was hard not to get the feeling that they really did like the idea of the end of the world. Maybe they thought that scaring people was the best way to get them to be good. And maybe they just liked scaring people. But what was it that made them like the idea of the end of the world? Did they really believe most people had gotten to be so bad that they were willing for the good people to be burned up too, just to get rid of the bad people? Were all the good people that ready to go to heaven? Maybe what the preachers liked most was the chance to show that they were ready, that they were not afraid. Maybe they thought that proved how good they were. Or maybe they thought the good people would be saved, and after all the fire and brimstone there would just be the preachers and a few other people left. Kite didn't think they would be as happy with that situation as they thought they would. It was usually pretty easy to see that the good people liked having the bad people around to compare themselves to. Kite wondered how God felt about all this, how God liked the idea of the end of the world. Had He let people get to be so bad just so He would have an excuse to burn them up? Was that the main reason He had made them in the first place?

He wanted to ask Ruth and Hampton what they thought, but he was afraid they would think he was being critical of Rev. Fairforest. Or critical of God. And he knew they would think that was blasphemous. He thought so himself. It almost always made him feel scared and guilty when he really tried to think about God. He supposed that was what it meant to be a God-fearing Christian.

When they got to the cemetery, it turned out to be a strip of land between the highway and the railroad tracks, with a billboard at one end of it and a John Deere dealer at the other. It had once been several times larger than it was now, Hampton said, but most of the graves had been moved when the highway was cut through. Now there were only about a dozen left, mostly Handegans and Nevilles. The layer of fine white gravel that covered the graves and the brick walkways in between were almost hidden by grass and weeds. Little Hampton's was one of the few that were cleaned off. His tombstone had a lamb carved on top of it and flowers and grapes carved down the sides. It said:

HAMPTON FIRBY LACEY, JR.
A Precious Lamb of God
Called Home to His Maker
January 9, 1954–December 11, 1958

Hampton leaned the gladiolas up against the left-hand side of the tombstone, so that they wouldn't cover up the writing; and Aunt Ruth looked down at the grave and held a Kleenex up to her mouth and nose, but she wasn't crying yet. After a minute or so of silence (except for the traffic behind them), Hampton put his hand on Kite's shoulder and guided him through a stand of Queen Anne's lace back toward the railroad tracks to a larger monument made to look like an open book and tilted up from the ground a little. On the left-hand page it said:

JESSICA HANDEGAN CUMMINGS
March 20, 1926
May 4, 1945

And on the right-hand page:

DAVID KITELY CUMMINGS
October 7, 1921
May 3, 1945

Kite knelt down and put the vase of roses right in front of where the pages came together. He stayed on his knees for a moment, wondering what was expected of him.

"I ought to come out here sometime and get these weeds cleaned off," he said.

He stood up and looked down at the marker, studying the dates. He knew that they had been in a car wreck when his daddy was home on leave from the navy, and he did not want to know anything more about that. What he wanted to know was what they were like when they were alive. Aunt Ruth had said his daddy was handsome and his mama was pretty, but he still didn't have any pictures of them in his mind. "Handsome" made him think of Tyrone Power, and "pretty" made him think of June Allyson. He knew they were not like that, but those faces got in the way of any others.

"What did people call my daddy? Kite, like me? Or David? Or what?"

"You'll have to ask your Aunt Ruth, son. I never did know your people at all. I didn't come along till afterwards."

"Do you think anybody has anything that belonged to them?"

"Not that I know of."

A few minutes later Aunt Ruth came up behind them and put her arm around Kite's waist and huggged him up against her side. And when she started talking, her voice was different: stronger than he had expected.

"It was not much more than six weeks ago, Kite, that your Uncle Hampton was laid up with his gallbladder, and I came out here by myself one Sunday. After I had put some flowers on Little Hampton's grave, I walked back here to your mama and daddy's, and I had no sooner looked down at this open book here, which I always think of as the Bible, you know, than the Lord spoke to me just as plain as I'm speaking to you right now. 'Kite needs a mama and daddy.' Those were exackly the words. 'Kite needs a mama and daddy.' And the funny thing was, it didn't surprise me one bit; it was like it was something I had known all along but just needed to be told.

"Well, when I got back home I didn't say a word about it to

Hampton. Not a word. But I prayed about it that night and every night for the next week. And when I came out here the Sunday after that I walked back here just like I'd done before. And I waited. And I listened. And I thought. And I prayed. But I didn't hear a sound. Not a word. Well—I'm ashamed to say it—but I began to doubt that I had heard it the first time. I should have known better than to try to test the Lord. That was His way of showing me how weak my poor little human faithfulness is. But then when I was driving back home—still full of doubt, still praying mightily for guidance—I saw two little fellas out in a field of broomstraw, flying their kites. And I knew that was a sign. And I thanked the Lord. And praised His Name.

"Well, I still didn't say a word about it to Hampton here. But by the next Sunday he was well enough to come out here with me again. And when we got out here, standing right on this spot, I told him what had happened, and he wasn't any more surprised than I had been; he said the exack same idear had come into his mind when he was lying at home in bed that Sunday two weeks before. So then there wasn't a bit of doubt in either of us's mind. So that evening after services we went to have a talk with Reverend Fairforest. And the next day we wrote a letter down to the Baptist Home. And here you are.

"Praise His Name."

"Praise His Name," Hampton said.

When they got back home, Ruth said, "Me and Hampton are gonna go take a little nap now. If you want to take a rest yourself, you'll be a lot cooler in there on the couch in the den than upstairs."

"No, ma'am, I'm not tired," Kite said. "I think I'll walk down in the woods, though. It's prob'ly cooler down there. And I just wanta see what it's like."

"Well, watch out for poison ivy with those short britches on. You know what it looks like, don't you?"

"Yes, ma'am."

The trees that bordered the driveway made a solid fence, but at the far end of the garden they were more open. Kite

headed in that direction and paused at the corner of the barn
to admire his uncle's garden again. There was not a stone or a
weed or a bug in sight. He moved even with the rows of corn
and bent over to peer down each splendid arrow-straight tunnel braided of curved green blades and sun and shadows. He
spotted a scattering of weeds so tiny it would have taken a
tweezer to pull them. He would get at them first thing in the
morning.

When he straightened up again he saw something moving
in the edge of the woods. He felt sure it was Boydy, and for a
second or two everything, even the bright sunlight, seemed
vaguely threatening; the picture of the Indians circling the
church flashed in his mind. Then two figures, one taller than
the other, came out onto the headland between the woods and
the garden, and he recognized Andrew and Chaplin.

They signaled to him.

"Where did you come from?" he yelled.

"Through the woods," Andrew shouted back. "There's a
path all the way to our house. Come on over here. We'll show
you."

Kite skirted the upper edge of the garden, beside the barn,
and walked along a narrow strip of fallow ground. He saw for
the first time that there was an especially fine view of the
mountains from the rise of land just behind the barn.

He joined Andrew and Chaplin and followed them into the
woods.

PART TWO

I did but taste a little honey with the end
of the rod that was in mine hand.

1 Samuel 14:43

Over the next couple of weeks, Kite got to know the woods and the fields and the orchards and the path to Andrew's house as well as he had known the streets and sidewalks in Thornton. He had definite responsibilities at home—he had to help in the garden whenever Hampton needed him to; he had to mow the lawn once a week; Ruth called on him sometimes for odd jobs around the house or yard—but for much of the time, for more of it than he had expected, more of it than he was accustomed to, he was free to go his own way, as long as he showed up on time for meals. Sometimes he explored with Andrew and Chap (Bass was a mama's boy who stayed home and read and drew pictures); sometimes he was by himself or with Clown. He was outdoors and on the move from early in the morning until after dark at night. He felt sure that this was the closest he had ever come to knowing what the preachers meant by being "born again." But he still had no idea what he had done to deserve it.

Ruth continued to worry and fret and pester him, but

Hampton had told him, when they were by themselves, "You can't let her make a little baby out of you, much as she wants to. I know you understand why she's like she is. Just try to be patient." Hampton had also warned him that he would not be nearly so free when packing started. But that was still several weeks away. In the meantime, the woods and the fields and the orchards lay waiting.

The woods, which Andrew told him were shaped like a Christmas tree—he had flown over them once in his cousin's new crop-duster—the woods took in close to fifty acres, though only about ten of those were on Hampton's property. They covered both sides of the shallow valley that separated Hampton's orchards from Mr. Crowley's pastureland. The path wound through them midway up the tree.

"We didn't make this path," Andrew told him that first Sunday afternoon. "It was here before my folks or your aunt and uncle moved out here."

"The Indians made it," Chap said.

"If you go by the path, it's just over a mile from our place to your's; but if you go by the road, it's a little over two miles. Mama says it'll be better if I don't ride my motorcycle over to your house for a little while. It makes your aunt too nervous. We can go back and forth by this path or we can ride bicycles. My old bike's still okay, and I'm pretty sure Connie's is too."

Chap wanted to know if he could ride one of them.

"They're both way too big for you," Andrew told him. "Besides, Mama's already told you that you can't go everywhere me and Kite go."

"Why not?"

" 'Cause it's too far. You'll get tired out. And we only got two bikes."

That same afternoon they went down into the Crowleys' cool clay-walled basement and hauled out the bicycles.

"I learned to ride on Connie's before I got mine," Andrew said. "That's why it's in such bad shape."

The handlebars were askew, both hand grips were gone, and the saddle was orange with rust. They took the bike into the back yard, washed it off with the hose, and Andrew raised and tightened the handlebars. Then he found some heavy black tape and wrapped it round and round the saddle and where the hand grips would have been. Then he pumped up the tires on Connie's and on his own.

"Let's give 'em a trial run back to your house. You wanta ride mine or Connie's?"

"Connie's is okay," Kite said.

Chap ran down the driveway behind them and stood still and watched as they headed down the road. Before they rounded the first bend Kite turned and waved good-by to him, and he waved back.

It was on one of those first afternoons, when they were out on the bikes, that a red Pontiac sneaked up on them just after they had crested a hill, blew two sharp little honks on the horn, and then zipped on by.

"Was that who I think it was?" Kite said.

"Shirley Dundean," Andrew said. "Do you know about her?"

"What about her?"

"Her mama died when she was just a little baby. She lives with her daddy, just the two of 'em, down near the river."

"I saw her at church Sunday, but I didn't know what her name was."

"She has a bad reputation," Andrew told him. "One time I heard your uncle say, 'Shirley Dundean makes grown men act like fed horses.' "

"How about growing boys?" Kite said.

"I don't think she fools around with boys much. Maybe rich boys. I know this football player that graduated from high school a year or so back, and he told me about one time when he went out on a date with Shirley Dundean, one of the first times he had ever been out with a girl. And they were parked out in the country somewhere and kissin' and grubbin', and he had gotten her blouse unbuttoned and pulled down around her waist, and she wasn't even wearing a brassiere or anything, but she wouldn't let him touch her; she kept turning way. And he kept saying, 'Aw, c'mon, please, just let me touch 'em, just let me kiss 'em.' And finally she said, 'Well, I'll have to pray about it. I just don't think it's right.' So she closed her eyes and bowed her head and just sat there right beside him with those big white boobs hanging out, and he was sitting there going crazy. So she prayed and prayed. For a long time. Maybe five or ten minutes. Finally, when she opened her eyes, she asked him how much money he had. He looked in his wallet and told her seventeen dollars. And she said, 'Well, the Lord says you can feel 'em and kiss 'em if you give me fifteen dollars to give to the church.' "

"Goddamn!" Kite said. "Shit! So what did he do?"

"I think he decided to save up till he could fuck her."

"Shit!" Kite said. "Goddamn! How much is that?"

"I don't know, prob'ly twenty-five or thirty."

"Shit!" Kite said. He had been standing up to pedal for the last half mile.

When they got back home that afternoon, Andrew said, "You wanta go fishing early in the morning?"

"Sure."

"We may have to let Chap come too."

"That's okay."

"Okay, then, let's go down to the branch and get some minners and some lizards."

The branch began in the far edge of the woods, about a quarter up the length of them. The earth all around that spot was soft and quick, and the undergrowth was rank there, the trees sparse and scrubby: small gray gums and water pines. Andrew said that in the winter when the underbrush died away you could see that the roots of the trees were exposed, as if they were having trouble holding on in that soft slimy mud; they seemed to be squeezing the water out of the soil. And there at the source earth and water were one: a live, dark-brown jelly. Then, here and there, you saw small shallows of stagnant water filmed with green scum—that's where the tadpoles were. And then, very slowly (you could hardly tell it at first), the water began to flow off; it trickled over a flat of hard red clay and into the actual creek bed. In the sunshine those tiny aimless runnels of water against the slick bright clay looked like so many snakeskins being shivered by the breeze.

The branch itself was narrow and winding. It quickly worked its way into the heart of the woods, and from there it divided them in half, running at the bottom of the wooded valley. It was surprising how quickly it gained force and volume, though there were, the whole length of it, only a couple of places you could not easily jump across. One of those places was a small pool not far from the mouth. It was about the size of a dining room table, several feet deep, and almost perfectly round. The stream entered the pool in a sudden drop, a little over a foot high. You could hear that splash of water, in the quiet of the woods, long before you got to it. On the bank above the pool, and reflected in it, was a wild azalea, close to ten feet tall. And on the bottom of the pool were layers of leaves—oak, hickory, azalea, pine needles—a dark, ancient, breathing quilt of leaves under the layers of clear water.

Where the water flowed out of the pool the creek bed narrowed and the banks were steep on both sides. That was where they decided one morning—Kite and Andrew and Chap—to build a dam. It was a perfect place for one. They made it out of rocks and limbs and a firm gray clay that they got from farther down the branch, from way up under the bank. The finished product was about two feet high and almost that thick—strong and well-constructed. They covered the whole thing, the top and the front side of it, with green moss.

While he was digging a rock out of the creek bed to use in the dam, Chap had found two arrowheads, just alike, small crystal-clear bird flints. He said they looked like little Christmas trees. "One minute," he said, "a bird was sitting in a pine tree, and the next minute this tree here was whizzing through the air, and then the tree was in the bird." He let Kite and Andrew look at the arrowheads and then he put them in his pocket.

Down below the dam, where the creek had gone dry now, except for one small stream that they let seep through to reduce the pressure and to keep the water from coming over the top, they built a village: houses made out of clay and pine bark, twigs of willow stuck in among them for trees, streets paved with white sand, and even tiny fences and bridges. Chap had been the one who started the village, but Kite and Andrew got as involved in it as he was. They ended up spending that whole morning down at the branch, working on the dam and the village.

At lunchtime they all three had to go home; but as soon as he had finished eating and had helped Ruth with the dishes, Kite headed back to the woods, eager to see if the dam had held. Andrew was already there, lying on his stomach on the bank above the dam, which was still in perfect shape. Chap had had to stay home to take a nap.

"Why don't you stop up that one place?" Andrew said. "And then we can see how long it'll hold."

Kite took up a handful of clay and sealed the single fissure in the dam, the safety flow, which had become enlarged while they were away. Then he lay down beside Andrew on the bank, and they watched the water rise very slowly and create its own breaches in the wall of moss, pieces of which began to lift off and float away. They could tell that the dam was being weakened because there were sudden shifts of it, sudden sinkings in places. In one or two spots the water began to come through with some force, but not before it had reached the top and begun to flow over, washing all the moss off. Then—very suddenly again—the whole thing gave way and a great flood of water fell through, loud and white, moving even the largest rocks, dissolving the whole mass of clay and wood, all of it caught up in that furious churning of water, which completely wiped away, obliterated, the village they had built.

Kite had to admit to himself that there was an undeniable satisfaction in witnessing that small spectacle of pure destruction, of which he and Andrew were the sole authors and the only survivors. He wondered if they had had that disaster in mind from the very beginning.

The branch got quiet again, and very clear and clean except for the debris and the mud along its edges. Then they heard

Chap coming back. He was bringing Bass along to show him what they had made. Kite and Andrew looked at each other and got up and moved quickly back into the trees, out of sight. Kite suddenly wished that there was some way to lure Chap away from the branch until they could get the dam and the village rebuilt.

Chap got within a couple of feet of the branch before he stopped. He looked down at the place where the dam had been, and the village of which there was now not a trace, with a funny open-mouthed expression, as if he thought that maybe he had dreamed the dam and the village, and the morning, and his whole life up to that minute. Then he turned around and began trudging back through the woods, crying, Bass trying to comfort him. Kite and Andrew—not looking at each other now—followed along behind them, but very quietly and far enough back not to be seen. By the time he got within sight of his house, Chap was crying so loudly, so bitterly, that Mrs. Crowley came out on the back porch to see what was wrong. Kite and Andrew stayed hidden in the edge of the woods and Kite felt guiltier still when he heard how distressed Mrs. Crowley sounded. He wondered if Chap was crying because the dam had been destroyed or because he had not gotten to watch it being destroyed. When Mrs. Crowley started yelling for Andrew, they moved back into the woods.

A day or so later, Kite and Andrew and Connie were playing basketball at the hoop that Mr. Crowley had put up in their back yard. The clouds over the mountains began to grow dark, as they often did in the late afternoons; they could see the lightning coming closer and hear the thunder getting louder. They kept playing even after the rain had started, but when lightning struck on the edge of the pasture and thunder exploded at the same instant, they ran into the house. While they were waiting for the storm to pass, Andrew said, "Come on upstairs and I'll show you something."

In the large bedroom that Andrew shared with Chap, Chap was lying on the floor coloring a picture in a coloring book. He didn't even look up when they came in. Andrew went into his closet and brought out a small black-walnut box with leather hinges. He and Kite sat down on the floor near the windows and Andrew opened the box and dumped out a pile of arrowheads, all very much like the ones Chap had found in the branch. There must have been several dozen of them.

"Damn," Kite said. "Where'd you get all these?"

"Different places. Some from outa the creek. Some from that big open field on the other side of the woods. Let's see how many we got." He pushed half of the pile toward Kite and began counting the other half himself. There were thirty-four, all told. Chap had come over while they were counting, and he began to line the arrowheads up in rows, all of them pointing in the same direction, so that they looked like an orchard of small glass Christmas trees. When the lightning flared, the arrowheads sparkled against the cherry-colored rug.

While Chap was arranging them in rows, Kite noticed for the first time that the fingers on Chap's right hand were all the same length: the top joints of the first three fingers were missing.

"You can have some of these if you want to," Andrew said, "or we can help you find some yourself."

"I guess it'd be better if I found some of my own," Kite said.

Before they went back downstairs, Kite knelt down beside Chap, who had gone back to his coloring book. "I'm sorry we tore up the dam, Chap. I'll help you build another one anytime you want me to."

"Okay," Chap said, as if it had not really mattered that much after all.

When he and Andrew were back outside again, Kite said, "What happened to Chap's fingers? I hadn't noticed that before."

"They got bitten off by a horse," Andrew said, "when Chap was about three years old. Connie had a horse then, named Joe-Boy, and one day she was letting Chap feed him some sugar, and the horse chomped down on the tips of his fingers."

"Damn," Kite said.

"He don't even remember it," Andrew said, "though sometimes he says he does."

They were sitting on the Crowleys' back steps looking out toward the mountains, which were especially clear and bright and blue after the rain, though the view from there was not half as fine as the one from Kite's room.

"You know old Boydy that works for your uncle?"

"I've seen him around, off at a distance. He won't ever come up close."

"Boydy thinks Chap has some kind of magic power. He thinks there's something special about him because of his bit-off fingers. Anytime he gets a chance he likes to touch Chap's hand, and one time he showed him this glob of hard clear plum sap, about the size of a big marble, and told him he was gonna make him a ring out of it. Chap told him he wanted to make the ring himself, so Boydy gave him the glob of sap. Chap prob'ly still has it somewhere."

Andrew turned and looked back through the screen door into the empty kitchen.

"I'll tell you something else—if you promise not to say I told you—my daddy thinks it was Boydy that locked Little Hampton in the corncrib and set it on fire. He thinks Boydy was jealous of Little Hampton. He even told your uncle he thought Boydy did it, but it made your uncle mad as hell. He thought my daddy was sayin' that just because Boydy's a nigger and not right in his mind. I'm just tellin' you so you can keep an eye on him. He might decide to get jealous of you too."

"Oh, I think he's a whole lot more scared of me than I am of him."

"Don't you tell your uncle I told you. I don't want him mad at me too."

"I won't."

"Wanta go down to the river? Sometimes the fish bite real good after a shower."

"It's gettin' close to suppertime," Kite said. "We better wait till after supper. I'll come back over."

During that second week, Kite and Andrew had gone fishing three mornings in a row without even getting a nibble. But the first time they went in the evening, after that afternoon storm, each of them caught two good-size catfish. Mrs. Crowley made a big catfish stew with a lot of fresh garden vegetables in it, and she sent two quarts of it to the Laceys. After that, Kite and Andrew went down to the river to fish several times a week, almost always in the evenings. Both families had supper between six and six thirty, so there were still at least two good hours of daylight left, even after they had ridden their bikes the mile and a half to the river. Sometimes they fished until after dark.

One night, on their way home from the river, they found a dead snake in the road. It was after dark, but there was a full moon that night, halfway up the sky, and they could see the whole countryside, all shadows. The snake, a shadow too, was not moving at all, and they figured he must have been run over by a car; but they poked at him with a stick, making sure

he was dead, because they could not tell what kind he was.
Then Andrew picked him up by the tail and draped him over
his handlebars, holding the tail against the right hand grip,
and they rode on home, Kite holding both fishing poles and
the snake swinging back and forth above Andrew's front tire,
looking alive. All around them cicadas were grating away, and
the thick smell of cotton dust plugged up their nostrils. Now
and again, Andrew's handlebars caught the moon.

When they got to Andrew's house, they turned on the
porch light and laid the snake on the front steps and inspected
him carefully. He was a copperhead, and they saw that his
body was torn in two places and was bleeding. He was a fairly
young snake and they coiled him into an empty mayonnaise
jar, and Kite took him on home with him. He kept the jar in
his room for several days, until Aunt Ruth told him he would
have to get rid of it. He carried the jar to the edge of the yard,
and when he unscrewed the lid the smell that poured out
made him gag—a hard, heavy, tainted odor. The snake had
bled more after they put him in the jar, and his body was
stuck to the glass. Kite pulled him loose and slung him into
the weeds and set the jar down in the grass.

They also went swimming in the river, in the afternoons,
mostly. But late in the second week—on a day when the temperature had hit 100 by noon, a day when everybody stayed
inside as much as possible, drinking iced tea, not moving if
they could help it—they waited until evening to head for the
swimming hole. Even then, close to sunset, the temperature
was still in the 90s, and as they coasted downhill toward the
river the air could have been coming straight out of an
oven—except that it was wet.

The best place to swim was about half a mile downriver
from the bridge. A wide sandbar curved out into the water
from the near bank, and on the other side the bank was sheer
and high and the water was deep enough for diving. Andrew
had made a sort of ladder by gouging a series of holes out of
the clay bank. Hardly anybody else knew about that spot,
Andrew said, except for a colored family that lived farther
downstream. But that evening, when they got to the bridge, a

red pickup truck was parked on the shoulder, and when they got to the swimming hole a man and a girl were there. They were sitting down in the shallow water just off the far end of the sandbar, so that all you could see of them were their heads and shoulders and arms. Each of them had both hands on the other's shoulders. It almost looked as if they were bathing each other. When Kite and Andrew first came out of the trees onto the bank, the girl squealed and giggled, but the man hushed her up. He raised one arm and waved to them and shouted, "Been a scorcher, hadn't it?"

"Yes, sir!"

"Sure is!"

Andrew gave Kite a quick nudge in the side with his elbow.

"You know who that is?" he said urgently, under his breath.

Kite turned and looked again. The girl had moved a bit now, so that her back was toward them. All he could see was blond hair and white shoulders. That was enough.

"Shirley *Dundean*," they said to each other, still whispering, eyes wide.

"You sure?" Kite said.

"I think so."

"Who is that with her?"

"If it's who I think it is, it's a guy named Mickey Woffert, and he has a wife and about half a dozen children."

"Damn."

They pulled off their T-shirts and sneakers and waded into the river off the near end of the sandbar. The water was cool and very muddy, almost the color of cream of tomato soup, Kite thought. At first they just floated lazily in the slow current, glancing now and then in the direction of the man and the girl, who seemed to be talking to each other but whose voices were muffled by the sound of the river, except for the girl's occasional giggling.

After a while, Kite swam across the river to the steps and climbed up the bank. The spot that was best to dive from was almost directly in line with the man and the girl, and Kite could tell for sure now that the girl was Shirley Dundean. She was facing him, and he had the feeling that she was watching him, though he couldn't be certain in the waning light. He stood still for a minute, very straight, breathing deeply, making his belly hard and hollow, then firm and full. Then he dived. When he came up he swam toward Andrew without looking in the couple's direction at all. After the third dive, though, he surfaced much nearer them than he had the first two times. As he wiped his hair out of his eyes, he saw that the man was signaling to him.

"How deep is it out there?"

Kite saw that the man was a good deal older than Shirley Dundean. He was balding and had a mustache that seemed to be almost in the middle of his round, red, foolish-looking face.

"There's one good-size hole about ten feet deep," Kite said, "but you have to dive at just the right spot."

"Ever see any snakes down here?" the man said. Shirley Dundean shuddered and squealed again, and Kite took his eyes off the man's face for a second or two.

"Sometimes. Not very often."

"How would you boys like a beer?" the man said.

"Sure," Kite said. "That'd be great."

"See that white-lookin' rock right up there?" He was pointing downstream. "We put some cans right on the other side of it to keep 'em cool. Just he'p yourself. Git one for your buddy."

"Thanks a lot," Kite said. "Much obliged."

He swam beyond them until he was even with the rock and then waded ashore. Four cans of Pabst Blue Ribbon were stuck halfway down in the sand just behind the rock, where the water was still. He took two of them and walked back upstream along the bank, toward Andrew.

"Thanks again."

"Sure thing," the man said, and Shirley Dundean turned and smiled at him. The man's hand looked red and hard against her smooth white skin.

"Hey! Wait a minute!" the man said. "See where we left our clothes at? Right up there behind you?" Kite had already seen the clothes. "There's a opener right on top of 'em."

"Okay," Kite said. "I see it."

A flowered towel was folded up on top of a pair of overalls

and what looked like a woman's blouse and shorts—and underwear. Kite opened both beers and then walked on up the
bank and out to the end of the sandbar. Andrew was standing
up waist-deep in the water.

"Wanta beer?" Kite was grinning delightedly.

"Sure. I guess so."

They sat down on the sandbar with their legs and feet in
the water.

"What was he saying to you?" Andrew couldn't figure out
exactly what was so funny.

"Just how deep was it. And do we ever see any snakes."

"And he just gave you the beers?"

"I don't think Shirley Dundean has anything on," Kite
said.

"Shit, Kite. Are you kiddin'?"

"I couldn't see any straps or anything, and it looks like her
underwear up there with the towel. I think that's why they
aren't moving. They must be gonna wait till it gets good
dark."

"Or till me and you leave."

"*I* ain't leaving," Kite said.

"Maybe we ought to. Maybe that's why he gave us the
beers. To get us to leave."

"I didn't make no such bargain. Do *you* wanta leave?"

"Hell, no." They both kept glancing downstream. "Maybe
she's got on some kinda strapless job."

"I don't think so."

The tops of the trees on the far side of the river and back
toward the bridge were now silhouetted against the pink sky.
The water had turned a dark caramel color and the flecks and
riffles of white stood out. Somewhere just behind them a
mourning dove was calling.

"Did you ever drink beer before?" Andrew said.

"Once or twice," Kite said. "Did you?"

"No. This is the first time. I don't much like it."

"I'll drink yours," Kite said. "Just gimme a minute or two
to finish this one."

They heard Shirley giggling again and looked downstream.
The man was standing up.

"He's as naked as a jaybird," Andrew said.

As he trotted up the bank to the pile of clothes, he waved at them very happily. And they waved back, laughing out loud. Shirley Dundean was still sitting in the water. The man took the towel back down to where she was waiting and held it up full-length in front of her, the bottom edge of it trailing in the water, and she stood up very unsteadily, grabbing hold of his arm. Then she took the towel and held it against her; it reached from her neck to her knees. And then she skittered up the bank, hopping and skipping and wobbling, and giggling louder than ever. The man was right behind her. The towel covered her in front, but the whole length of her naked backside gleamed and glowed in the dusk like a stack of full moons.

"Look at *that!*" Andrew said. "Lordy, lordy."

"Jesus!" Kite said. "God A'mighty!"

She ran on into the trees and out of sight, and the man followed her, snatching their clothes up on the way.

"Let's go!" Kite said, already on his feet.

"What're you doin'?" Andrew said. "You gonna rape her or something?"

"Hell, no. I just wanta see that ass again."

"You gonna see Mickey Woffert's fist in your face if you don't watch out. Sit back down."

"I *can't* sit down," Kite said. "Not after that."

He stood staring at the trees where the couple had disappeared. Then, half a minute later, he turned, strode manfully into the water, fell forward onto his belly, swam furiously downriver and to the opposite bank, climbed the clay ladder, and dived like a kingfisher. And he did that five more times.

On the way home, just after they had turned off the highway, Kite was momentarily blinded by the headlights of an oncoming car, swerved too far to his right, and plunged down a steep embankment into a thicket of blackberry bushes. Andrew was some distance behind him and was also blinded by the lights. He had no idea where Kite had disappeared to until he heard him laughing. He had been thrown over the handlebars, but he said he wasn't hurt, just scratched up all over. They had a hard time getting the bike untangled—they were laughing like loonies, and Kite kept imitating the way Shirley Dundean had been giggling all evening—but when they finally had it back on the road, it was still in one piece and could still be ridden.

"I thought you were used to drinking beer," Andrew said.

"I'm just not used to jacking off on a bicycle," Kite said.

When they got back to the Laceys' house they went in through the back door, and as they headed up the hall Kite saw that the lights were on in the living room. Just as they got to the bottom of the stairs, Uncle Hampton called out to him.

"Kite? Is that you? Come on in here."

When he got to the living room doorway and Aunt Ruth saw the scrawls of blood on his chest and arms and legs—he had not yet looked at himself in the light—she let out a little gasp and put her hands over her face and started whimpering. And it was not until after that that Kite saw who the company was. Rev. Sills and Rev. Fairforest were sitting side by side on the sofa with the curved back.

"It's just scratches," Kite said. "I'm okay. I just fell off the bike into some blackberry briars."

Hampton had moved over to Aunt Ruth and put his arm around her shoulders and was repeating what Kite had just said. Rev. Sills and Rev. Fairforest had stood up and were shaking hands with him; and then Rev. Fairforest turned away and stooped down on the other side of Ruth's chair.

"It's good to see you, Kite," Rev. Sills said. "You sure you're all right?"

"Yessir, I'm okay."

Hampton said, "Maybe you should run upstairs and get cleaned up a little and give Aunt Ruth a minute or two to get quieted down."

"Yessir."

When they got upstairs to the bathroom Kite started sponging off the blood with a wet washrag, and once he got the blood cleaned off, Andrew began swabbing him with alcohol.

"Jesus Christ!" Kite said. "That stings like shit. Lemme do it."

"Shhh!" Andrew closed the door at the head of the stairs and then the bathroom door.

Then, while Kite applied the alcohol, Andrew stood by fanning him down with a towel.

"Do you think they can tell I been drinking?"

"Not if we douse enough alcohol on you. But I wouldn't kiss 'em good night if I was you."

"You know what I'm afraid of. When I get back down there, they're gonna wanta have prayers, they're gonna want me to pray. What am I gonna say?"

Andrew clasped his hands under his chin, closed his eyes, and tilted his face toward the ceiling.

"Dear Lord, please help me learn how to jack off on a bicycle without falling into the briar patch. Amen."

They had to bite down on the towel and the washrag to keep from laughing out loud—and they ricocheted from wall to wall of the tiny bathroom, elbowing each other in the ribs and writhing with choked-back laughter, until tears were streaming down their faces.

Once Kite was back downstairs in the living room, wearing blue jeans and a clean T-shirt, sitting in the straight chair just inside the doorway—Andrew had gone back out the way they came in—Hampton said, "Rev. Sills had to come up to Willisburg this afternoon, so he was kind enough to stop by over here to see how you been getting along."

"I'm getting along real good," Kite said.

"That's exactly what your aunt and uncle have told me, and I'm just so happy to hear it."

"Yessir, I love it up here."

"I think that's just wonderful. Not that we ever had any doubts about it, you understand." Widening his eyes at Ruth and Hampton.

"Kite's a real big help to us," Aunt Ruth said.

Kite was aware that Rev. Fairforest had hardly taken his eyes off him since he came back into the room, and his smile seemed to be getting sweeter and sweeter—but he was surprisingly still and quiet.

"I'm sure he is," Rev. Fairforest said. "I'm *sure* he is."

"Everybody down at Baptist Home certainly do miss you, Kite," Rev. Sills said. "They all said to tell you hello."

"I miss them too," Kite said. "Is everybody all right?"

"Everybody's just fine."

"Are Jimmy and Jarlene okay?"

"Fine and dandy."

Soon after that, Rev. Sills began to talk about how much good the Baptist Home did and what a fine Christian institution it was and how much it cost to keep it going. And pretty soon it was almost as if he was preaching a sermon. It was a sermon Kite had heard many times before. He sat with his right ankle on his left knee, jabbing the end of his shoelace through the hole in the side of his tennis shoe and into the tender flesh of his instep. Every so often he tried to smile at Rev. Fairforest as sweetly as Rev. Fairforest was smiling at him.

Rev. Sills must have let the time slip up on him, for when he happened to glance down at his watch he did a sort of double take and then said, "I declare. I'm afraid I'm outstaying my welcome. Besides, I've got a long drive back tonight. Let us have a word of prayer together."

They all bowed their heads.

"Our Kind and Gracious Heavenly Father. It does our heart so much good to see this family of good Christian folks whom Thou hast made a wholeness out of separateness and despair. It does our heart so much good to see so much happiness and helpfulness and closeness where before there was need and heartsickness and aloneness. We pray for Thy continuing blessing on this Christian household and on this community and on this fine mother and father and this fine young man and on all the mothers and fathers and children in this community and on all those down at the Baptist Home who have given of their lives and talents to help make this fine young man—and so many many others like him—a true serving and believing member of this family and Brother Fairforest's church and this community. We pray that Thou willst guide us in the paths that Thou wouldst have us walk in. In Jesus' dear sweet name we pray. Amen."

"Amen," Rev. Fairforest said.

Kite had decided that he would pray only if Uncle Hampton did, but he felt nervous and sweaty because he was afraid that as punishment for drinking and lusting (and lying and stealing) the devil would take hold of his tongue and make him say, "Dear God, thank you for Shirley Dundean's ass. And thank you for letting me get a look at it. Amen."

There was a long uneasy pause after the Amens, but nobody else said anything. Then Rev. Sills coughed and stood up and then the rest of them stood up, and they all moved toward the front door.

The next day, Saturday, while he was mowing the lawn, Kite kept thinking about the expressions on their faces when he had first come into the living room. Aunt Ruth was the only one who had cried out, but the others had looked at him exactly the same way Chap had looked at where the dam was supposed to be. He only hoped that they had been so shocked by the sight of the blood smeared all over him that they hadn't noticed that he had had two beers. He had tried to hold his breath when he shook hands with the preachers, and he had brushed his teeth before he came back downstairs. Surely if Rev. Sills had noticed that he had been drinking he would have taken him aside and given him a talking to. Or else he would have said something to Ruth and Hampton. But if he had, surely they would have said something to *him* by now. And at breakfast and lunch they had seemed the same as always. There was the possibility, though, that Rev. Fairforest had smelled the beer on his breath. That could have been what he was smiling about. That smile might have meant, "This is our little secret." Rev. Fairforest was still young, after all; he probably remembered how hard it was to resist temptation when you were young. Still, Kite knew that he was going to have to try harder from now on. Now that he was living with the Laceys. Now that he had so much to lose. He ought to throw away those dirty pictures that he kept hidden under his socks and underwear. What would happen if Aunt Ruth ever came across those? She'd have a fit. He wondered if she and Hampton had ever taken a drink. They probably thought that even beer was a mortal sin. They probably . . .

That was the only thing Kite really disliked about mowing the lawn: it was so repetitious—back and forth, back and forth, or around and around, around and around—that the same thoughts (and sometimes the same tunes) kept going back and forth and round and round in his head.

Hampton still had just an old-fashioned push mower, but he kept it well oiled, so it wasn't much harder to use than a gas mower; and he also kept the blades sharpened, so that it cut clean and smooth. Kite liked being able to see the soft shower of grass spraying back over the wooden roller, and he liked the quiet whir of the long undulating blades much better than the roar of a motor, and the melony smell of the fresh-cut grass much better than the smell of gas fumes. He also liked the lawn itself—the fact that it wasn't just one kind of grass all over, but a mixture that varied from one part of the yard to another and that included clovers, mustards, chickweed, dandelions, plantain, wild onions, ground ivy, honeysuckle, even daisies and strawberries.

He had cut the strip of grass along the driveway first, then the patch of fine and sparse wire grass on the lower side of the house, and now he had started on the much larger spread of lawn between the house and the garden. That lawn was bordered on the upper side by the pinewoods that lined the driveway, and on the lower side by the valley woods and the orchards. When he paused at the upper corner of the lawn, near the barn, to wipe the sweat out of his eyes, he saw some-

thing that made him think he had been out in the sun too long
already: in the edge of the woods on the far side of the lawn,
just beyond Aunt Ruth's hollyhocks, a gray tree trunk moved
out of the sunlight and into the shadows—even though not a
breath of air was stirring. Then he realized it must be Boydy.
It was the first time he had seen him in over a week—although once or twice, coming home from the Crowleys at
twilight, he had had the spooky feeling that someone was following him along the path or perhaps lying in wait just ahead.
He remembered what Andrew had told him about Little
Hampton, and now he decided that he ought to go ahead and
try to make friends with Boydy. It was getting on his nerves,
glimpsing him slithering around in the woods and the bushes
without ever even coming out in the open enough to be waved
at. It was like trying to talk to somebody that stuttered. Like
Bullard Thurman down at Baptist.

As he pushed the mower toward the lower side of the lawn,
he made a point of not looking exactly at the spot where he
had seen the tree move; instead, he watched it out of the corner of his eye. But there was nothing to see. Every leaf stayed
still. As he trudged along in front of the hollyhocks he kept
his eyes on the spinning blades of the mower and whistled
between his teeth, but a prickly chill peppered his shoulder
and arm and ribs on the side toward the woods. When he got
to the corner where he turned and headed up the side of the
lawn nearest the house, he glanced back again, very nonchalantly—and that time he was certain that the darkest hole
among the dark green shadows was Boydy's face. He kept on
mowing. He would cut one more swath around the yard, and
then . . .

When he drew even again with the hollyhocks, he came to a
casual stop, bent down and tightened the lace of one sneaker,
then straightened up and sauntered toward the woods, as if
perhaps he was only going to step out of sight to take a leak.
Just to the left of the spot where he had seen the tree move, a
break in the leaves made it look as if there might be a path,
though he knew there wasn't. Even so, he stepped across the
flower bed and moved toward that break.

The first thing he was aware of when he entered the woods was how cool and dark they were. He felt the sweat turn cold all over his body, and it took a long moment for his eyes to get used to the contrast between the bright green sunstruck lawn and the deep green and gray dusk of the woods, where the sunlight was just a distant sparkling in the tops of the trees. He looked from side to side, but everything was still and quiet, though he could not see far in any direction. Nor, because of the tangled underbrush, could he easily move very far in any direction. He suddenly realized—sensed, almost—that the huge leaves only inches from his face were not the leaves of a tree but the leaves of a poison ivy vine that wreathed a tree trunk. He took several quiet steps farther into the woods and then shouldered his way through the leafy branches of two medium-sized dogwood trees growing only a few feet apart. Just as he eased the last branches aside, holding his forearm at an angle in front of his face, he saw the old man moving toward the trees on the other side of the clearing that he himself was now at the nearer edge of. Kite stood still for a moment and watched him. There was something aimless and uncertain about his movements and about the whole set of his body.

"Hey! Wait up!"

Boydy didn't even look around. He must be deaf, Kite thought.

"Hey!" He shouted much louder. And that time Boydy turned around and looked in his direction, but didn't seem to see him. The way he tilted his head back made Kite think of an animal that has just picked up a scent.

Holding his hand up—as if he was saying "How" to an Indian—Kite moved closer. Boydy had on baggy overalls, faded and grimy, a long-sleeved gray shirt, and a green greasy-looking baseball cap. It was not until they were less than ten feet apart that Kite was sure the old man saw him.

"My name's Kite." He held out his hand.

Boydy said something that he couldn't understand (it sounded like "Moccasin"). Kite wondered if the old man called himself by some name other than the one everybody else—white people, anyway—called him. He was barefooted. He raised his arm but kept it close to his body, and they shook hands.

"I been seein' you around," Kite said, "but I just hadn't had a good chance to say hello."

"Yessa."

"I'm Mr. Hampton's nephew. He told me you watch out for the place for him sometimes. He appreciates that."

"Yessa."

"I guess you must live around here somewhere."

Boydy looked at him more directly than he had before, but his eyes were empty, as if he hadn't heard what Kite said or didn't understand. Then: "I know where some dewberries is ripe at already."

"Yeah?"

"Big uns. Sweet as sugar. Juicy."

"Sound good."

"You want me to show 'em to you?"

"Whereabouts?"

"Just back yonder." He tilted his head back again. "Backside of this same woods here. I'll show you. Come on. Come on."

"I guess I better finish cuttin' the grass first. Maybe then, if I'm not too tired out. I thank you anyway."

"Yessa. You holler for me."

"Okay."

"You holler for me."

"If I finish up in time. If it's not too near suppertime."

When Kite got to the dogwood trees, he turned and looked back and saw that Boydy was still standing where he had left him. And once he got started on the lawn again he kept wondering if Boydy was still waiting for him or if he had wandered on home. Maybe he had even come back to the edge of the woods and was watching him again. Up until then Kite had thought that he didn't like the idea of being watched, but now he decided that he *did* like it; it was just Boydy he didn't like. What if it was Connie Crowley hiding down there at the edge of the lawn and watching him cut the grass? What if just now when he had walked into the woods it had been Connie

Crowley standing there instead of old Boydy? What if she had deliberately let him catch a glimpse of her so that he would follow her into the woods? But why would she want him to? *Why would she want him to!* That was a dumb question. What other reason could there be? She wanted him to fuck her. But he was not sure if he could do that or not. He didn't think so. Not Andrew's sister. But he might not have any choice. She might be like Jarlene. She might be able to get him so heated up that he wouldn't care whose sister she was. But she really wasn't very much like Jarlene. He had thought about fucking Jarlene for a long time before they had done it. He had never thought about Connie that way. Not in a way that got him excited. Not until now. Connie was prettier than Jarlene, there was no doubt about that. But he never had thought about her the way he thought about Jarlene. Jarlene, it seemed to him now, had somehow or other, without his even being aware of it, let him know that it was all right to think about her that way. And Connie never had. How did they do that? he wondered. Or how did they not do it? Maybe Connie didn't want anything but to kiss. He would have settled for that. That would have been better than old Boydy.

When he finished the lawn he didn't think twice about Boydy. He cleaned the mower, put it back in the barn, and then went inside and took a long cold shower. When he got out of the tub he wrapped a towel around his waist and went into the kitchen—Aunt Ruth was outside working in her flower beds—and took three Hershey's kisses out of the cellophane bag that was almost always stuck back out of sight on the lowest shelf of the refrigerator.

Upstairs, he pulled the spread off the bed and lay down on his back, completely naked. He set the kisses in a row of three cold circles across his chest and ate them one by one, following the same slow ritual with each of them: First pulling loose the tiny strip of paper that said *shey's kisses Hershey's kisses Her.* Then deliberately unwrapping the foil until the little dark brown cone was completely naked. Then rolling the foil into a tiny hard ball between his fingertips, putting it down

on his chest, and flicking it across the room. Then biting off
the tip of the cone. And then putting the whole dark waxy
sweet piece in his mouth.

When he had finished all three he looked down at the sharp
line across his belly. He had never been so brown there. But
between that line and the tops of his thighs he was almost as
white as the sheet, so that he looked as if he'd been sawed in
two. He wished Jarlene could see him now. If she saw how
dark and sleek he was, she would want to lick him all over.
Like a Sugar Daddy. He remembered, all of a sudden, the
way Boydy had looked and sounded when he told him about
the dewberries—and that made him think about the way he
had finally persuaded Jarlene to go back down to the river
with him. After that first time, the time she washed his hair, it
was several weeks—seemed like several months—before she
would sneak off with him again. It wasn't that she was teasing
him or playing hard to get. And it wasn't that she thought it
was sinful and shameful the way they had both been taught
to. They both had sense enough to figure that much out: the
whole human race would have died off long ago if everybody
really felt the way they were supposed to. It was just that she
was so afraid of getting caught. "I'm afraid of what they
might do to us. I'm afraid they might send one of us off somewhere else. When I think about how I would feel if I didn't
get to see you, just to look at you, I can't think of a feeling
worse than that. I couldn't stand to feel so bad."

It was funny that at the beginning he had wanted to make
Jarlene feel sorry for him the way she seemed to feel sorry for
the animals—and now, more and more, he had begun to feel
sorry for her, just because she seemed to have gotten to be so
crazy about him. She knew better than to make a nuisance of
herself the way some girls would have, but he could tell how
she felt from the way her face lit up every time she saw him,
and the way it clouded over sometimes when she started
thinking about how different things would have been if they
were going to a regular school and had their own mamas and
daddies and houses to go home to. She liked to talk about the
kind of house she was going to have some day, and how many
children, how many boys and how many girls, and what their

names would be, and how she would take care of them. Sometimes, when Jarlene talked about those kinds of things, it all
became so real that Kite thought of himself as one of the children (the boy named Bolton) and thought of Jarlene as his
mama. And it always seemed strange and surprising to him
that thinking about Jarlene as his mama did not make him any
less horny. It made him hornier than ever.

It was one of those times, he remembered, when he had
said to Jarlene, "You know what? I had to go back down to
the pasture yesterday with Mr. Tupp, and the watermelons
are swole up like striped pigs lyin' out in the sun. They're
gonna be truckin' 'em off in a day of so. We'll've missed our
chance."

"Seems to me like they could give us a watermelon party
once a year."

"You know better than that. They can sell those melons for
enough to keep us in canned peaches all winter."

"I'd rather have just one slice of watermelon."

"Listen—we could sneak off early in the mornin', get us a
melon and put it in the river, and it'd prob'ly be cold by ten
o'clock. So we could still be back in time for lunch. Not that
we'd have much appetite."

She had given him a look like the one he gave to Boydy.

"Miz Massingale knows you and Peggy and Nessa always
go downtown on Saturday mornin'. If she misses you she'll
just figure that's where you've gone to. Peggy and Nessa
won't let on if you tell 'em not to, will they?"

"I don't reckon so. That's not the main thing I was wonderin' about." She gave him another look. "What're we gonna
do while we're waitin' for the melon to get cold?"

"I'll be good," he said. "I'll be as good as you want me
to be."

"It's me as much as you," she said.

"Shoot, Jarlene, you know you can be good if I can."

She smiled at him.

"You don't believe I can be good, huh?"

"I believe you can be good—that's just the thing of it. I
know you can. But I know how you look when you're tryin'
so hard to be good."

"I can be good," he said, "but I can't be not good to look at. Unless you want me to wear Billy's Wolfman mask."

He remembered how pearly gray the sky was the next morning, except for a smudge of pink where the sun would come up. They stood in the edge of the woods and looked down across the field of melons, slick and shiny with dew. There must have been a hundred or more. Kite thought about a picture he had seen once of a parking lot at a Volkswagen factory. Beyond the line of trees that bordered the lower side of the field, a bluish-white mist, like skimmed milk, rose off the river.

They moved down along the fence a ways, and then into the field, trying to step as lightly as deer. Kite thumped his knuckle against a medium-sized one they liked the looks of. It sounded like a single clap of muffled thunder. He turned it so that he could see the pale underside and then cut the vine with his pocketknife. He straightened and scanned the woods and the pasture before he picked it up.

As they moved, more gingerly now, down the narrow dirt road toward the river, Kite held the melon balanced on his right shoulder, his right hand spread against the deep-feeling side of it.

"You didn't know you had a date with Jojo the two-headed boy, did you?"

Jarlene laughed. "What would you do if Mr. Tupp was suddenly to come around a bend in the road?"

With a smooth easy motion Kite tilted his shoulder, lowered the melon to his waist, and pushed it up under his T-shirt, holding it there with both hands and patting his fingers against it. "I wish you'd look here what this wicked girl has done gone and done to me, Mr. Tupp. She done gone and got me in trouble, and I didn't even know what was happ'nin'."

Jarlene laughed again—but she also looked a little embarrassed and uncomfortable.

And later on, after they had put the melon in the river and walked along the bank for more than a half a mile, Kite said, "Maybe we better head on back and see how our baby's doin'."

"Don't," Jarlene said, and he saw that she looked sad and troubled.

"I'm sorry. I was just cuttin' fool with you."

"I know it. But it makes me feel bad."

He moved closer and put his arm around her shoulders and kissed her on the cheek.

"It's not your fault," she said. "The reason is, I don't remember anything at all about my mama and daddy, but I can remember clear as day a little baby in a cradle. I can remember standin' and lookin' down at it for a long long time. I asked Miz Massingale and Miss Terrell and Reverend Sills, but they all say I didn't have any brothers or sisters. I don't believe 'em."

"Where were you before you came to Baptist?"

"Lesley-Rankin. In Georgia. That's where Nessa was too, and I asked her if there were any babies there, but she says there weren't any. But I'm sure I've got a brother or a sister *some*where; I just don't know how to find out where."

"Maybe I could break into the office some night and look at the records they keep and see if maybe they tell anything."

"I don't want you to do anything like that, Kite. I'll find out someday, one way or another. I'll just have to be patient."

When they got back to where they had left the melon, they sat down on the bank and gazed across at the field of cotton on the other side of the river.

"How much longer do we have to leave it?" Jarlene said.

"Oh, a good while yet. It'll make you sick to eat it warm."

"It prob'ly cooled off a good bit during the night."

"Some. Not a whole lot. But that's why it was a good idea to come early in the mornin'."

"Do you remember anything about your mama and daddy, Kite?"

"Not a single thing. Sometimes I have dreams about 'em. But I don't really remember anything. Jimmy does. He remembers his daddy. He says his daddy could spit a watermelon seed twenty-five feet, and if the ground was soft he could spit one out so hard it would go an inch deep in the ground."

"Did you tell Jimmy we were comin' down here today?"

"Yeah, but he won't tell anybody, don't worry about that."

"Did you tell him about last time?"

"Lord, no. I didn't tell anybody." He felt bad about lying to Jarlene, but he could tell she already felt uneasy and he didn't want to make her feel any worse. He wished he could think of some way to cheer her up, but he didn't know what to say.

The sun was higher now; it was getting warmer. Kite moved away from the shade tree they were under and took off his T-shirt and his sneakers and lay down on his back in the clover with his eyes closed. Jarlene stayed in the shade. He felt sure that she was looking at him. Maybe just that would be enough to make her feel better.

"What else do you remember about when you were little?" he said.

She didn't answer for a minute. Then: "I remember we lived out in the country, and we had a mailbox that stood on the other side of the road from the house. We never did get much mail, I don't think; and one springtime the door to the mailbox got left standin' open for several days or more, and a pair of wrens built a nest in it. I remember my daddy takin' me down to the road and liftin' me up so I could look inside and see the nest. He put a note on the mailbox and told the mailman not to shut the door and just to lay our mail on the ground or blow his horn and we'd run get it. The nest was so far back in the corner that we couldn't see well enough to see when there were eggs in it, but my daddy knew when it was about time, and so we were watchin' for the baby birds. Then late one night some boys came by and put cherry bombs in the mailbox (ours and some other people's too) and blew it to smithereens. I was already asleep, but it woke me up. I went out on the front porch. My mama and daddy were standin' out there in their underwear. Down by the road little wisps of white smoke were lying in the air just above the tops of the weeds."

Kite lifted his head and looked over at her. He wished he hadn't asked her to remember anything else, but how could he have known that was what it was going to be? She was staring at the muddy water, looking sadder than ever. He wanted to get up and go over and put his arm around her again. But then the thought came to him that maybe she had made up that story just to get him to do exactly that. So he closed his eyes again and lay still.

"That's a mighty sad story," he said.

Jarlene didn't say anything else. A few minutes later Kite began to feel sleepy. Then she said, "You know what we forgot?"

"What?"

"We forgot to bring any salt."

"Mmm-hmm."

"I don't like watermelon near as much without salt."

"I'm working up a good sweat," he said, "so you can take a lick of me and then a bite of melon, and then another lick off me and another bite of melon. Only trouble is, even sweaty I'll prob'ly be sweeter than the melon."

"Now you said you were gonna be good, Kite."

"I'm just trying to be helpful."

He still had his eyes closed, and all he could see was a slow, mesmerizing flow and swirl of lava that pulsed red black red black red black. . . . All he could hear was the river lapping at the bank and a squirrel fussing way back in the woods. The steady warmth of the sun made his body feel heavy and light at the same time; his back and legs and arms could feel the curve of the earth even as the sun seemed to be lifting him into the air . . . floating him down the river. . . .

When Jarlene put her hand on his stomach he wondered if he was dreaming. He knew that he could open his eyes, but he didn't. Her hand was so light that after a few minutes he was no longer sure it was still there. Then he felt her fingertips move along his ribs. He kept breathing evenly and deeply. He could smell her. Then she put her hand over one of his tits. He thought about how it would feel to put his hand on her tit. But he just kept breathing. Kept his eyes closed. Pretended to be dreaming. After all, he was the one who had loved her the first time—after she got things started she had let him take over, except that some of the time she had her hands in his hair and was guiding his head up or down or in or out. She sure wasn't asleep—but she didn't eat him up like

a puppy that hadn't been fed in a week either. So maybe turn
about was fair play. And besides, he really had meant it when
he promised to be good. But when he felt her breathing on his
stomach, warm and cool at the same time, and when she
started kissing his navel—his cock forgot all about that promise, never had heard of it. He jammed his hands behind his
head and locked his fingers together and raised his hips, and
she took his pants off again, just the way she had the first
time. He dug his heels into the ground, his knees were bent
and far apart, his eyes clenched shut, he was breathing
through his mouth. She let his balls bounce against her open
hand several times, until he put his ass back on the ground
again; then she held onto his balls very gently and began to
stroke his cock with the side of her face, first one cheek, then
the other, up and down, up and down.

Jesus! Jesus! Jesus!

Later on, when they were eating the melon, which was ripe
and sweet but not nearly cold enough, Kite said. "How did
you learn to do all that? How did you know how to make me
feel like that?"

"Like what?" She looked off across the river.

"Like I was goin' crazy and to heaven at the same time."

She hesitated for a moment, biting her lower lip. "My
Uncle Jacky taught me."

"Who?"

"You know. Uncle Jacky. Who I spend Christmas with.
Down in south Georgia."

"Does his wife know about it?"

"Oh, sure." She was trying to smile, but it looked a little
sickly, Kite thought. "Sometimes she just watches, other
times she like to kiss his face and neck while I'm doing that to
him. Uncle Jacky says all she really knows how to do is tease.
She's always been real nice to me, though. The both of 'em
have. They have this real pretty mobile home down in this
great big trailer park down there. There's even a swimming
pool for everybody that parks there to use. But I never have
been down there when it was warm enough weather."

Kite felt disappointed and sad to know that Jarlene had

done things like that with somebody else, especially an old man named Uncle Jacky. She was the first girl that he had ever fooled around with at all. The only way he knew about things like that was from Jimmy.

Jarlene kept talking about the trailer park and the skating rink, but Kite didn't want to talk about that or anything else. After they finished the watermelon, he lay down in the shade and went to sleep. Jarlene didn't let him sleep for any more than about ten minutes, but he dreamed that they were in a big white bed together and that Mrs. Massingale and Rev. Sills were peeping in at them through a window.

"Tell Andrew I need you two boys to paint the sign on the shed tomorrow," Hampton said. "Better plan to get a early start."

"Yessir," Kite said.

They were at the supper table.

"And do be careful," Ruth said, frowning at him as if she might never see him again.

"Andrew's helped me paint before," Hampton said. "He can show him how."

"Just be careful."

"Yes ma'am."

The shed had a tin roof, and on the side that faced the highway the words LACEYS PEACHES had been painted in large block letters. And just below the S P was a huge peach with a stem and a leaf, like one you would see in a child's coloring book. The words and the peach had faded badly since the previous painting two springs before, but the outlines were still clear; it would just be a matter of filling in fresh colors.

Hampton waked him at five thirty the next morning, and when they got to the shed a few minutes before six Andrew was already waiting for them. Hampton unlocked the storeroom at the back of the shed, and they brought out the cans of paint he had bought the day before. Then they followed him up into the loft to get the ladder. It took several seconds for Kite's eyes to get accustomed to the dim dust-fogged air. "Mind your head," Hampton said. The loft was crowded with stacks of bushel baskets and lids, half-bushel baskets, piles of cloth sacks, cardboard boxes, machine parts, tools, lengths of pipe. The ladder had to be maneuvered out, like working a Chinese puzzle. Twice, Kite banged the back of his head against the timbers in the roof. "Good thing you got a hard head," Hampton said.

After they got the ladder down and out and had it propped against the side of the shed, Hampton said, "Look back up there in the storeroom, Kite, see if you don't see a old broom. Then you climb on up and give it a good sweeping, just get the loose paint and the rust off, and me and Andrew'll start mixing."

"Yessir."

The roof was not steep at all, or very high, and he was wearing his tennis shoes for traction—even so, it felt funny to be up there, especially with the broom. The licks on the head had made him a little dizzy. He wished that he had eaten more breakfast. He moved slowly to the peak of the roof and stood with one foot planted on each slope. There was a grove of pines between the shed and the house, which he could not see at all; but just beyond the tops of the pines were the mountains, looking even closer than usual, though they almost always seemed closer in the mornings, especially on mornings as clear and bright as this one. To the south he had a fine view of a stretch of countryside that could not be seen from the house: woods and fields and orchards. And to the east, toward town, he could see half a dozen houses a mile or so away.

Once he started sweeping he realized that the letters and the peach and the roof itself were all larger than he had thought: the job would probably take them a good part of the day. It also occurred to him that he and Andrew could easily change the sign to read LACEYS PEAS or LACEYS CHEESE or LACEYS ASS. Or they could paint the peach to look like an apple or a target. He wondered what Hampton would say to that. Or do.

As he moved down the roof, the tin sheeting occasionally buckled musically under his weight. He thought of how nice it would be to lie up in the loft on a rainy night and hear the rain on the roof right above his head. He thought of how nice it would be to take Jarlene up there. Or Connie Crowley.

He had swept about three quarters of the front side of the roof when he heard a car on the road beyond the house. It came into sight less than half a mile away; it looked like the Dundeans' red Pontiac. He was sure it was Shirley Dundean driving her daddy into town to his job at the grocery store. He moved diagonally across the roof, up toward the front edge, and straddled the broom like a kid playing horsie. Bending his knees and bouncing his ass up and down a little, he held onto the handle with one hand and waved heroically at the car with the other. It looked like Mr. Dundean riding shotgun. He could not tell for sure who was driving, but whoever it was blew the horn at him: two quick little honks. If the car had slowed down at all, or if he had thought of it sooner, he would have moved to the crest of the roof and done a tightrope walk, balancing the broom. He watched the car disappear.

By the time he finished sweeping, Andrew had climbed up with a long piece of string and a disk of chalk.

"I just saw Shirley Dundean go by," Kite told him.

"Was that her blew the horn?"

"I think so."

"Well, how do you s'pose she knew I was here?" Andrew said.

"Shit," Kite said. "I hate to tell you, but she didn't."

Together they marked the letters off into four horizontal

sections, Andrew explaining that they would work down from the top, one section at a time, moving from opposite ends toward the center. Hampton had climbed three fourths the way up the ladder holding two small coffee cans, each a third full of red paint. Andrew took them and handed one to Kite, and Hampton took the brushes out of his back pocket.

"We'll do the red today," Andrew said, "and then come back tomorrow and add the black that makes 'em stand out."

"What about the peach?"

"The yellow today and the pink and green tomorrow."

Hampton had climbed down and moved several yards back from the shed, so that he could look up at them.

"You fellas all set?"

"Yessir."

"Then I'm headed back down to the garden for a spell. Take your time and do a good job for me."

"Yessir."

There was no place to set the cans of paint; they each had to hold a can with one hand and paint with the other. It was hard to find a comfortable stance: after fifteen or twenty minutes Kite began to feel as if he might fall over on his face.

"I wish we had bigger brushes."

"Your uncle thinks we wouldn't be as neat."

Kite also understood why they had gotten an early start; already the morning sun was heating the tin roof up like a griddle. They took their T-shirts off.

"We should've started earlier."

"I wish we had," Andrew said. "We'll be getting up that early when school starts. But by then it'll still be pitch-black dark at six o'clock."

Kite found it hard to believe that such a time would come. But he liked the idea of riding to school in a bus. At Baptist the classrooms were in the same building where they slept and ate.

"You remember my buddy Jimmy I told you about?"

"I love pussy?"

"I think that's what we oughta paint on the other side. In big red letters."

"I'm game if you are."

"Shit," Kite said. "I'd get unadopted so quick I couldn't see straight."

Andrew was at the end of the shed nearer the road. "I think I see Shirley coming back," he said.

Kite moved down the length of the roof to just beyond the L.

This time Shirley drove by very slowly, and she was by herself. She was wearing dark glasses, and her shoulders and arms were completely bare. She waved at them lazily, just moving her wrist, her elbow propped in the open window. She also seemed to be moving her lips, but they could not tell what she was saying. They raised their cans of red paint, as if proposing a toast. Once past the shed, the car speeded up again.

"Lord," Kite said.

"I guess she knows I'm here now," Andrew said.

"I don't know whether she noticed you or not."

"Didn't you hear what she was saying?"

"No, and you didn't either."

"You mean you can't read lips? You really couldn't tell? 'Fuck me, Andrew. Fuck me, Andrew.' "

"More likely it was 'Fuck *you*, Andrew. Fuck *you*, Andrew.' "

"Shit, I bet she's going home and put on her bathing suit and put a quilt down on the grass in her back yard and rub baby oil all over herself and lie out in the sun all morning with a little radio on."

"And let the sweat trickle down between her boobs." Kite was groping down into the front of his jeans. "And dream that I'm coming to lick it off."

"We better get back to work," Andrew said. He turned back to the letters.

"Wait! Here she comes again."

"Damnation!"

This time she drove by very fast, but just as she got in front of the shed she blew the horn again—those same two quick little honks. Seconds later she was out of sight.

"What the hell is she up to?" Kite said.

"Just prick teasing, if you ask me."

They stood watching the farthest stretch of road toward town. Waiting. Listening. Watching.

"I'm not gonna stand here gaping," Andrew said. "That's just what she wants. Let's keep working. We ain't never gonna finish at this rate."

"Hell, she's gonna be back any minute," Kite said. "And *she's* gaping at *us* as much as we are at her."

Still holding the can of paint in one hand and the brush in the other, he moved gingerly up to the peak of the roof, and then out to the front edge, and sat down very carefully right behind the lightning rod, one leg on either side of it, both legs dangling. On one side, under one thigh and buttock, the tin felt warm as toast, right through his jeans; the other side was cool.

"You better watch out, Humpty Dumpty. You gonna break your goddamn neck."

"It's not my goddamn neck that feels most goddamn breakable right now."

He waited.

And watched.

The road and the trees were already turning shimmery in the heat.

"Andrew," he said, "see that patch of red in the middle of those woods yonder? See where I'm pointing to? Where is that?"

Andrew straightened up and shielded his eyes.

"I think that's prob'ly where Tom Lester has his watermelons. He has about ten acres of 'em every year. We'll have to take a little hike over that way in a month or so. My daddy's not foolin' with melons this year."

It occurred to Kite that the dark green pinewoods with that hole of red clay in the middle looked like a plugged melon.

"Look back *up* the road," Andrew said.

Kite turned and saw that this time she had come from the same direction as before. She must have taken a right just beyond the bend, onto Ansel Mill Road, which circled behind the orchards and came back into Bridge Road just this side of her daddy's place.

"Damn," Kite said. "She is playing with us."

This time she was driving so slowly that the car was in sight before they heard it. And even after they saw it, it was hard to tell if it was actually moving.

"Damn," Kite said.

Andrew kept on painting. "I'm not going past the halfway mark," he said.

"Okay. That's okay. We got all day."

"You're gonna need it."

The car was still just a red car.

"I don't think she's moving more than ten miles an hour."

"I bet she'd stop for a while if you painted a big red twenty on the front of the shed."

"Only trouble is, I don't have a big red twenty. I don't even have a big red ten." He did not take his eyes off the car. "Are we gonna get paid for this paint job?"

"I am," Andrew said. "But I think you're prob'ly just earning your keep. If I know Mr. Lacey."

Now Kite could see her sunglasses and her bare shoulders. But just at that instant the windshield caught the sun and he was blinded by the dazzling dizzying pinwheel of light. He shut his eyes automatically, but the moment he did he felt himself losing his balance. He groped for the lightning rod and caught hold of it with the hand that held the paintbrush, but in the process he swiped the brush across his cheek and slurped a splash of paint out of the can and onto his jeans.

"Goddamn," Andrew said. "You're making me nervous as hell."

"I'm okay, don't worry."

He looked down just in time to see her gliding by. She waved to him again, even more lazily than the first time, and then she slowly moved that hand to the back of her neck, lifting her bright blond hair off her shoulders, showing him the smooth tender ivory-colored hollow of her armpit.

He grinned down at her and then moved his tongue back and forth across his lower lip.

This time, once past the shed, she did not speed up; if anything, she went even slower. Kite imagined himself climbing quickly down the ladder, running down the road, hopping into the car with her, and heading for the Cherokee Motel.

Instead, he went back to work. But he looked up every time he heard a car. The Dundeans' red Pontiac did not reappear.

By eight thirty Kite's back and shoulders and legs were aching, especially his calves and the tops of his thighs; sweat was burning his eyes and dripping off his nose; the sun was baking the top of his head and blistering his back; and he felt as if the blazing tin roof was melting the soles of his tennis shoes and the soles of his feet. Andrew assured him that football practice in late summer was far worse than this. When he went down to refill the paint cans, Kite soaked both their T-shirts under the spigot at the front of the shed, and they worked for a while with those draped over their heads and shoulders.

By nine thirty Andrew had finished the top three sections of his half of the letters, and Kite had started on the third section of his half. Hampton came ambling out of the pines and shouted up to them, "Why don't you fellas take a break and come back and finish this afternoon when it's cooled off some?"

"Yessir."

"Yessir."

"Looks like you boys picked the hottest day of the year so far."

They agreed to start again at four.

Andrew got on his motorcycle, and Kite and Hampton headed back through the pines. They had gotten to the edge of the yard when Kite heard two quick little honks of a horn. If Hampton had not been with him, or if he could have thought of an excuse fast enough, he would have turned and raced back to the road. Instead, he kept on walking.

"Who is that keeps blowing that horn?" Hampton said.

"Some friend of Andrew's," Kite told him.

When they came into the kitchen, Ruth said, "Lord help, boy, you've got more paint on you than you did on the roof."

At his aunt's insistence, he took his jeans off in the kitchen and then went down the hall to the bathroom, where he stood

underneath an ice-cold shower until his teeth started chatter-
ing. Then he went upstairs and got out his pictures.

At six o'clock that afternoon Kite lay flat on his belly on the
northwest slope of the roof of the shed, directly above the
point of the A in LACEYS (now completely repainted except
for the black shadow borders to the left of each letter). He
had his fingers hooked over the ridge of the roof, but he did
not have to hold on (not yet), and he eyed the road like a
sniper, waiting for Shirley Dundean to drive back into town
to fetch her daddy. He was sure she was coming.

After a big noonday meal of fried pork chops, fried okra,
boiled potatoes, green beans cooked with ham hock, corn
bread, and iced tea, and after he had helped clear the table and
dry the dishes, he had wandered out into the yard and lain
down in the hammock.

Later, Hampton had called up to him, "Kite, me and your
Aunt Ruth have to go to a funeral over in Willisburg this afternoon, so we may not be back till after dark. I'm leaving the
keys to the shed here on the TV set, so you and Andrew lock
up for me after you finish."

"Yessir, we will."

Ruth said, "And there's plenty of leftovers in the icebox if
you get hungry before we get back."

"Yes ma'am."

"And be careful, now."

"Yes ma'am."

He was surprised that they had not wanted him to go with
them. He reckoned Hampton just wanted the sign finished.
He liked the feeling of having the place to himself, but he also
felt left out. He wondered whose funeral it was, anyway. He
might have been able to say something comforting, especially
if there had been children or kids his own age there. "Just be
thankful you had a mama and daddy as long as you did," he
would have told them. "I never had either one. And I've only
had Aunt Ruth and Uncle Hampton a few weeks now."

But maybe it wasn't really a funeral at all; he did not remember hearing them mention it earlier. Maybe they had to
go to a meeting with somebody from Baptist—to talk about

how he was getting along. Maybe they weren't too happy with him after all. But why not? How could they not be?

He went into the bathroom and looked at himself in the mirror. There was still a faded smudge of red paint on his cheek, but he was so tan now that it was not very noticeable. There were tiny beads of sweat in the edge of his hair and underneath his eyes and on his upper lip and in the hollow at the base of his throat. His hair looked even darker and curlier than usual. He wished Shirley Dundean could see him up close like this. She would love the way he looked right now. So horny-looking. Maybe if he just called her up . . . and told her that Aunt Ruth had some sweet pickles she wanted to give to the Dundeans . . . and would she just stop by on her way back to town. And then when she got there, he would go to the door with just his cut-offs on . . . and when she saw how he looked, and when he told her nobody else was at home . . . the next thing they knew she would be sucking *his* sweet pickle for all it was worth.

"You're crazy," he said to his reflection in the mirror. Besides, Ruth and Hampton probably didn't go anywhere at all; they're probably hiding down there in the edge of the woods, just watching to see what kind of mischief I'll get into.

He went downstairs, where it was cooler, and wandered idly from silent room to silent room. He turned on the television set, but there was nothing on but soap operas. He went outside and lay down in the hammock again.

When he heard Andrew's bike, he headed back to the shed.

"I had to come back early and finish up," Andrew said, " 'cause Mama and Daddy had to go to that funeral over in Willisburg and I have to be back home in time to look out for Chap and Bass when Connie leaves. She has a date tonight. Mama said she was leaving enough supper for you too if you'd like to eat with us."

"No, that's okay. Thanks anyway. I guess I better stay around here."

"You must be expecting hot Shirley to come over."

"Yeah. Like shit," Kite said.

"She zipped right past me when I was riding back home this morning. I don't think she even saw it was me."

"What time does her daddy get off work?"

"Prob'ly six or seven on Fridays."

It seemed a little cooler on the roof than it had been that morning. There was a slight breeze now.

"Whose funeral is it anyway?" Kite said.

"It's Reverend Pelly. He used to be the preacher at the church for a long time. Until his mind went kaflooey. He used to have this little dog, a little Chihuahua named Feisty, that he was crazy about. The Sunday after Feisty got run over and killed, Reverend Pelly prayed for him in the pulpit for about fifteen minutes, told about his whole life. Then he started crying and cursing. And not just cursing the woman that ran over him, but cursing God and Jesus too. I was scared shitless. I thought we were all gonna get struck down by lightning."

"Damn!" Kite said. "I wish I could've been there."

By five o'clock, Andrew had finished his half of the letters.

"We'll do the peach tomorrow, okay?"

"Sure," Kite said.

"Can you get the ladder back in the loft by yourself?"

"Sure."

"Maybe Shirley'll come by and lend a hand."

"Sure."

Andrew was at the bottom of the ladder now. Kite walked down to the edge of the roof.

"Who's Connie going out with?"

"Dale Diebold. I don't guess you know him."

What a sissy-sounding name, Kite thought.

"See you later."

It took Kite another half hour to finish the bottom section of his half of the letters. Then he climbed down off the roof, cleaned the brush, and put the lid on the paint. He carried the paint and the brush back into the storeroom and closed the door behind him. Listening intently for the sound of a car on the road, he pulled his tennis shoes off without untying them and skinned his cut-offs and his underpants down his legs. He stood still for a moment, completely naked in the small hot room, feeling himself begin to get hard. Then he pulled his cut-offs back on, folded his underpants to the size of a hand-kerchief and stuffed them into one of his shoes. Next he went up to the loft and got two of the cotton sacks the pickers used. He liked the velvety feel of the dusty wood floors under his bare feet, and then the edge of each rung of the ladder against the arch of his foot, and even, after the first few seconds, the scalding tin of the roof. He climbed quickly to the back slope, even hotter now than the side where the sign was, spread the sacks out, and lay down on them. The cloth was worn smooth and soft, and the hard heat of the roof came through like a rosy glow against his stomach. He twisted around to look behind him again, but there were only woods and orchards on that side of the shed. Then he turned slightly onto one side, unsnapped and unzipped his cut-offs, widened the fly, and slowly rolled back onto his stomach, laying the belly of his hard cock against the smooth hot sacking. His whole body shivered and jerked with pleasure, but he forced himself to lie still. He did not want to come until Shirley Dundean was right there below him.

He knew that she would not be naked, of course; he told himself not to hope for that. But he also knew that he could remember the evening at the river—and would wait to remember it—at just the right moment. Bracing his toes and elbows against the roof, he lifted his hips and let his shorts slip down a more comfortable quarter of an inch. The sun was behind him now, smiting his back, but it would light up the front seat of the car as Shirley drove toward town. And lying down like this would give him a much better view than when he was standing up. He thought of himself sitting in the back seat of that old red Pontiac, massaging Shirley's bare shoulders and then slipping his hands down to hold her boobs. He thought of himself sitting in the front seat, right beside her, and leaning over and putting his mouth on her tits. Then he thought of her without any pants on, his face nuzzled between her legs, tonguing and tonguing and tonguing, until he lifted her right up off the seat with just the strength of his tongue—until her ass was against the top of the seat, his arms hooked around her knees, his hands pressing against the insides of her thighs, her torso hinged back so that *her* hands were resting on the back seat, and her stomach and breasts and neck as rigid as a table.

Jesus, Jesus, Jesus.

He twisted onto his back, his cock vibrating in the air like the diving board after the fat boy jumped off. The sun blinded him: he squeezed his eyes shut and saw colors and curlicues of color, just like in the comic strips and the cartoons. Think about something else, he told himself. Think about something else. But what he thought about was the first time he saw Shirley, that first Sunday morning at Calvary Baptist, wearing that lavender dress and that black ribbon around her throat. And what he saw next was Shirley down at the river, running up the bank, her backside glowing and glistening like a waterfall. A snowfall. And he thought about the couple of times he had talked to her after church, how nice she had seemed.

A *car*! He twisted onto his side again and squinted up the road. Everything—including the car—was bleached of color. He scrubbed his knuckles against his eyelids. When he opened his eyes, the car was black . . . and full of colored people. He watched it slide by.

His face and hair and hands and armpits were wet. But his cock was warm and dry. He tugged the top sack toward the crest of the roof, so that he could blot his face against it. And now—Lord!—his cock was right against the tin, nothing in between; he quivered and whimpered. It was hard to tell which was harder or hotter, his cock or the roof.

Then he saw Shirley's car. It was halfway to the shed. He grabbed hold of the ridge of the roof with both hands and flexed his legs until only his toes were touching—only his toes and his cock and his stomach and his hands. And now he could see her sunglasses. And now her naked shoulders. And now her blond hair. Jesus. Jesus. He could hear the tin sheeting buckling and burping underneath him. And now the steering wheel, framing and cradling and caressing her boobs. Closer. Closer. Sweat spattered his arms. Closer. Closer. She was slowing down . . . getting slower. . . . He in turn speeded

up. *Uh- uh- uh- uh- uh- uh-* She was stopping! *Uh- uh-*
Good Lord! *Uh- uh-* She was turning in! She was *uh- uh-*
stopping at the shed! Jesus. *Jee- Jee- Jee- Jee-* JEE-SUS ...
JEE-SUS ... *Jee-*sus ... Jesus.

His whole body went limp—except for his cock—and he
slumped against the roof. The cum felt like a warm poultice
under his belly. He kept his head down, his forehead pressed
against the cotton sack. He heard the car door slam. Shit.

"Hey up there!"

He didn't move.

"Hey! Kite?"

He would pretend to be asleep.

"Kite? You playin' possum up there?"

But what if she climbed up the ladder? He would not put it
past her.

He raised his head.

She was wearing a crinkly white top that left her shoulders
and the upper part of her chest completely bare, not even any
straps. And tight red shorts. She was standing so close to the
shed that he could not tell how short the shorts were.

"Oh. Hey, Shirley. I didn't hear you drive up." His voice
sounded like somebody else's.

"You been up on that roof all day, seems like."

"Just about it."

"It's a wonder you ain't burnt to a crisp, hot as it's been."

"Naw."

"Well, I guess you're just gonna have the best tan of anybody."

What if she asked him to come down? He thought about
trying to reach down and pull up his shorts and somehow get
them zipped up and fastened—but he knew it was impossible,
as hard as he still was. Besides, something told him to keep his
hands in sight.

"Well, the reason I stopped by," she was saying, "was to
see if you'd like to ride into town and get supper at the Clock
with me and my daddy. When I took his lunch in to him at
lunchtime he said why didn't I stop by here this evening and
see if you wanted to ride in and have supper with me and him

at the Clock. He figured Mister and Mizriz Lacey wouldn't be back from the funeral. And I just hate to have to cook when it's as hot as it is."

"I appreciate that a lot," Kite said. "Tell your daddy. But I guess I better stay around here, since my aunt and uncle told me to watch out for things."

"You real sure?"

"I guess I better not."

If he could have stood up and walked down to the edge of the roof he could have looked right down between her boobs.

"I'd be glad to let you drive if you're scared to ride with me."

"I guess I better not. Thanks just the same."

"Well, then, maybe we can do it another time," she said, looking disappointed.

"I sure hope so," he said.

"Your sign sure does look pretty. You boys done a good job."

"Well, it didn't take much but time."

She seemed to be waiting for him to say something else, but he didn't know what else to say.

"I reckon I better be goin' now," she said. "We'll see you all Sunday."

"We'll see you. Thanks again."

She turned around and walked back to the car. She was barefooted. And the red shorts were very short, cuffed right up under her ass, squeezing it; and the backs of her heavy thighs looked damp with sweat.

She got into the car, backed cautiously into the road, blew two little honks on the horn, and drove away.

Kite felt so tired and hot and heartsick that he couldn't move, except to lay his head down again. He felt like cursing. And crying. But he didn't. This must be how Preacher What's-His-Name had felt when his little Chihuahua got killed. The difference was that he had nobody to blame but himself—he never should have done such a stupid thing as jack off on top of the shed. Maybe God was trying to teach him a lesson by having Shirley stop by like that. That was certainly what Hampton would have said. Maybe there was some sort of rule about not jacking off outdoors. He wondered if there was something in the Bible about that. He did not know anybody he could ask. And the thought of trying to find something like that in the Bible made him feel even more miserable than he already felt. It looked like God could give you a clue, a hint, when there was something like that you needed to know, needed to look up. But of course God wanted you to read the whole thing. That was the whole point.

He got up on his hands and knees and began to wipe off his cock and his stomach and then the roof. He felt that maybe he should ask God to forgive him, but if God wanted to be asked for forgiveness—he knew full well that God knew what he was thinking—it was up to Him to let him know what was wrong. And why. And not punish him in such a mean way when he didn't even know any better.

For supper that night he had cold potatoes, cold beans, bread and butter, iced tea, and a piece of lemon meringue pie. It felt strange to be sitting at the supper table by himself, the house so quiet and empty. It had not occurred to him that he had already gotten to know his aunt and uncle well enough to miss them the first time they went off, but that was how it seemed. What was even stranger was that he suddenly missed Baptist, too. He thought of everybody having supper down there in the raftered dining hall and how crowded and noisy it always was. He thought about Andrew and Connie and Chap and Bass having supper together at their house. And then he thought about Shirley and her daddy at the Clock. He would have seen other girls there, too, he was sure; girls he never had seen before, some probably even better-looking than Shirley, and wearing tight shorts and halters and T-shirts—and barefooted.

"Shit!" He slammed his fist down on the porcelain-topped table, and the dishes jumped and rattled.

After he finished eating, he washed and dried the dishes and put them back in the cabinet; then he fed Clown. The sun was behind the woods now, and the yard was striped with broad shadows and shafts of orange light. He hooked up the hose and watered Ruth's flower beds with a fine easy spray.

After that, he went back inside and drifted solemnly from room to room. He did not know what he was looking for. In the living room he turned on one of the small lamps. Then he went outside again and walked down the long driveway and up the road to the shed. It was the first time he had really looked at the sign from a distance; it looked so bright and new that he felt almost foolishly proud of it. The tarred and graveled road was still very warm, but the tar did not stick to his feet, as it sometimes did during the day. When he got back to the driveway the powdery dust felt cool and soft by contrast, and the grass in the yard cooler still. He sat down on the back steps and watched the bats and the swallows circling and tumbling just above the tops of the tress. A few minutes later he got up and ambled across the back yard and around the side of the barn. The garden looked especially rich and clean and beautiful in the dusk, even more beautiful than it looked early in the morning. The sight of it gave him the same satisfaction that the sign had. He stood gazing at it for a while and then walked down between two rows of corn, the soil dry and coarse under his feet, the broad blades stroking his bare legs. When he got to the far side he turned and moved up the gentle slope away from the woods. That rise of land between the back of the barn and the west orchard gave a fine view of the mountains. They were only a long sharp silhouette now, blue-gray against the shiny sky; and the countryside in between was all shadows.

When he heard the sound of a motorcycle he moved around the hillside so that he could see the stretch of road that climbed from the bridge and then rounded toward the Dundeans'. At first he had thought it might be Andrew, but then he remembered that Andrew was baby-sitting. Then he wondered if Connie's date rode a motorcycle. Not with that name, he thought; and then the sound snored on beyond the Crowleys'. By the time the single red taillight had come into view he felt sure it was Mickey Woffert on his way to see Shirley. The light had no sooner appeared than it disappeared. And then the sound faded way too. It made him think of the ventriloquist he had seen at the fair who held a lighted cigar between his teeth and then suddenly flicked it around so the whole thing was inside his mouth and his mouth was closed and the dummy was singing "Home on the Range" from far away.

A few minutes later he turned and headed back toward the house.

When he came downstairs the next morning, he saw at once that something was wrong. Hampton was standing at the stove and Aunt Ruth was sitting at the table on the porch. It was usually the other way around. More unusual than that, Ruth was still wearing a bathrobe and she had not brushed her hair.

Hampton said, "Good morning, boy," and Kite thought that his voice was louder and cheerier than it generally was first thing in the morning.

Ruth had her fingertips against the rim of the full cup of coffee that was sitting in front of her. She did not look up or say "Good morning" when he sat down.

"Feels like it's gonna be another hot one," he said, and poured himself a glass of milk.

After a moment she said, "It is unseasonable." But her expression did not change. She looked worried, and it seemed to Kite that the two sides of her face did not quite match. He tried not to look at her.

"I slept good, though," he said.

He thought back to the night before. It was almost nine thirty before they got home. They had seemed tired and went to bed right away, but he had not been aware that anything was wrong. Hampton had asked him how much of the sign they got finished, and if they had had any problems, and how much paint was left, and did he lock up good. Now that he thought about it, maybe Ruth had been quieter than usual. Ordinarily she would have asked him if he had had enough for supper and would have tried to get him to eat another piece of pie. The only thing he could remember her saying was that her neck and shoulders were aching.

"I watered the flower beds last night," he told her. "I thought they prob'ly needed it since we haven't had a good rain all week."

He was not sure that she had heard him until she said, "I expeck so."

"Here we go, boys and girls." Hampton brought out a platter of scrambled eggs and bacon and a bowl of hominy. He set them down and then stood behind his chair with his hands on the top rung and bowed his head. Kite looked down at his plate.

"Our gracious and wise Heavenly Father, we give thanks for this food set before us for our nourishment. And for our many other blessings. We give very special thanks that we have young Kite with us now as a part of our fam'ly and that he is such a fine boy and a hard worker. We know that we poor human beings cannot always understand the infinite wisdom and justice of Thy holy ways, but we pray for Thy help and guidance to accept these things that we cannot understand and go on faithfully with our life as Thou wouldst intend for us to do. We pray for this in Jesus' name and for His sake. Amen."

When Kite opened his eyes and looked up he could not tell that Ruth had moved at all or changed expression. Hampton put some eggs and bacon and hominy on her plate, then helped himself, then passed the food to Kite.

"You know, Kite," he said, "I was just thinking the other day about when I was your age, maybe a little bit younger, and me and my sister Helen would spend the summertime, or a good part of it, with our Grandaddy and Grandmama Mosier. That was our mama's mama and daddy. I don't know what made me think of it. I reckon just seeing what a good time you and Andrew and Chap have, roaming around and about."

Kite could tell that his uncle was only pretending that nothing was wrong so he tried to go along, but it was hard not to keep glancing at Ruth. She was eating now, but absent-mindedly, as if she didn't really know or care what she was doing; and she certainly didn't seem to be listening to Hampton, although Kite had the feeling that he was talking to her as much as to him.

"They lived just outside Columbia. In a big fine house. Grandaddy Mosier had made a pile of money selling farm machinery and then lost most of it in the Depression. But back when I was a little tyke they lived in that great big house, red brick, with the mortar struck back. And with a yard three times as big as this one, and full of shrubs and flower gardens—camellias and roses and azaleas; fruit trees and fig bushes. Your Aunt Ruth would have loved that old place."

It was almost as if he was trying to catch her off guard, and perhaps he did. She turned and looked at him—but her frown only deepened; she didn't say anything.

"I remember, in particular," he said, "what a fine yard it was to hide Easter eggs in. Me and Helen and our cousins—about fifteen of us, all told—would go there with our fam'lies for Easter weekend, and Grandma Mo would hardboil dozens of eggs for us to dye. Then Grandaddy would do the hiding the first time." He paused for another bite of food and a sip of coffee. "Out of that whole yard, the part that Grandaddy was proudest of was the fishpond. He had built it himself. Just hollered out a little basin, about the size of a tractor tire, then took all these nice flat rocks he had collected from riverbeds up in the mountains and sort of inlaid those into the cee-ment. And then made a double border around the top with bigger rocks, round and loaf-shaped. Then he planted mint and periwinkle around it, and some shrubs, and then put in half a dozen fine big goldfish. Well, one Eastertime us children got it into our heads to dye the goldfish. I don't know whose idear it was. Not mine—I never had that much imagination; but I was always willing to get in on somebody else's mischief, so I went along with it. We mixed up some blue Easter-egg dye—prob'ly put half a dozen tablets in about a gallon of water—and then poured that into the fishpond. Well, of course it tinted the water a little, so the fish looked a shade purplish, but every time we dipped one out it was still the same color it always had been. Finally, out of impatience—and determination—we went back inside and swiped a bottle of Sheaffer's ink from Grandaddy's desk and poured that in. Well, that turned 'em blue all right. But that wasn't all it did. The next morning—it was Easter Sunday—when Grandaddy went out to sprinkle those little flakes of food on the water, all the goldfish were dead as a doornail. Blue as violets and dead as a doornail."

Hampton was laughing, but he didn't sound the way he usually did when he laughed; Kite wasn't sure whether his uncle had to force himself to laugh because the story really wasn't too funny or because he was worried about Ruth.

"What did your grandaddy say?" Kite asked him.

"He prob'ly threatened to give us all a good sound spanking, but I guess there were just too many of us. It would have worn him out."

Kite glanced at his aunt. She was eating very slowly and carefully and pausing frequently, seeming to study the food—or the tabletop, or her own hand—for several minutes at a time.

"Tell Kite that story your grandaddy used to like to tell so," Hampton said to her.

She gave each of them a quick look, blank as a wall, and then looked back down at her plate.

"You," she said.

Kite thought his uncle looked extremely sad then. Defeated. And when he started talking again his voice sounded tired, and much flatter than before.

"Your Aunt Ruth's grandaddy was prob'ly even richer than mine," he said. "But no more of it sifted down to her than did to me. Her grandaddy was a very sporty dresser and always smoked a big expensive cigar. And when he was courting Ruth's grandmama he used to get all decked out and take her for rides in a fine horse and buggy.

"Well, one Sunday afternoon—and she was as dressed up as he was: a fancy frock on and a big hat with flowers and ribbons on it—they were out for a ride—this was down in Cannonsburg—and Ruth's grandmama said, 'Will, I believe I smell something burning.' And he said, 'Oh, I expeck it's just my cigar.' So they rode on a little ways. And then he said, 'You know, Edna, I think you're right. I smell something too now.' Well, they both looked all around, but they didn't see anything on fire anywhere, so they kept trotting along. And then Will noticed a man on the street waving at them and pointing to the air just above his head.

"Well, at first they didn't know what to make of it, but then they heard what the man was yelling to them: 'Yer hat, miss! Yer hat!' And when Ruth's grandaddy looked up at Edna's hat, it was a-smoking away, just about ready to burst into flames. She had to snatch the pins out quick as she could and jerk it off and throw it down on the ground. I guess it was pretty much ruint. The only thing they could figure out was that Will had flicked his cigar ash a little too careless, and it had landed on Edna's hat."

"Dad-gum," Kite said.

Hampton didn't even try to laugh this time; and Ruth, as far as they could tell, had not been listening. Kite tried to think of something else to say, but nothing came. The stories had saddened him, because they made him more aware that he had never known his grandparents or his cousins—or even if he had any—so he had no stories or memories to exchange. The three of them ate in silence for what seemed a long time. Then Ruth got up, moving very slowly, and went into the kitchen; and Kite, through the window in the porch wall, could see her moving through the dining room as silent as a ghost.

After a few more minutes, even more uncomfortable, Hampton said, "I have a big favor to ask of you, Kite. I'm afraid your Aunt Ruth is not gonna be much like herself for the next few days, so we'll both have to be specially thoughtful of her." Kite thought his uncle might be going to cry, he sounded so worried. "It was a bad mistake for us to go to the funeral yesterday. I thought it was all along, but you know how Ruth is when she gets her mind fixed on something. It was the first funeral we had been to since Little Hampton's. That's why I thought it might be better for us not to take you along with us. I was afraid it would trouble you if your aunt took a turn for the worse. And I knew she would regret it even more afterward if she knew you had seen her get all upset."

"Yessir," Kite said. "That's all right."

"Well, now, the favor I have to ask you is this. I feel like I should go on into town and talk with the doctor a little bit, and then stop by and see Preacher Fairforest and see if maybe he can come over for a visit. So the favor is, I need for you to stay here, just to keep her comp'ny or in case she needs anything. I'd feel much easier about it."

"Yessir," Kite said. "I'll stay here. I don't mind."

"I'll stop by and explain what it is to Andrew."

"Okay."

Hampton was standing now and moving toward the screen door.

"I don't think she'll even notice I'm gone," he said, "but if she asks just tell her I'll be back tereckly."

"Yessir."

"I can't say how much I appreciate you helping me out this way. I hate to ask it of you."

"I'm glad to," Kite said.

He watched his uncle cross the yard and get into the car. Then he started clearing the table. When he had all the dishes stacked in the sink, he walked through the dining room and stood in the doorway that led into the living room. His aunt, still wearing her bathrobe, was sitting on the sofa with the Bible, unopened, on her lap.

"Is there anything I can get for you, Aunt Ruth?"

He thought for a moment that she was not going to answer. Then: "I don't believe so."

"Well, you call me if I can. I'll be back in the kitchen."

She seemed to be watching him so closely that he was reluctant to leave, but after another moment of silence he turned around and headed back to the kitchen.

He was just finishing the dishes when he heard somebody knocking at the back-porch door.

It was Boydy. He had on his bib overalls, a long-sleeved gray shirt, and his green baseball cap.

"Hey, Boydy. What is it?"

He touched the bill of his cap. "Is Mr. Lacey to home?"

"No, not right now. He's gone into town."

Boydy took a step back, looked down at his right foot, and then, tilting his head back like a chicken, eyed the far corner of the house, as if he thought perhaps Hampton was hiding just around the corner.

"Can *I* do something for you?" Kite said.

"I needs to talk to Mr. Lacey hisself."

"Well, I reckon he'll be back in a hour or so."

Moving closer to the screen again, Boydy seemed to be looking at him in an even stranger way than usual, almost the same way Aunt Ruth had looked at him. Kite stood and waited for him to have something else to say or to make up his mind to leave, but he just continued to peer through the screen at him for a few seconds, then looked away, then back again. Finally:

"I seen you humpin' yo' daddy's barn yesterdy."

Kite was not sure he had heard him right.

"What now?"

"I says I seen you humpin' yo' daddy's barn yesterdy."

"He's not my daddy," Kite said. "And I was painting the barn."

"I knows what I seen. I knows that much difference."

"What would I be doing a dumb thing like that for?"

"I watches out aroun' this farm." He tilted his head back again and squinted toward the corner of the house. "We's decent folks aroun' here. Christian folks."

"Is that what you wanta see Mr. Lacey about?"

"I knows my respons'bilidies."

"Well, he's not here now. I told you. And Miz Lacey is sick today, so I don't think Mr. Lacey is gonna wanta be bothered by your made-up tales."

"I knows what I seen."

"Then you musta been drinking yesterday."

"Nawsuh. Nawsuh."

"Well, today's a bad time to bother Mr. Lacey. And he's not here anyway."

"Then I'll just wait outcheer by the well house." And after giving Kite another look, he moved off across the yard.

Kite felt a little queasy, and as if he was having a bad dream. He also felt a hateful impulse to run after Boydy and beg him not to say anything to Hampton, but he couldn't bring himself to do it. He kept thinking of Boydy standing off in the woods or the orchard and watching him up on the roof. The thought that somebody had been watching him without his knowing it made him feel creepy and dirty. And mad.

That damned old fool, he said to himself. Hampton's not gonna believe that old black fool. Why should I worry myself about him?

He went back into the kitchen, dried the dishes, put them in the cabinet, and wiped off the stove and the countertops. Then he stood at the kitchen window, gazing out across the bright green lawn, wondering what would happen when Hampton got home. He could see Boydy's bare feet and the ends of his overalls sticking out from behind the well house.

"I thought I heard somebody knocking." Aunt Ruth was right there beside him before he realized it.

"Just Boydy," he told her.

She stood there for a few seconds, watching him again, then she went to the icebox, took out the bag of Hershey's kisses, and headed back toward the living room, moving slow as molasses, slower even than Boydy. Kite followed her. He stopped in the doorway and watched her sit down right on top of the Bible, which she had left lying on the sofa; instead of getting up again, she tugged it out from under herself—and with such prolonged and strenuous effort that he was on the verge of offering to help, but thought better of it. She put the Bible back in her lap and put the bag of kisses on top of it. Kite sat down in the pink armchair.

"Well, we got another hot one," he said.

She did not reply, or even look at him.

"Oh, but I don't mind the hot weather," he assured her. "I like the hot weather better than the cold weather."

He remembered how cold it got in the bunk room down at Baptist in the wintertime. And that's probably where I'll be come wintertime (he thought), if Boydy shoots off his loud mouth.

"I like being outdoors a lot," he said. "I guess that's why."

He thought of what it would be like to be in prison, and never be outdoors again. And he wondered if there was some kind of law against jacking off on a barn, jacking off on somebody else's property. Not a rule in the Bible, but a law like a traffic law. For all he knew, there was a law against doing it anywhere, even in your own bedroom or bathroom.

"And I don't like to wear so many clothes, either," he said. "The way you have to in the wintertime. Of course, now, I like it when it snows. But it never did snow too much down in Thornton. Do you all get much snow up here?"

She didn't answer, but she looked at him and held out the bag of kisses to him. He took a couple.

"Thank you." It was like playing a game: he felt that he had made a point, but he wasn't sure how, and so he wasn't sure how to make another one, how to get a streak going.

"It sure was hot up on that roof yesterday," he said. "But I think the sign's gonna look real good. Did you notice it yesterday when you all were leaving?"

Nothing. There was no way to tell if she had heard him or not. He thought she didn't look quite as sad as she had at the breakfast table, but there was not much expression of any kind. She put another piece of candy in her mouth.

"How many people will be working up at the shed when the packing starts?"

She didn't answer. He felt more and more nervous. If he kept on talking about the shed, she might want to know why he was not up there. What could he say? And why couldn't he think of something else to talk about? He wished he knew some stories like Hampton's. A good long story to tell.

"You know what's orange and goes click-click?" She didn't

even look at him. Then he heard a car coming up the driveway.

"I'll be back in a minute," he said, and got up and went
through the dining room, into the kitchen, and out onto the
porch. There was no car in sight. And no sound of one, not
even on the highway. He went back into the kitchen and put
the two kisses down on the table. From the window he could
still see Boydy's black feet against the green lawn, like two
burnt spots in the grass. What if Hampton went by Preacher
Fairforest's and the preacher decided to come right on over
here with him this morning? And what if Boydy was right
there waiting for them when they got out of the car and told
both of them what he had seen? The preacher too. Oh, shit.

He went back to the living room and sat down again. Don't
think about it, he told himself. Don't borrow trouble. He became aware that his aunt was watching him again; she seemed
to be waiting for something. But what?

"I remember one snowfall we had down at Thornton," he
said. "I guess it was the biggest one we ever had while I was
down there. Maybe six or eight inches. It was a good many
years back. Anyway, some of us took cardboard boxes, and
some of the rest of us took trays out of the dining room, and
we went over to this big hill not too far from Baptist to do
some sliding.

"Well, we had been sliding for a good while, and then, just
as I got about halfway down the hill one time, I heard a kind
of a squealing squeaking noise. So when I got to the bottom I
walked back, up to where I thought I heard it at, and looked
all around. And then, sure enough, I saw something moving
in the snow. Just barely moving. And when I stooped down
to see what it was, it was this little baby rabbit. It seemed almost froze to death. And it was just a little one. I could hold it
in my hand. It had sort of brownish fur on its back and white
on its stomach. And its ears were laid back against its head,
the way they do when they get scared. So I wrapped it up in
my scarf and took it back to school.

"At first I didn't tell anybody about it. I put my scarf down
inside of an old shoebox and then put it down in there and put

the top on so it wouldn't hop out and punched some holes in the top. When I told my best friend Jimmy about it, he said we'd have to get a little baby doll's milk bottle to feed it with, that that was the way his big brother had fed a pet coon of his one time. So we found out one of the little girls in the grammar school had a little doll's baby bottle with a nipple on it. And so we put some milk in it and sat it on the radiator to get it warm.

"At first the rabbit wouldn't even open its mouth, but we kept on trying. We'd put a little milk on our finger and sort of smear it on his mouth, and then pretty soon he got so he wasn't scared of it. The only thing was, though, that it seemed to tickle his nose; he would drink for a few seconds and then pull back and twitch his nose and then shake his head from side to side so fast it was just a blur. Then he'd drink some more. So that was how we gave him his name. Milkshake."

He had thought that maybe she would smile at that, but she didn't. She was looking at him, though, and she seemed to be listening.

"Well, I kept him for a good while," he said. "He got to be a pretty good-size rabbit. Of course, the other boys in my bunk room knew about it, but hardly anybody else did at first. Then, little by little, other people got to know about it and would sneak up to our room at night to look at him and play with him. During the day we kept him in a big box underneath my bed, but at night we let him out and let him hop all around. And we brought him lettuce and carrots from the dining room. It was the only real true pet most of us had ever had. Sometimes I would let him get up on the bed and sleep beside me at night.

"Then one afternoon I came back to the bunk room and the box was empty. Eli, the janitor, told me he had seen Mr. Cudd taking Milkshake downstairs, and he said he was holding him by his hind legs, upside down. I went right down to Mr. Cudd's office and asked him what he had done with Milkshake, and he told me that it was against the rules to keep a pet in the bunk room. I told him that if I couldn't keep him in the bunk room then I would build a little house for him out by the barn, or I'd just take him out and let him go in the woods. But he said he had already given Milkshake to the cooks in the kitchen to make rabbit stew out of. He said that was what I would have for my supper. He said that was my punishment for breaking the rules.

"I never had felt so bad before. I went back up to the bunk room and cried and cried. I didn't think it was fair to be punished for something I didn't even know was wrong. Nobody never had told me what the rules were. I just didn't know any better. And Milkshake never had done any harm."

He had to stop. He had surprised himself. And part of the surprise was that he had made himself feel so sad. He felt almost like crying just thinking about it, almost as if it really had happened that way. He glanced at his aunt. If he felt so sorry for himself, then she should be feeling sorry for him too, but there was no way to tell. She wasn't even looking at him anymore. She had opened the Bible and was turning the pages very slowly. He thought maybe she was hunting for something to read to him to make him feel better. The empty kisses bag lay on the floor at her feet. He couldn't think of anything else to talk about, and he was tired of talking. The room seemed very quiet now; the only sound was the turning of pages.

He wondered why it was taking Hampton so long, and he wished he would come on back and get it over with. Waiting like this was like waiting in the dentist's office. He didn't know if Hampton would believe Boydy or not. Even if he did, it would just be Boydy's word against his own; all he would have to say was that he was up there sunbathing. Then he wondered if he had left a stain on the roof. If he had thought about it sooner he could have gone up there and washed it off. But now it was too late. He felt like Bluebeard's wife.

Aunt Ruth was still turning the pages, though not so slowly now; several pages at a time. She was hardly even looking at them. Kite watched her go all the way through to the end; she closed the Bible and stroked the cover with her hand. Then she looked at him again, her face sad and worried.

"I'm sorry you feel so bad today," he said.

He watched the tears rise in her eyes, just like water in a

sink, and then they began to slide down her cheeks. She was still looking at him, and she hadn't made any sound at all.

"I'll get you a Kleenex," he said, and stood up to go look for one.

"I have one," she said, fumbling for the pocket of the robe. Then, bending over almost double, she put her face into her hands and began to cry out loud. He sat down beside her on the sofa, put his arm around her, and patted her shoulder.

"That's all right," he said, "that's all right." He felt that she was the one whose rabbit had been killed, and that he was comforting himself.

Moments later, she took her hands away from her face, and looked down at her robe, and smoothed it with her fingertips. She said something he could not understand because she was still stobbing. Then she started to get up.

"What is it?" he said.

"I have to go put some clothes on," she whimpered. "I have to go put some clothes on." She went across the hallway and shut the door of the bedroom behind her.

At that same instant he heard the sound of tires against the driveway. He got to the back porch just as Hampton was getting out of the car. He was by himself.

"I'm sorry I been so long," Hampton said.

"That's okay."

"How's Aunt Ruth?"

"She's just gone to put some clothes on. She started crying."

Hampton put a little brown bottle on the kitchen table, filled a glass with water at the sink, and then took the bottle and the glass of water down the hall. He closed the door behind him.

Holding his breath, Kite moved to the window. Boydy's feet were still right where they had been all morning. He must have fallen asleep.

Or maybe died.

He quickly asked God to forgive him for having thought that thought at all, much less with such relief and joy. "Dear Lord, I do truly thank You for letting Boydy fall asleep. I don't want him to be dead. I swear it. Sleeping's fine." He just hoped he would go on sleeping for a long time.

A few minutes later, when Hampton came out of the bedroom, he said, "I believe your Aunt Ruth's feeling some better, Kite. I don't think we need to be so worried now." He had the empty glass in one hand and a piece of paper in the other.

"I sure am glad," Kite said.

"We both of us had so much on our mind we forgot all about this." He handed Kite the piece of paper; it was a picture. "We ran into your Aunt Ruth's Cousin Nan at the funeral, and your Aunt Ruth thought to ask her if maybe she had a picture of your mama and daddy, and she said yes she thought maybe she did, and so we went by her house afterward, and sure enough she had found this picture, so she sent it along for you to have. We don't know exackly when it was made, but either not too long before or after your mama and daddy got married."

"I sure do appreciate it," Kite said. "I'm real glad to have it." But it was not at all what he had expected. It was a brownish photograph but the faces had been tinted with color—the lips and eyes and cheeks and hair—so that it looked halfway like a photograph and halfway like a not-so-good painting. And the man and woman—only they were closer to a boy and girl—looked stiff and scared, sort of halfway alive and halfway dead. Kite didn't know what to say.

Hampton reached into his pants pocket, took out a wad of money, peeled off two one-dollar bills, and handed those to Kite too.

"Why don't you go up and ask Andrew if he'd like to ride the two of you boys into town on his motorcycle to get yourselves some lunch? I don't wanta ask Aunt Ruth to fix for us today."

"Yes, *sir*!" Kite said. "I sure will. Thanks a lot."

"Just let me be the one to tell Aunt Ruth about it. Sometime later."

"Yessir."

"Then you boys can finish up the sign when you get back."

"Yessir. We'll see you later."

Kite ran up the stairs to his room and put the picture, face down, on the top of the chest. Then he went into the bathroom and looked at himself in the mirror. He didn't look anything at all like his mama and daddy. Thank goodness.

When they got to the Clock that day all the seats at the counter were taken, so they sat at one of the tables near the back, where they got the full effect of the air conditioning. Andrew ordered a cheeseburger with coleslaw and chili, french fries, onion rings, and iced tea.

"I'll have the same thing," Kite said, "and a chocolate milk-shake."

"Instead of the ice tea?"

"No, ma'am. Ice tea *and* a chocolate milkshake."

The waitress was a thin woman with gray hair; Kite thought she looked like a nurse or like somebody's mother.

"Sue Bee, this is Kite Cummings," Andrew said.

She nodded at him without smiling.

"I'm glad to meet you," Kite said.

Andrew had spoken to half a dozen people at the other tables as they made their way to the back, and once they were seated he waved at the man behind the counter. Kite had the feeling that Andrew knew everybody in the place, and he

looked forward to the time when he too would know everybody and would feel as much at home here—in the Clock, at
the school, in the town—as Andrew did. Most of the people
eating lunch looked like businessmen or workingmen or farm-
ers; there were far more men than women, and there was
hardly anybody his and Andrew's age. He was disappointed.

"This is the coolest I've been since last winter," Kite said.

"Yeah, me too."

"Riding on your motorcycle was the next coolest, I guess.
Except for swimming. I sure wish I had one."

"You can ride mine anytime you want to," Andrew said.
"By yourself, I mean—if you want to."

"I think this was just a special occasion. Aunt Ruth's not
even s'posed to know about it. So you might better not say
anything to your mama."

"I wish she didn't get so scared about everything," Andrew
said.

"Me too—but I guess it's because of what happened to Little Hampton, and since they got me to take his place I have to
try to be understanding and patient."

"Do you think she's gonna let you play football?"

"Not this year. I hope maybe next year. There's a lot of
privileges I have to earn by being a good son. And a good stu-
dent. I'm already having trouble with the son part. When
school starts I'll prob'ly be sunk."

"Aw, school's not so hard here. I'll help you out if you need
me to."

Kite could tell from Andrew's grin that he was often in
need of help himself. "Thanks, Andrew. I expect I'll need all
the help I can get."

Kite did not hear what Andrew said next because a girl
with a bright tan and short black hair was coming through the
front door, followed by a heavyset bald man in a seersucker
suit and a red necktie. The girl was wearing blue jeans and a
pink T-shirt that was too short to tuck in and showed a
mouth-watering sliver of smooth brown stomach when she
waved at the man behind the counter.

"Hey, turn around and see who that is that just came in,"
Kite said. "She's so cute. Jesus."

As if searching hungrily for their waitress and their cheeseburgers, Andrew twisted around just in time to see the girl and the man sit down at a table nearer the front than the back. They spotted him at almost the same moment he spotted them, and the three of them waved and smiled.

"That's Lynette Baker and her daddy. He runs Topp's Department Store."

"She sure is cute," Kite said. "What grade is she in?"

"She'll be in tenth too. She's real smart. She's in the band. Plays the clarinet. And she has a beautiful horse that they keep out at Dub Long's place. She rides it in the horse shows."

The girl and her father were sitting across from each other, so that Kite saw them both in profile and could gaze at the girl without her being, at first, aware of it. But after she—and her daddy, too—had looked back in his direction several times, he began to feel that they were talking about him—or, more likely, about Andrew—and he looked away.

"How well do you know 'em?" he said.

"Oh, not real well. I know Mr. Baker from the store. And they come to all the football games, since Lynette's in the band. Every time I see Mr. Baker after a game, he says something to me about it. Says I looked good if we won. Or makes a joke about it if we lost. I reckon I know *him* better than Lynette."

"I wanta get to know her better than anybody."

"She's not exactly Shirley Dundean." Andrew nudged Kite's elbow with his own.

"She has such a cute little face, though. And she's a whole lot younger than Shirley. She'll fill out some."

He glanced back toward the front, but the waitress was standing between him and Lynette, taking their order. When she moved away, Lynette said something to her daddy and then stood up and headed toward the back. Kite assumed she was going to the restroom. Just the chance to see her closer excited him; he suddenly felt emptier and hungrier and wished that he had ordered two cheeseburgers. As she moved through the crowded tables, she was looking down toward the floor, but when she raised her eyes she was looking right at

him, and he realized that he was staring at her again. He
turned and looked out the window into the parking lot, where
the cars were shining and sparkling and shimmering under
the white-hot sun.

"Hey, Andrew." She was right there beside the table. "You
havin' a good summer?"

Her voice made Kite think of how she would sound talking
to her horse: soothing him, stroking him; very firm but very
gentle.

"No complaints so far. How 'bout you? Come on, sit
down."

"Just fine."

"This is Kite Cummings. Mr. and Miz Lacey's nephew.
This is Lynette Baker. Her daddy runs the Topp's Department Store."

They smiled at each other and nodded.

"I'm glad to meet you," Kite said.

"Daddy said he thought that was who you were," she told
him. "That's why I wanted to come say hello."

"I sure am glad you did," Kite said.

Up close, her hair was not black but dark brown and looked
neat and tousled at the same time; there was a little tendril of
it that curled under each of her ears and tickled the sides of
her neck.

"I also have a favor to ask of the both of you." She ducked
her head a little. Even so, Kite could not understand why he
continued to think of her as shy when she had walked right
up and sat down and started talking to them as if they were all
three old friends.

"Shoot," Andrew said.

But before she could tell them the favor, the waitress was
there, plopping down their food.

"Don't let me interrupt your lunch," Lynette said. "You all
go on and eat. What I wanted to ask you"—and now she was
looking directly at Kite, who looked back very solemnly, all
the while churning his milkshake with the straw—"is
whether or not your uncle has already signed up everybody
for the shed for this summer."

"I don't think so," Kite said. "Not as far as I know."

"Then do you think there might be any chance of me gettin' on?"

"Not a chance," Andrew said. "Unless me and Kite put in a good word for you with the boss."

She gave them a playfully pleading grin. "I sure would like to work out there with you all. I can work for Daddy if I have to, but I been working at Topp's all winter on the weekends."

"I'll ask my uncle soon as I get back home," Kite said. "You want me to call you?"

"I sure would appreciate it."

"You ever worked at a shed before?" Andrew said.

Kite had uncapped the bottle of catsup and was holding it in midair above his open cheeseburger. But the catsup wasn't coming. After a few seconds, he hit the bottom of the bottle with the heel of his hand. The bottle cracked open all the way down one side, and most of the catsup gushed onto his plate, covering the burger and the french fries and drooling onto the table, while he carefully held the two halves of the bottle together, as if hoping for some sort of magic mending.

"Oh, shit!" Kite said. Then, glancing at Lynette and blushing: "Excuse me." But when he saw how hard she was trying not to laugh, he laughed out loud himself; and then she and Andrew did too, but louder and longer than he had. He didn't think it was all that funny, and he felt like everybody in the place was looking at him. Even so, he was glad that Lynette was not giggling or covering her face with her hands the way girls sometimes did; she was laughing out loud, her mouth wide open. There was not much he could do but sit there, still holding the bottle with both hands—horizontally now, so that no more catsup would spill out, though there wasn't much left to spill. Then the waitress came up and stuck a tray under the bottle, and he put it down, very gently.

"I guess you want another order," she said, as if soaking the first one with catsup should have satisfied his appetite.

"Yes, ma'am," he said, "I sure do."

She maneuvered his plate onto the tray. Lynette and Andrew had stopped laughing and were looking at him more sympathetically. Lynette started wiping off the table with paper napkins. Kite had so much catsup on both hands that he started licking some of it off before trying to use the napkins. Lynette reached over and took his left hand by the wrist and pulled it toward her and started wiping the catsup off. A sudden stinging at the base of his thumb made him lift his hand away from hers; but when he did that she misunderstood (he guessed): she raised his hand toward her mouth and started licking the catsup off, her dark eyes twinkling at him. That made Andrew start laughing again, and Kite felt himself blushing even hotter than before. He reckoned his face must be as red as the catsup. But he didn't care, even though he was sure that the feel of her tongue on his fingers was going to give him a hard-on any minute. Then she suddenly pushed his hand away from her mouth and turned his wrist as if she were going to take his pulse.

"You're bleeding," she told him. And he saw then that the streak of red on the side of his hand was both darker and brighter than the catsup. "You cut yourself."

He pulled his hand away from hers so that he could examine it himself. When he pressed the cushion of flesh at the side of his palm, the blood flowed more freely.

"I better go wash it off," he said. Andrew had stopped laughing. "I'll be right back," and he smiled at the sober looks they were giving him.

The man from behind the counter intercepted him before he got to the restroom door.

"You okay, son?"

"Yessir. I just cut my hand a little bit. I didn't even know it at first."

"I sure am sorry. It's not bad cut, is it?"

"No, sir." He held his hand up. "Just a scratch." He felt like the hero in a cowboy movie.

"I'll go get you a Band-Aid," the man said.

Kite went into the restroom and turned on the cold water and washed his hands off. He still couldn't see or feel where the cut was—until a trace of blood seeped out again. He

rinsed it off and then folded a paper towel and held it against
the cut.

He looked at himself in the mirror. His face seemed a little
mottled, but his eyes were shining and dancing, the way they
did when he had a fever. He felt so hungry and light-headed,
and everything seemed so much more real than usual—that it
seemed unreal. When he thought about Lynette licking his
fingers, and when he thought about her working at the shed
all summer, he felt himself getting hard. Then he imagined
for a moment that he was back in the restroom on the bus. He
looked around to see if there was anything written on the
walls, but there wasn't. He turned back to the mirror and
sang to himself under his breath:

> Oh sweet Lynette Baker,
> I'd like to take her
> Home with me right now

Somebody tapped on the door, and the man from behind
the counter came in.

"By the way," he said, "my name's Roy Grazandos."

"I'm glad to meet you. Kite Cummings."

"I couldn't find any Band-Aids, but I did find a little anti-
septic." He pulled a half-empty half pint of bourbon out from
under his apron. "Hold your hand over the basin here. Now,
where's it cut at?"

He sloshed a little bourbon onto the spot Kite pointed to.
"That sting?"

"Little bit."

"I don't think there's any glass in it, do you?"

"No sir."

He looked at Kite's reflection in the mirror. "You look a little green around the gills. You want a slug?"

"No thanks."

"Well, I think you're gonna be okay, don't you?"

"Oh sure, I'm fine," Kite said.

When they came out of the restroom, Lynette had gone

back to her daddy's table, but she waved at him and smiled. Andrew had almost finished eating.

"You okay?"

"Sure."

He sat down, and in a few minutes Sue Bee brought him a whole new order and a little bowl of catsup with a spoon in it.

Farther down the branch from the spot where they had built the dam, the creek bed widened into a shallow, sandy-bottomed oval almost ten feet across and half again that long.

"This is Chap's swimming hole," Andrew said, though it was not really deep enough for anybody to swim in. "I used to come down here to go wading before I was big enough to go down to the river."

On the higher bank at that spot, growing on two tremendous hickory trees, was a muscadine vine, one of dozens in the woods. One thick rope of it, hanging as it did between the two trees, made a perfect swing. You could swing from one bank to the other or drop off in the water. Andrew had been swinging on it for a good many years; the bark was worn off in places and the blond wood was smooth and shiny. Chap, on the other hand, had just started swinging.

"When do the grapes get ripe?" Kite asked.

"Not until early fall. They're not very big, most years, but they're good and sweet. You have to climb up in the trees if you wanta get 'em before the birds do. One day last fall—it was a real hot day—me and Chap had been up in these trees for about an hour eating muscadines. Chap always says he's supposed to have the ones that fall on the ground or in the branch because he can't pick 'em as fast as I can, but he does pretty good. Anyway, that day he ate so many he got sick and couldn't climb down, and he started vomiting and just about fell out of the tree.

"In the late fall, after the grapes are done and the vines have dried out some, you can cut off pieces of the vine about the size of your finger and smoke 'em just like cigarettes. And you can almost taste the grape in 'em. You can smoke 'em in the spring and summer too, but when the sap's up they're hard to draw on and hard to keep lit."

That afternoon, after the three of them had been racing crawfish in the wide, shallow part of the branch, Andrew and Kite tried swinging on the vine at the same time, and their combined weight caused it to give a little, so that it hung a bit lower and was not quite as good for swinging as it had been. Chap told them they would have to stop swinging on it at all, even one at a time; they had gotten too heavy for it. So they stopped, and Chap soon got used to the vine being lower; it seemed just as good as ever. But the next day Kite was chasing Andrew downhill through the woods and Andrew, without even thinking, grabbed onto the vine to swing across the creek—but the vine pulled loose somewhere high up in the trees, the whole thing. Andrew landed in the middle of the branch with his jeans and his tennis shoes on, still holding onto the vine, green leaves all around him. Kite busted out laughing. And then Andrew did too. But Chap, who had been following along behind, started crying as loud as he could bellow, because now the swing was ruined for good.

Soon after that they began to wander farther down the branch in hopes of finding another such vine and another good place to wade in. Just a day or so before Andrew had pulled the swing down, just as they got to that spot one afternoon, they had seen a cottonmouth slide off the bank and into

the branch and up under a large rock. They waited for him a
long time that same day, but he never did show. The next afternoon they sneaked up on him: he was lying on the bank in
the sun again, stretched out straight as an arrow; and Andrew
crushed his head with a rock almost as big as the one the
snake had hidden under the day before. And even though his
head was crushed and pinned under the rock, his body wrig-
gled and switched back and forth for a long time, violently at
first and then it got still and only shivered a little now and
then. Chap said he didn't see how anything with a cotton
mouth could hurt you, that if anything with a cotton mouth
bit you, you wouldn't even feel it. Andrew told him you
might not feel it right off, if you had been playing in the water
and your leg was cold and you had been scraping it on
branches and rocks—you might not feel it any more than a
bee sting, right when it bit you. But it wouldn't be long, he
would guarantee, before you began to feel it all over—inside
your head and your stomach and your arms and legs. That
cotton mouth could kill you quick as anything, Andrew said.
After that, Chap was afraid to go wading in that part of the
branch.

But the section of the branch from the hickory trees down
to the narrowest part of the woods, which was also the edge of
Hampton's and Mr. Crowley's property, had little to offer;
much of it was choked with honeysuckle, blackberry bushes,
or kudzu. More than once, Kite, Andrew, and Chap found
themselves standing at the barbed-wire fence that enclosed
Mr. Duncan's pasture and pigsty, gazing wistfully at the far
side of it, where the woods widened again. There were signs
along the fence that said NO TRESPASSING, and Andrew and
Chap had been told not to cross that fence. All three of them
knew there was something especially sinful about trespassing,
because every Sunday morning for as long as they could remember they had prayed in church to be forgiven for it. And
yet, that also made it seem almost inevitable: surely, after all
those Sunday mornings, they had accumulated enough forgiveness to take care of one single trespass. They also knew
that Mr. Duncan went to church and prayed the same prayer,

and had therefore forgiven them all in advance, just as they had agreed to forgive anybody who trespassed on Hampton's or Mr. Crowley's property.

Andrew said, "Why don't you get your aunt and uncle to let you camp out down here in the woods one night with me and Chap? We've done it before—in the fall, usely, or early spring, before the mosquitoes get too bad—but we could talk 'em into letting us do it now. Then we could get up early in the morning before anybody else wakes up and follow the branch all the way to the river."

"Is that where it goes to?" Kite said.

"Well, sure. Where did you think it goes to?"

Kite had never given much thought one way or the other to where the branch went after it disappeared into Mr. Duncan's woods. He tried not to act too surprised, but that bit of information had struck him as very oddly special and satisfying. The water that he waded in and caught crawfish, minnows, and tadpoles out of one day was the same water that he went fishing and swimming in the next day. Or maybe that very same evening. He felt a shiver of delight identical to the one he had felt when he suddenly realized that the muscadine jelly he had been eating on toast for breakfast every morning had been made from grapes off the same vines that he climbed on and swung from down in the woods. Everything was connected.

But when the camping-out was mentioned, Aunt Ruth, right off the bat, said, "Absolutely not. No telling what might happen."

Uncle Hampton, on the other hand, thought it was a fine idea (at first they were even afraid that he might want to join them), so it was two against one. Not that that necessarily meant anything. But when the Crowleys said okay, that made it four against one; and Mrs. Crowley's word carried considerable weight because she was the one who had eased Aunt Ruth's mind about the motorcycle.

For the campsite—in spite of the cottonmouth they had killed nearby—they decided on the open and level spot near the wide and shallow part of the branch. Aunt Ruth had heard that if you laid a rope all the way around the camp no snake would crawl over it, so they promised her they would do that.

They spent a good part of the day gathering firewood and hauling sacks of pine needles to spread thick where their quilts would be placed. Late in the afternoon, while Andrew was fixing rocks in a circle for the campfire and Chap was raking leaves out of the branch and scooping out a place for them to put their canteens and Coca-Colas to keep them cool, Kite went back to the house to get his supplies for the night. When he got back down to the branch, Andrew and Chap were standing a few feet apart and gazing down at the pieces of a big black snake that had been chopped into several pieces.

"What happened?"

"I was back up the hill looking for some rocks," Andrew said, "and this poor old snake crawled across Chap's foot, and I guess it just scared him so bad that he hacked it all up with the hoe."

"It did not scare me, either," Chap said.

"What did you kill it for then?" Andrew said. "It's just a blacksnake; they won't hurt you." He nudged one of the sections of the snake with his toe. The belly was white, and the inside of the body looked tough and grayish, with white strings running all through it. The blood looked dark and thick.

"I know that," Chap said. "I know what kind it is."

"Why'd you kill it then?'

"It didn't have to crawl right over my foot like that," Chap said.

"You didn't have to butcher it all up, either. When it's dead it's dead."

"It sure is dead now," Kite said.

That night they built a fire and roasted weenies and warmed up the chili that Mrs. Crowley had made for them. Each of them ate two hot dogs, a deviled egg, a whole cucumber pickle, and potato chips and drank a Coca-Cola. After that, they toasted marshmallows over the embers of the fire. Kite lay back and watched the smoke drift up through the gently bobbing leaves. It was already dusk at the bottom of the woods, but the tops of the tallest trees still held the copper-colored sunlight. Moments later, when he sat up again, the red sunset made it look as if the woods were on fire at the crest of the hill.

They went to bed early because they were planning to wake up at dawn, but they had trouble falling asleep. They lay on the quilts side by side, talking softly, and with longer and longer silences, slapping at an occasional mosquito and gazing into the throbbing darkness all around them. Directly overhead, they could see small patches of bright stars.

"What was it like where you lived before, Kite?" Chap said.

"It was okay. Just like living at school. Like if you stayed at school all the time instead of coming home every afternoon the way Andrew does and the way you will next year. There was a great big bunk room, where me and most of the other fellas my age slept. And you ate supper and breakfast together, not just lunch."

Andrew said, "That dudn't sound too bad, does it?"

"Were there any woods?" Chap said.

"Not nearby. Not like these. And there weren't any mountains, either. Not even any hills. Just flat. I never had seen any mountains till I got up here."

"You ever seen the ocean?" Andrew said.

"Nope."

"Me neither."

"Me neither," Chap said.

"I never did see it that I can remember," Kite said. "I may have seen it when I was a baby, but I don't remember it—and there's nobody now to tell me what I did see and what I didn't."

They got up the next morning before sunrise. The air was so damp, close to the creek, it was almost chilly, but Andrew uncovered the coals of the fire and soon had it blazing again. For breakfast they had cereal, to start with, and ate it right out of the boxes, which could be made into little rectangular bowls if you opened them up just right. Then they made toast—fried it in a big black frying pan that Chap said looked and felt as big and heavy as a manhole cover. And they had muscadine jelly to spread on it. And cool milk that tasted tinny because it had been in the canteens. And up at the houses they were all still asleep.

When they finished breakfast, they cleaned the pans in the creek, scouring them with sand. They put out the fire, rolled up the quilts, and put them up in a tree. Then they headed downstream. For some reason—excitement or overconfidence or perhaps just to make it a greater challenge—they took no hatchets or knives with them, nothing like that. Each of them had two nickel boxes of raisins, and Kite and Andrew carried canteens.

When they got to the barbed-wire fence, Andrew said, "Okay, now, Chap, you sure you wanta go? It's no turning back after this."

"I'm sure," Chap said. "I can keep up."

Kite, holding on to one of the posts, had already climbed over. Andrew picked Chap up from behind, holding him just under his arms, and lifted him across the top strand of wire to Kite, who took him with both hands at his waist and set him down, surprised at how light he was. Kite thought for a moment that this was going to make Chap angry, but if it did he didn't show it. Maybe Andrew had been hoping it would make him mad and provide an excuse to leave him behind.

They were out of the woods now, although still in their long blue shadow, and they were off their own land. Mr. Duncan's pasture took in about ten acres. A few weeping willows grew along the branch there, and a large cedar on the hillside; no other trees. They moved into the pale sunlight. The grass was white with dew, and their shoes and socks were soon soaking wet. There were no cattle in sight, so they must have been on the far side of the hill, at the barn. But the lower corner of the field, near the branch, was taken up by a pigsty, and a tremendous reddish-brown sow lowered her head and followed them with eyes they could hardly see for all the mud caked around them.

When they entered the woods again, there were far more oaks and hickories and fewer pines than in their own woods. At ground level these woods were more open and spacious but also darker, because the foliage was much denser, like a high green ceiling. A smooth, narrow path ran alongside the branch, and it was easy going for almost three quarters of a mile. The air was still cool and sweet, and the birds and squirrels were making a companionable racket. Kite and Andrew and Chap were not talking much at all. Here and there they saw pools that looked as if they might be good places to find arrowheads, and they promised themselves they would come back to them. They kept an eye out for vines that might be good to swing on, and once or twice they stopped to test those that looked promising, but each time they were disappointed.

They came next to a section of woods where a great many trees had been cut down and there were countless stumps, each about a foot high. For almost fifty yards Kite and Andrew made their way by jumping from one stump to the next, never touching the ground. And even Chap could make five or six jumps in a row before he missed one.

Soon after that, though, they found themselves at the edge of a swamp. They could still see the course the creek followed, but the ground was pudding soft under a cover of kudzu, which was strangling the smaller trees and would devour everything in sight by midsummer. In order to skirt the swamp they had to move away from the branch, and that led them out of the woods and into a field of broomstraw. About midway through the field—they were moving parallel to the creek again—they came to a place where the blackberry bushes were so dense and tangled there was no way to get through them.

"I tried going through a briar patch like this on a bicycle one time," Kite said. "I ain't about to try it on foot." He and Andrew laughed.

They had to veer uphill and away from the branch again to get around the briar path. A few berries were beginning to ripen, but they didn't find any that were sweet-ripe yet. They were almost at the top of the hill before the vines thinned out and they saw a place they could get through and turned again toward the river. Directly ahead of them, a little higher than they were and perhaps a mile and a half away—though it seemed much closer because they saw it just over the tops of the trees at the near edge of the woods and could not see the stretch of land in between—directly ahead of them they saw a large field planted in a grass crop of some sort. Andrew said it was probably barley but it could be clover; it was hard to tell from this far off. At any rate, it was an awfully good stand to have been growing on the slope of a hill, and a fine sight to come across unexpectedly. They all three stopped and looked at it as if it were a bird or an animal that they did not see very often. It was as green and fresh-looking as a bed of mint, and it was bordered on the far side by a pinewoods, which was almost black beside the bright shiny greenness of it. And above the pines, in front of the sky, the lilac mountains, appearing taller and closer at hand than usual and for the same reason that the field seemed close at hand.

When Andrew and Kite turned and started downhill again, Chap said, "Let's see if we can make it to that field, want to?" And Kite could tell that for Chap, even more than for himself, the field, unlike a bird or an animal, which would have taken flight at once and at once become a memory—the field was like an object; not a goal at all, in spite of their wanting to get there, but an object, something that could be touched and owned. Like an arrowhead.

"That field's across the river," Andrew said, heading on downhill. Chap was standing still, getting one last look at the field. Kite had known, of course, that the river lay in that general direction, but he had thought it was much farther away. It had not occurred to him until then that this was a much more direct route to the river than the roads they took when they went on bicycles.

"How do you know?" Chap said. He was coming along after them, now, but still lagging some distance behind.

"You don't think the river's that far away, do you?" Andrew said over his shoulder. "Anyway, we have to get to the river first. That's the main idea."

"Okay," Chap said, "but then let's go on to that field, okay?"

"Okay by me," Kite said.

"Okay," Andrew said.

When they got to the river—it must have been close to ten o'clock—they walked up and down the bank looking for a place to get across. But the river was much wider and swifter here than it was below the bridge where they went swimming and fishing, and they could not tell how deep it might be. Andrew and Kite saw places where they felt they could make it across without too much trouble—but not with Chap.

"We'll have to go on down to the bridge and cross there," Andrew said.

The bridge was fairly close compared to the distance they had already come, but they had a hard time getting to it. They could not stick very close to the river because the bank was too steep in places or the mud so soft they would have sunk in it up to their knees. They had to fight their way through thickets and underbrush. Earlier, after they had circled the swamp and the briar patch and had come back down into the woods, they had been able to follow the creek all the way. All they had to do was jump from one side to the other whenever the going got rough; but there was no choice of that sort by the river. They trudged along single file, talking even less than before, Andrew in front, then Chap, then Kite. From the back Andrew's head and Chap's head looked almost exactly alike, except of course that Chap's was much smaller; but their heads were the same shape and their dark brown hair—walnut-colored, really—grew just the same way. Every time Kite saw somebody who looked a good deal like him, in any way at all, he wondered if the boy was perhaps his twin brother, even though they had told him at Baptist Home that he did not have any brothers or sisters; and even though, most of the time, he knew that that was true.

Before they were even halfway to the bridge, Chap began to get tired and cross and started whining that he wanted to stop for a while. The other two ignored him for a time, but they were tired too; it was very hot now and there was little or no shade. Finally, they sat down on the trunk of a large fallen tree, all three of them slumped over with their forearms on their knees. Three different times, when they were close to the river, they had seen large brown water moccasins slide off

the bank and out of sight when they felt somebody coming.
Each time, Kite thought of his Aunt Ruth: he never left the
house, regardless of where he was going, that she didn't say,
"Watch out for snakes"—though of course he seldom did. It
was no good watching out for snakes: you would have to keep
your eyes on the ground all the time, and even then there was
no guarantee you would see one.

It was while they were sitting there resting that Kite looked
and saw Boydy moving at a snail's pace along the opposite
bank, heading upstream. He had on his baseball cap.

"Look yonder."

Andrew and Chap looked in the direction he was nodding.

"Hey, Boydy!" Andrew yelled. "Hey, Boydy!" But the old
man couldn't hear him.

"Where do you reckon he's going to?" Chap said.

"He don't know," Andrew said.

Moments later he disappeared behind some trees.

Kite had decided that Boydy must not have said anything
at all that night to his uncle about seeing him up on the shed.
It had probably gone right out of his head while he was
sleeping behind the well house. But even if he had said something, Kite doubted that Hampton would have spoken to him
about it. He would have been too embarrassed. Kite was
pretty embarrassed himself. Maybe he would tell Andrew
about it sometime—but not when Chap was around.

By the time they got to the bridge they were not moving
much faster than Boydy had been. They sat down in the
shade by the side of the road and took their shoes off, and
shook the grass and the sand out of them, and then started
picking the beggar lice and the cockleburs off their socks.
Chap was slow at that because he made a point of not using
his right hand, where the tips of the fingers were missing.
When Kite and Andrew had cleaned off their own socks and
had started inspecting the scratches on their legs, Chap lay
back and propped one foot across Andrew's knee, so that he
and Kite could pick the beggar lice off that sock while Chap
continued to work on the other one. In return, Chap divided
his second box of raisins with them; they had eaten all of

theirs before they even got to the river. Kite, in his sock feet, walked halfway across the bridge, leaned over the railing, dropped the empty raisin box into the water some eight or ten feet below, and then moved quickly to the other side of the bridge to watch it float past. It was still afloat when he lost sight of it. Then he yelled back to Andrew and Chap and dared them to dare him to jump off the bridge.

"Soon as we get cooled off and rested," Chap said, coming onto the bridge, "we're gonna go find that green field we saw from back yonder."

"Don't you think you're too tired out for that today?" Andrew said. "Me and Kite'd rather go on down the river and go in swimming for a while."

Chap looked surprised and sad, and Kite could not be sure how much of the disappointment that he himself felt was his own and how much of it was for Chap.

"I'd rather go find that field," Chap said. "You said we could. You promised."

"I didn't know how tuckered out we were gonna be. It's just too hot."

They could not see the field from the bridge, of course. It might have been as much as two or three miles away now, and Kite was not at all sure of the best way to go about getting there. He wondered if that was why Andrew had backed out, because he didn't know how to get there either. Or maybe it was just because he couldn't see the field any longer.

"You all can go swimming anytime," Chap said.

"We can go to that field anytime, too."

But Kite knew that the field might not look the same if they waited too long.

"I can go by myself," Chap said.

"No, you can't," Andrew told him, making his voice very gentle now. "It's too far. You don't know the way. You have to wait until me and Kite can go with you."

"No, I don't, I can find it." He walked back to the end of the bridge and leaned against the railing long enough to pull his shoes on. Kite and Andrew were sitting on opposite sides of the bridge, their backs to the water, and Chap walked right down the middle, looking very determined, not glancing at either one of them.

"You can't go by yourself, Chap," Andrew said again.

Chap kept walking and did not look back when he got to the end of the bridge and started up the road. Andrew didn't move. He looked at Kite and shrugged his shoulders. Kite would have liked to follow Chap and go along with him, but he stayed where he was.

"He won't go far," Andrew said under his breath.

"You really wanta go swimming?"

"Don't you?"

"I don't much think so." Kite turned and gazed up the road to where Chap, looking very small, was about to disappear around the first bend.

"The skinny-dippers might be back down there again," Andrew said.

"I don't see the red truck anywhere."

"He might have let her out on his way to work. She might be down there by herself."

"Holler if you need any help," Kite said. If Andrew left, he would set out after Chap. But Andrew still hadn't moved.

Kite eased down off the railing and turned and gazed down at the brown water. On the nearer bank, not far from where they had sat down to take their shoes off, he saw a reddish snake sunning himself; then, as he looked more closely, he decided it was only a stick. Moments later, when he glanced back at that spot, the stick was gone. He moved to the other side of the bridge, where Andrew was still sitting on the railing, and looked upstream, the direction they had come from. He thought about climbing one of the taller trees on the higher bank to see if he could see the green field. The sun was very hot. His stomach felt empty.

"I think we oughta go get little Chap to come back," Kite said.

"I guess we better," Andrew said. They put their shoes on.

As they rounded the first curve they saw Chap sitting on the bank in the shade not far ahead of them. When they got close enough, Chap said, "I need somebody to tie my shoes for me." Kite knelt down and tied his shoes, even though he knew that Chap could have done it for himself if he'd had to. Chap did not mention the green field. Instead, he stood up and walked back toward the bridge with them.

As they headed for home, trudging now, not talking at all, Kite thought about the evening the week before when the Crowleys had asked him to eat supper at their house. After supper he and Andrew were walking back to the Laceys when suddenly Clown appeared on the path in front of them, tossing his head as if was giving a challenge, and they decided to race him home. The dog won easily, of course, and Kite and Andrew came chugging across the back lawn breathing hard and fast, their knees and calves like Jell-O. They collapsed into the glider that Hampton had moved off the porch and onto the lawn, under the trees. The sun was just going down behind the violet mountains. Clown came and lay down in front of them. He was a beautiful dog, Kite thought, but at the same time he was often somewhat foolish-looking, slack-jawed and with a puzzled profile and a tongue too big for his mouth. Lying in the grass, he looked much redder than usual, and the grass looked greener. And Kite noticed that Andrew's brown skin, like his own, was dark and glowing because they were lying in the sunset light.

Andrew spotted a tick on Clown's eyelid and got down on the grass to try to get it off, kneeling and straddling the dog's body. He had to be careful not to pinch the eyelid, and Clown, who thought it was a game, kept twisting from side to side, his head slipping out of Andrew's easy hands like a big bar of soap. Once, when Clown turned a certain way, Kite saw the sunset for a moment in one of his rolling chestnut-colored eyes. Andrew finally got the tick off and pinched it between his thumbnail and fingernail. His hands were wet, and the blood smeared and made a small sunset on the ball of his thumb. He held it up for Kite to see and then quickly wiped his thumb down Kite's nose, making a mark like Indian war paint. And they had started wrestling in the wet grass.

"I know you don't want the rest of 'em to think you got the easy job 'cause you're kin," Hampton said, "so I figgered I'd start you out loading this first week; then what we usually do is swap around later on, so nobody has to do the same job the whole time."

"That's fine," Kite said.

"Here, have some more eggs and hominy. You got to eat a workingman's meal this morning."

Ruth said, "Most of the boys and girls that come from town bring their lunch or supper with 'em, and I suspected you'd perfer to eat with them instead of coming back down here, so I made up some sandwiches for you. They're in there in that paper bag in the bottom of the icebox."

"Great. Thanks a lot."

"Just put 'em in the cooler when you get to the shed," Hampton told him.

"Yessir."

"I better get on back up there, I guess. You come on when it suits you; I told the rest of 'em eight thirty."

"What time did the pickers get started?"

"Oh, we got 'em out a little after six. Those of 'em showed up."

"He's gonna wash off the front porch for me first," Ruth said. "Then he'll be along."

"You prob'ly better wear long pants, too," Hampton said. "For loading."

"Yessir."

By the time Kite got to the shed, most of the others were already there. It seemed strange to see cars parked all around, and they had raised a lot of dust; an orange haze hung in the air. The first two truckloads were being emptied at the rear. Most of the workers were milling around on the far side, in the shade, waiting for assignments and talking about how sleepy they were.

Kite spotted Lynette's dark hair; she was standing with two other girls at the bottom of the wooden steps. She had on blue jeans and one of her daddy's or brother's old striped dress shirts, with a frayed collar, the cuffs rolled up, and the tail hanging halfway down to her knees. He came up behind her.

"Hey, Lynette."

When she turned around he saw that the dress shirt was unbuttoned down the front and she had on a dark blue T-shirt under it.

"Hey, Kite," she said. "I been looking for you."

She introduced him to the other two girls and then to a boy named Pruitt Gibson, who was sitting on the bottom step and who eyed him with a sort of lazy sneer and stuck his hand up. Pruitt had a narrow face and a pile of wet hair, which he had combed very elaborately with a big-toothed comb. Kite thought that if one of the girls put her hand down on top of his head, streams of water would run down his face.

"You been back to the Clock lately?" Lynette gave him a cunning little grin, which he gave right back.

"Not lately," he said, and stuck out his tongue and licked his fingers.

She laughed exactly the way she had at the Clock. It almost gave him goose bumps.

The other two girls looked mystified, and Pruitt looked resentful. A few seconds later he stood up very casually and nonchalantly draped his arm around Lynette's shoulders.

"You worked here before?" he asked Kite.

"Nope. First time."

"You know whatcha gonna be doing?"

"Loading, this week."

"Loading, huh?" Pruitt's smile was first cousin to his sneer; he looked Kite up and down. "Well, you have yourself a good time."

That smile, as it turned out, stuck with Kite all day long; by midafternoon he hated Pruitt's guts and felt little affection for anybody else, least of all his uncle.

His job was to take the half-bushel baskets full of peaches off the end of a conveyor belt and carry them across the back of the shed, down a ramp, and into a refrigerated truck-trailer, where they had to be stacked up higher than his head. It didn't seem too bad at first, but once everything got all cranked up, the baskets just kept coming without any break at all; he wasn't accustomed to working so steadily. There was only one other guy helping to load, an older man named Wallace, who wore mirror glasses, whistled under his breath, and had nothing to say. As far as Kite could tell, Wallace had been doing this all his life.

The baskets had small wire handles at each side, and it was not until after he had loaded a dozen or more that Kite realized that Wallace had gloves on.

"Know where I could get some gloves?"

Without looking at him or breaking stride, Wallace yelled toward the front of the shed, "Hey, Coble! Pair gloves!"

Coble was one of his uncle's gofers: fat, red-faced, bald, stupid-looking.

Kite had loaded a dozen more baskets before Coble showed up with a pair of cloth gardening gloves.

"These all I could find," he said.

They reminded Kite of the gloves they wore in minstrel shows, but they were much better than nothing.

Before the baskets came down that last conveyor belt, they had gone through a long low tunnel where they were sprayed with ice-cold water. That made the baskets heavier, and they were still dripping wet when Kite picked them up. For the first hour or so he held each basket out in front of him, about level with his waist. But before long he found himself letting the bottom edge of the basket rest against his legs at mid-thigh, so that he could lift and push it a little with each step he took and—on the ramp—to help him keep from falling forward. Long before noon the front of his jeans was soaking wet and his legs were itching. He understood all too well why Hampton had told him to wear long pants. Even so, he had the feeling that the tops of his thighs would be black and blue by the end of the week.

What made it all even worse was that Lynette and Pruitt, along with half a dozen others, were just culling. He could see them on the far side of the shed, standing up on a platform, just watching the peaches roll by, picking out the ones that looked rotten or bruised or too green or too small, and dropping them into the trough at the side. You could do that all day and not even work up a sweat. And you could talk while you were doing it. Lynette and Pruitt had their backs to him, but they were standing side by side, and more than once he saw Pruitt's hand on her waist or her arm or shoulder. He saw Pruitt's possum smile again and wondered how Lynette could even stand to let him touch her. He guessed he did have the kind of face some girls thought was handsome, but Kite thought he looked like a shit-eater.

Hampton came back to the loading door several times, and always said the same thing: "You doing okay, boy?"

"Fine," Kite said. The first time he came back, Kite asked him where Andrew was. He hadn't seen him all morning.

"I had to send him out with the late-shift pickers. One of my drivers got bit by a snake."

Driving the pickers didn't sound like such a hard job either. Easier than this, anyway.

Twice, late in the morning, as he came back for the next basket, he saw that Lynette had turned away from the culler and was looking in his direction. The first time he just waved;

the second time he spread his white-gloved hands in front of his face and moved them back and forth like windshield wipers, the way he had seen Al Jolson do in a movie. That made Lynette laugh. But he couldn't hear her because of the racket the machines made.

When they broke for lunch at noon he decided to go home and put on dry pants. He took his lunch with him and sat down at the kitchen table. Ruth was not at home, but he didn't know where she had gone; he reckoned Hampton had taken his lunch up to the shed with him. He gulped down the sandwiches, one ham and cheese with lettuce and tomato and one peanut butter and jelly, and drank most of a quart of milk, right out of the bottle. Then he went outside and lay down in the hammock and fell sound asleep. The next thing he knew Andrew was standing at the end of the hammock, shaking it and grinning down at him.

"Come on, Kite, they already started back. You gonna get fired the first day."

"Good," Kite said.

The afternoon was longer, hotter, and harder than the morning had been. He soon realized that he should have taped his hands and fingers when he went to the house—and he should have put socks on; his feet were hurting now as well as his hands. By the time his jeans were soaked through again with water dripping from the baskets, his T-shirt and hair and face were soaked with sweat. By three o'clock, sharp pains were streaking down his arms and prying under his shoulder blades every time he picked a basket up and every time he put one down. The hardest part was when the stacks in the trailer got five high and he had to raise the basket to arm's length.

He tried to keep his mind off the work by thinking about Lynette. But that made him think about Pruitt. And that made him as miserable inside as he was outside. He had spotted two or three other girls among the workers who looked as if they might be worth thinking about, but he hadn't had a chance to look at them long enough or close enough to know what to think. And it wasn't all that easy to get Lynette off his mind. But he wasn't sure why it wasn't. Who did she remind him of? he wondered. Somebody in the movies? He couldn't remember. He couldn't even think straight. All he was sure of was how bad his hands and feet and arms and back were hurting. And how much he hated Pruitt Gibson. He didn't even glance in that direction anymore. It made him mad to see how easy they had it, and to watch the two of them rubbing up against each other.

He didn't see Hampton all afternoon—and he was just as glad he didn't—but one of his straw bosses, Sidney Somebody, wandered by once or twice and nodded to him. And after the last load was brought in, Andrew came over to see if he was holding up okay.

"You look about wore out," he said.

"Just about."

"Well, the first day's always the hardest."

"I sure hope so," Kite said.

"Besides, you got stuck with one of the shit jobs."

"Hampton said he didn't wanta play favorites."

"Why don't you go get yourself a Coke?" Andrew said. "I'll take over for a while. I've had it easy today."

"I sure would appreciate it. Want a Coke, Wallace?"

Wallace shook his head. "I might get one when you get back."

The Coke machine was at the front of the shed, against the wall of the storeroom. Coble was propped up against it in a cane-bottom chair, half asleep.

While he drank the Coke, Kite sat on the edge of the porch and looked out across the cars and the road at the green hillside and the green trees.

"I'm glad to see you takin' a breather," Coble said. "You been goin' mighty hard."

"Yessir," Kite said. "Not much other way to go back there."

"That loadin'll make you a muscleman quick."

There *was* that. Kite nodded. "Where's Mr. Lacey gone to?"

"He's up the road to check with ol' McGowan. See how much work we got tomorrow."

After that break, and with Andrew to help him out and to

talk to, the last hour and a half was the easiest part of the day. Since they were at the end of the line, the others finished first, and Lynette came by to tell him good-by. She had taken the dress shirt off and had the sleeves tied around her waist. Kite set down the basket he had just picked up and wiped the sweat off his face with the bottom half of his T-shirt, giving her an even better look at his smooth brown stomach than she had given him that day at the Clock.

"We looked around for you at lunchtime," she told him.

"Yeah?"

She was barefooted and held a brown loafer in each hand.

"We thought maybe you had gone to the Clock."

"Oh, no."

"Somebody told me they got real good catsup there."

"And plenty of it," Andrew said.

Kite smiled from one to the other.

"You all wanta eat lunch with us tomorrow?" she said.

"Sure," Andrew said.

She looked at Kite. He didn't know who "us" was.

"Okay."

"Okay." She flashed her happy, bright-eyed smile at him. "See you all in the morning."

She padded off toward the front of the shed, and Kite wondered who she was riding home with, or if she had her own car.

"You know Pruitt Gibson?"

"Sure," Andrew said. "Plays basketball."

"What kind of a claim has he got staked out on Brown Eyes?"

"Lynette? What kind does it seem like?"

"I can't tell yet. Could be just a big-brother act."

"So . . . be a little brother. That's a start."

"May be a stop, too."

"Hell, you can take on Pruitt Gibson. He's not so tough."

"I told you before, though: I gotta be good."

"If you can't be good," Andrew said, "be careful."

When Kite got home he took a long shower—first hot, then cold, then warm. Then he went up to his room and lay down on his bed stark naked and gazed up at the ceiling. He was too tired even to jack off.

At supper that night he had little to say. It took all the energy he had left just to eat. Now that packing had begun, Ruth would fix the big meal, the hot meal, for supper. That night it was fried country ham, mashed potatoes with red-eye gravy, biscuits, collards, creamed corn, and pear salad. And iced tea. Kite drank four glasses.

"You cert'ly worked up a appetite," Hampton said.

Kite kept on eating.

"The first day seems like the hardest, I reckon."

Kite shrugged.

Nobody said anything for a while.

"If you want me to," Hampton said, "I can find something else for you tomorrow. Get somebody else to load."

Kite did not look up from his plate.

"I'll load," he said.

He was in bed that night by nine o'clock, sleeping like a baby.

They were partly right about the first day. It wasn't really as hard after that, though he was stiff and sore for at least half an hour every morning. The problem was that once he got used to the work itself—the lifting, the lugging, the clammy jeans—the job got more and more boring. Wallace might as well have been deaf and dumb, and there was rarely anybody else near enough to talk to; nothing to break the monotony. Moving back and forth at the same steady pace between the end of the belt and the back of the truck, he felt like an animal pacing a cage; on a chain. Every day of that first week seemed longer and slower than the one before.

What made the mornings go especially slow was looking forward to lunch. Starting the second day, he and Andrew, Lynette and two of her girlfriends, and Pruitt and two of his buddies collected their lunch bags from the cooler, crossed the road, and climbed the hillside pasture to sit in the shade of half a dozen big broadleaf oaks. Kite had started wearing swimming trunks under his jeans, and when they got to the trees he would take off his tennis shoes and socks and jeans and put them in the sun to dry out some while he ate lunch. By Friday, just as he had expected, there were greenish-purple bruises across the front of his thighs.

"Does it hurt?" Lynette said, gently tracing the broad stripe on his left leg with the tip of her forefinger.

"Little bit."

"My *heee*-ro," Pruitt said in a Minnie Mouse voice.

Kite stuck his bare foot toward Pruitt's face. "Wanta kiss it and make it well?"

"Go to hell," Pruitt said.

Kite went on unwrapping his lunch and laying it out in front of him: fried chicken, cold biscuits, and half a cantaloupe.

Pruitt, in between bites of his livermush sandwich, said, "I hear you been doing such a bang-up job, they gonna let you keep on loading all summer, Kite."

"That's not the way I heard it," Kite said. "I heard you been begging old Coble to let you load next week."

"You got it mixed up," Pruitt said. "Old Coble's been begging *me* to let him *take* my load." Pruitt's buddies guffawed and one of the girls, not Lynette, giggled.

"Shit," Kite said.

"I bet you didn't even know old Coble was a cocksucker, did you?" Pruitt said. "I guess you'd've had an easier job if you had."

"That how you got yours?"

"You two just shut up," Andrew said. And then, looking steadily at Pruitt: "Else I'm gonna kick you and your foul mouth back down the hill."

"You and who else?" Pruitt said.

"He doesn't bother me," Lynette said. "I've been around dumb animals before."

"Is that how come you like Kite so much?" Pruitt said.

Kite lunged in Pruitt's direction and ended up with his knees on Pruitt's bony chest—but quickly eased up because Pruitt looked as if he was choking on his potato chips; before he could do or say anything else, Andrew had pulled him off. "He ain't worth it, Kite. You remember what you told me."

Pruitt's two friends had quickly gotten to their feet and were now making threatening noises and gestures, completely ignoring Pruitt, who was on his hands and knees and seemed to be looking for something in the grass. As soon as he had his breath back, he stood up too and glared fiercely at Kite, who had already sat back down to his lunch.

"Why don't you all just go on back down to the shed?" Andrew said. "We only got a thirty-minute break, and I don't wanta waste my time and energy breaking up fights. You two been working up to this all week, and the sooner you realize Lynette ain't either of you's personal private property, the better off you're gonna be."

"Come on," Pruitt said, looking first at Lynette and then at his buddies. The three boys started slowly down the hill, trying to look if it was entirely their idea. Then Pruitt looked back at Lynette again.

"You coming?"

"After I finish my lunch I will."

Pruitt turned away, took a couple of more steps, and then moved quickly to the right and at a slight angle back up the hillside; he snatched up Kite's jeans and then cantered back down the hill, holding the jeans by the bottom of one leg and swinging them in a circle above his head.

Kite looked disgusted but didn't move. When Pruitt got to the bottom of the hill, Kite yelled after him, "I knew you been wanting to get into my pants, Pruitt."

Pruitt crossed the road, trailing the jeans in the dust now, and disappeared into the shed.

"What an asshole," Kite said.

"He didn't used to be like that," Lynette told him, and her girlfriends murmured agreement. "I don't know what's got into him."

"I bet you don't," Andrew said.

Lynette looked wounded, Kite thought.

"I never have said anything to make him act like that," she said.

Kite put the chicken bones and the cantaloupe rind back into the paper sack. Then he sighed wearily and lay back in the grass and gazed up through the jigsawed leaves interlocked by sunlight and shadow. Then he closed his eyes. The next thing he knew, Lynette was kissing him softly on the lips and had her hand on his stomach. The first thing he saw were her dark eyes, almost black in the bright sunlight.

"Time to go back down to work."

He sat up slowly, groggily, and squinted down at the shed broiling in the sun. The glassy waves of heat rising off the tin roof and the tar-and-gravel road made everything look unreal, dreamlike. He felt that he was gazing down from heaven onto hell. Andrew and the other two girls were already at the bottom of the hill. Lynette had fetched his shoes and socks for him. The socks were still damp.

While he was putting on his shoes, he said, "Some of us from the church me and Andrew go to are going up to the mountains a week from next Saturday to go swimming at a lake up there. You wanta go with us?"

"I sure would," she said. "I'd love to."

"Will it be okay with your mama and daddy?"

"We won't be real late getting back, will we?"

"I don't think so. When I asked Uncle Hampton about it this morning, he said he thought we were just gonna work half a day on Saturdays, so we'll prob'ly leave around three or four."

"I'm sure they'll let me," she said.

When they got back down to the shed, neither Pruitt nor Kite's blue jeans were anywhere in sight. Kite went up and down both sides of the shed, looking for Pruitt and cursing him under his breath; then he went up into the loft; and then he walked all the way around the outside of the shed. Near the ramp at the back where the peaches were unloaded, Pruitt's two buddies were leaning in the doorway talking to a couple of girls.

"Where's Pruitt?" Kite said.

"Pruitt who?"

When Kite moved toward them with his fists clenched at his sides, one of the girls gave a little smirk and said, "I think he threw your pants up inside the water tunnel."

"That son of a bitch," Kite said.

When he got back up to the front of the shed, Coble was al-

ready bent over at the entrance to the tunnel, shining a dim
flashlight into the darkness.

"I think my pants are in there," Kite said.

"You better scoot in there and get 'em out, then," Coble
said. "They'll play hell and high Josie with this machin'ry.
And it won't do them no service neither."

"I wasn't the one put 'em in there," Kite said.

"I can't he'p that."

"Well, *I* can. I can find that son of a bitch Pruitt Gibson
and shove his ass up that tunnel."

"Well, you better have him in your pocket, boy, 'cause I
ain't got no time for a search party. We got to get started up.
What's Mr. Lacey gonna say if he gets back from his dinner
and we ain't runnin'?"

"Goddamn," Kite said, and hoisted himself up onto the
ledge at the mouth of the tunnel. The opening was a little
over four feet high and wide enough for two half-bushel baskets to go through side by side. He started out on his hands
and knees, but the metal rollers hurt his knees so bad that he
quickly flattened out onto his belly. That was not much better. His T-shirt slid up under his arms, and the rollers were
cold and slimy as well as hard. When he tried to pull himself
along with his hands, his fingers kept getting pinched and
caught between the rollers; he had to push himself forward
with his feet. But the toes of his shoes could not get much of a
hold and kept skidding off in a way that cracked his knees and
shins against the metal. The tunnel was little more than
twenty feet long, but the light from the other end blinded
him; he could see almost nothing in front of him except the
glow of his own hands and arms, and he had to keep reaching
out on both sides, feeling for his pants. Coble and whoever
else was standing at the entrance blocked out the light from
behind now, and other figures had begun to gather at the far
end, casting long wavery shadows toward him. What if his
pants were not in here after all? he kept thinking. What if that
was just another part of the joke? He could hear somebody
laughing. Goddamn that son of a bitch Pruitt.

He was almost halfway in when his left hand, sweeping at
arm's length toward the side of the tunnel, snagged his jeans.

Just as he pulled them toward him—and in a shuddering split-second he realized he should have known this was coming—he was enveloped by a flood of water and by the hollow, deafening roar of the ocean. He had seen pictures of guys on surfboards swallowed up by huge towering waves and held down under tons of water—that was the image that flashed into his head. Even though he knew with one part of his mind what was happening, he kept telling himself that he would soon come back to the surface. Then he realized that he wasn't rising; wasn't floating; wasn't moving; that the pressure and pain and thunder of the water were not subsiding at all, were constant and continuous: pounding and stinging his head and back and arms and legs and ass. He yelled out—not a word, just a sound—but he could not even hear himself. His ears and eyes and mouth were stuffed with water. And there also seemed now to be a thick layer of water between him and the rollers, so that it was harder than ever to move. He managed to hang onto the jeans and to get them wadded up under his forearms, and it then became slightly easier to pull himself along. He tried to be sure from the feel of the rollers that he was still moving straight ahead and would not bang his head against the side; he could no longer see anything at all, only darkness. It occurred to him that there might be doors that had slid shut at the ends of the tunnel; that he was trapped; that the whole space was filling up with water. He tried to crawl faster, banging his elbows and knees against the corrugated surface underneath him, ducking his head close to his chest and trying to suck some air out of the water. He felt certain that he was drowning.

Then the water stopped. At first the silence was so odd, so sudden, that he could not have named it; it was something entirely new. A light rain was falling all around him, but so light and gentle after what had come before that it did not even exist for him. Then lights and shadows blurred into view again. He was much closer to the end than he had thought. He heard his name being called. He lay still for a few seconds, trying to catch his breath. Then he crawled on out. When his vision cleared—he was still stretched out on his belly, his head at the edge of the tunnel—the first face he saw was Hampton's, frowning. And then, some little distance in back of Hampton: Pruitt Gibson, grinning like a possum.

Once he was on his feet again, leaning against the belt where the baskets were lidded, shivering, shuddering, he looked around for Lynette but he didn't see her. Pruitt had disappeared again too. He knew that people were watching him, talking to him, but their voices sounded far away and unimportant.

Hampton put a cotton sack around his shoulders. "You better go put some dry clothes on, boy. You okay now?"

"Yessir."

The sun felt terrific. Like a nice warm fire in midwinter. He was halfway through the pines when Lynette caught up with him.

"Kite? Are you okay?"

"Sure," he said. "Just good and clean."

She put her hands on his shoulders and pulled herself up enough to kiss him on the lips. He put his arms around her and kissed her back this time.

"You're so cold," she said.

"You're so warm." He put his face against her hair. "I bet you could warm me up quicker than I could cool you off."

She pulled back a little, and he let his arms slide away from her. She looked at him very solemnly. "I'm not gonna have anything more to do with Pruitt," she said.

"Okay by me."

She kissed him again, very quickly, and then turned and ran back through the trees.

Fifteen minutes later, when he got back to the shed, Hampton was waiting for him, leaning against the grille of the truck that was being loaded.

"Why don't you go on over to the other side and do some culling for me the rest of today, Kite? I got somebody else loading."

"Yessir. That's fine with me."

Then he saw Pruitt come out of the back of the truck and move slowly toward the conveyor belt. Kite stepped up onto the ramp and moved up close behind him but did not say anything until Pruitt had picked up the next basket and

turned around. Then he grinned at him. He tried to make it
the same kind of grin he would give a cute girl.

"You must not have had very much to show old Coble," he
said.

Pruitt didn't even look at him, just kept on moving. Then
Kite noticed he wasn't wearing gloves. At almost the same
moment he noticed that Lynette was watching them over her
shoulder, from the other side of the shed. He waved to her.

"You better get Coble to get you some gloves," he said.

Then he headed for the culler.

Kite walked up the path with a piece of glass, like a small windowpane, in one hand and the picture of his mama and daddy in the other. He had studied the picture several times a day ever since Hampton gave it to him, but it was only in the past week that he had begun to believe that those two somber-looking, old-fashioned people were really his parents, not just two people in a picture Ruth and Hampton had come across somewhere and had given him to try to make him feel better.

When he had showed Andrew the picture, Andrew told him he ought to make a frame for it. Andrew said he had made picture frames in the woodworking shop at school and would show him how. Hampton had brought the piece of glass back from town and had told him there were some scraps of molding he could use in the storeroom up at the shed.

He went around to the front because sometimes Coble lingered after everyone else had gone, hoping to sell a small bas-

ket or bag of peaches to somebody passing by. Kite didn't
want to be mistaken for a prowler, but neither Coble nor his
old tan pickup was anywhere in sight.

It seemed strange, almost spooky, that the shed, which just
a few hours before had been full of workers and noise, was
now so quiet and still. When they had stopped work, around
four thirty, the shed was out in the broiling sun; but now,
since the sun had sunk behind the woods, it was all in
shadow—so that walking inside was like walking into the
woods at this time of day: it was already twilight there. And it
was like the woods at evening in another way, too: as the
colors and shapes faded and blurred, sounds and smells got
sharper. The smell of peaches and dust and heat and sweat
seemed thicker and stronger than it had at midday; and as
Kite moved slowly through the empty building he was aware
of the squeak of his sneakers, and of the plunking sound of the
tin roof as it cooled off, and of the sorrowful burbling of a
dove up in the loft.

He put the picture and the piece of glass down on top of a
stack of upside-down baskets and unlocked the storeroom
door and turned on the light. The room was a jumble of odds
and ends, most of it junk, Kite thought. He remembered the
first time he had gone in there, to get the broom to sweep off
the roof. And the second time. Now he looked around more
carefully. In addition to rags and sacks and boxes and baskets,
there was a small generator, a section of broken rollers, the
rusted hub of a small tractor wheel, an old-fashioned ceiling
fan with half a blade cracked off, a mildewed stack of hard-
bound ledgers, a wreath of baling wire, and a dozen or so
blackened smoke pots. In the back corner, a big cardboard box
held scraps of lumber, wooden spindles and rollers, some pine
logs, and some kindling and shavings. Kite began to rummage
through the box, looking and feeling for strips of the same
width. He found two lengths of finished pine molding, only
slightly beveled, and each with a double groove. One piece
was long enough to make the two shorter sides of the frame,
the top and the bottom, and the other strip was long enough
for one of the longer sides; now he needed only one more
piece. But he could not put his hands on it. He seemed to keep

fishing the same wrong pieces out time after time, always thinking he had the right one. And he kept getting splinters in his fingers. If he could have dragged the box closer to the light or emptied it onto the floor, that might have been quicker and easier, but the room was too crowded.

He heard a muffled noise just behind him and turned in time to see the door close, as if of its own accord. And before he understood what was happening—so that at first he didn't even recognize the sound—he heard the key turn in the lock. He glanced around the room, as if he thought somebody else might have come in; and when he said "Hey," out loud, he hardly recognized his own voice, and he felt foolish, as if he were talking to the door and the key. He was still standing at the box, one hand resting on the ragged top edge of it, and only half turned toward the door. "Hey! Who is that?" And he still didn't move; but waited. . . . He seemed to be expecting to hear the key turn again and to see the door swing open. Open, Sesame, he thought to himself, and felt more foolish still. When he was finally able to make himself move, he walked toward the door in as deliberate and confident and nonchalant a way as the clutter would allow; as if somebody might be watching him, and as if by simply ignoring what he had seen and heard, by refusing to believe it, he could will the door to open. But even as he turned the knob he could feel and hear that it was not going to open, and as he pressed his shoulder against it he knew that it was more than just stuck.

He continued to lean against the door. He felt stupid and tired; that brief effort of will and the futility of that effort had compounded his bafflement. He pressed his ear to the door and listened. He expected to hear someone chuckling, snickering—but there was nothing, just his own breath, his own heartbeat. He realized now that what he had expected to hear was Pruitt; he could see Pruitt's possum grin. But at the self-same instant he was equally certain it wasn't Pruitt. Pruitt could not have kept quiet this long. Pruitt *would* have been giggling and snickering. Pruitt couldn't have resisted taunting him. And, anyway, what would Pruitt have been doing back out here this late? He knew who it was. Who else could have followed him into the shed without making a sound? Who

else would have been lurking around to see *him* come in? He
wished to God he could believe it *was* Pruitt.

"Boydy." He tried to make his voice calm and reasonable,
but authoritative. "Boydy. Now listen to me. You come back
here and unlock this door." But the words sounded hollow
and pointless. He was sure that Boydy was already back outside, soaking rags with tractor gas. He was probably crawling
up under the shed, so that he could start the fire directly
below the storeroom. Would he have matches with him? Did
Boydy smoke? He couldn't remember. He didn't think he had
ever seen him smoking. And he wouldn't have planned this,
after all; it would have been a spur-of-the-moment hateful-
ness, just the way it must have been with Little Hampton. He
might have to go somewhere to get matches. That was Kite's
only hope.

He stepped away from the door and heaved his shoulder
against it. It gave hardly at all, and a sharp pain shot across his
back and down his arm. He cursed under his breath and
rubbed his shoulder with his other hand until the pain faded
to a gnawing ache. He felt for a moment that he was back in
the washroom on the bus. The room seemed to be moving. It
was getting hotter every minute. He felt dizzy. And in a cold
sweat. He leaned back against the door and scanned the room
for an ill-fitting board that he might be able to pry loose, but
the room looked tight and solid—unlike the outside of the
shed, which was weathered and rotting. It would go up in
flames like a cracker box. Like a corncrib. He wondered if
there was any point at all in yelling for Hampton. More than
likely he was in the house with the TV on, or out in his garden. He never would hear him from that far away. And they
would not begin to expect him back for quite a while either;
he had told them he was going straight on over to Andrew's,
since Andrew had the tools he needed. The shed would probably burn to the ground before Hampton or Ruth even
smelled the smoke.

"Boydy! Goddamn you, Boydy, you better get your black
ass back in here and unlock this door!" Yelling so loud sent
the pain shooting through his shoulder again. He bit his lip.

Silence.

"Boydy! . . . Boydy!"

He was wasting his breath.

Just calm down and use your head, he told himself. You're not a helpless baby like Little Hampton.

With all the junk in here there ought to be something he could make use of. He looked all around him again, desperately now. The broken fan was much too large and heavy and unwieldy to serve as either ax or crowbar. There was nothing he could do with the tractor wheel. Or the baling wire. . . .

The baling wire. He saw now that the hoop of baling wire was fastened in two places with smaller-gauge wire. Maybe he could use that to pick the lock. His fingers felt stiff and numb and slippery with sweat as he worked to unwind the piece of wire nearer the top of the large circle. He seemed to be back in a nightmare again, moving in slow motion. Maybe this *was* a nightmare. Maybe he would wake up. Before he burned up. At last he had the piece of fine wire untangled.

He moved back to the door and stooped down to put the keyhole at eye level. He inserted the wire slowly and carefully and then tried to turn it clockwise, the way the key would have turned. But the wire was so fine and his hands so slimy with sweat that he seemed to have little control of it. Maybe he should twist the wire into a key shape. He pulled it back out, quickly bent it double, and then shaped it into something like the form of the real key. Then he eased it back into the keyhole. Holding his breath. Hoping. Praying. This time he had more control, more leverage; it felt more like a genuine key in his fingers. He felt the wire come up against something; it wasn't just wavering in space, antennalike. He pressed a bit harder and tried at the same time to turn it. It would not turn; instead, it slid farther into the slot and became harder to keep hold of, but he kept gently pushing and turning. Then he felt something give; for a thrilling instant he almost shivered with relief and delight and accomplishment; he felt delivered. Then he heard the real key drop to the floor outside.

He pushed against the door with his shoulder, held onto

the wire with one hand, and turned the knob with the other—but the door did not budge; and now the wire was just stabbing into nothingness again. He pulled it out and doubled over until his face was almost touching the floor, hoping there might be a crack under the door big enough to snag the key through (he had seen that once in a Western movie—though the hero was in a jail cell, which had made it a whole lot easier); but the bottom of the door was tight against the raised sill. That scheme was hopeless. He felt defeated. Furious. He wanted to scream or cry. Like Little Hampton.

Then he smelled smoke. He jumped to his feet and stood sniffing the air, just the way he had seen Boydy do that day in the woods. The smell was not as strong when he was standing. Was it really smoke? He blinked his eyes and looked toward the light. Was there a slight bluish haze? Or was he seeing things? Smelling things. Maybe smoke was coming in under the door. He got back to his knees and bent over again. The smell was stronger there—but was it smoke or just the accumulated dust and dirt ground into the wood floor? His eyes were burning—but was that from smoke or sweat? He looked up at the light again, at the small naked bulb in the ceramic fixture—but now, from this angle, he saw that there was a slight crack, a wonderful black fissure, at one side of the fitting. If he could pry the fixture out, he might be able to enlarge the hole and then climb into the loft. He wasn't tall enough, though, to reach it; he would need something to stand on and something long and pointed to force into the crack.

He shoved the stack of bound ledgers across the floor toward the center of the room and then placed the tractor-wheel hub on top of the ledgers. Then he went back to the box of wood in the corner.

"Kite?"

He froze.

"Kite? You in there?"

The voice was so familiar. It sounded beautiful. For just a split second he thought it might be his daddy's voice.

"Andrew?"

"What're you doin' in there?" Andrew was trying the door-
knob.

"I'm locked in. Listen. Listen now. The key's down on the
floor right there near the door. Can you see it?"

"Just a minute."

He could hear Andrew's hands brushing the floor.

"There's a light switch back there beside the loading door."

"How'd you get locked in there anyway? Are you okay?"

"I'm okay. Can you find the key? Go turn the light on."

"I got it. I got it."

And then Andrew was opening the door. And standing
there looking at him as if this was some kind of joke he was
playing.

"How the hell'd you get in there?"

"I told you, I got locked in. That old black bastard was out
to get me the same way he got Little Hampton. I guess he just
didn't have any matches on him." Kite had come out of the
storeroom and was looking up and down the shed, but there
was no sign of fire. It was almost dark now.

"What makes you think it was Boydy?"

"Who else would have been around here and done such a
thing?"

"It's a good thing I came on over. I didn't know whether
you had changed your mind or what."

"I was on my way. I was in here looking for—oh, shit. Oh
shit!"

"What? What is it?"

"The picture's gone. My mama and daddy. I put it down
right here on these baskets, with the glass on top of it. Now
the piece of glass is here, but the picture's gone."

Andrew slowed up, turned onto a narrow dirt road, drove
down it for several hundred yards, and then came to a stop.

"I think we better walk the rest of the way."

He and Kite pushed the bike into the bushes at the side of
the road.

"How far is it from here?" Kite said.

"Maybe half a mile. Give or take."

The road turned into two narrow paths, with a row of weeds in between and with pinewoods thick and dark and high on both sides.

"How far would it be as the crow flies?" Kite said. "From the shed, I mean."

"Maybe two miles. Two and a half."

"That's the way he comes and goes, idn't it? Cross country?"

"Most of the time, I reckon. I don't keep up with him that much. He's at your place more than ours."

"He usually comes out of the woods. Out of the woodwork."

The crickets were chirring away as if their lives depended on it, and the mosquitoes' pestery whine was like something that might have been real or might not have been, like the smoke in the storeroom. The sound made Kite think of the fine wire he had used to try to pick the lock with—only now that wire was sliding into his ear.

"What's that?" he said. Up ahead, in the middle of the path, something white seemed to be floating several feet off the ground.

"I don't know." Andrew slowed up a little.

Kite thought it was going to be the picture of his mama and daddy . . . but they were close enough now to see that it was nothing but a piece of rag tied to the top strand of a barbed-wire fence that stretched right across the road. Instead of crossing it, instead of climbing over or under, Andrew moved off the path into the woods, and Kite followed. They stayed right beside the fence, where the trees had been thinned out some, but it was still much darker there than on the path.

It seemed strange to Kite that the picture had become so important to him now, from the moment he realized it was missing. For days and days after Hampton gave it to him he had felt guilty because he couldn't make himself believe that they were really his mama and daddy; he had been disappointed in the way they looked; he wished the picture never had turned up at all. But now he felt ashamed; he felt he had betrayed them, had done them some hurtful injustice, by losing their picture, by letting Boydy get ahold of it. What did he want with it anyway? What was he going to do with it? Had Boydy known his mama and daddy? Did he remember them? Was that why he had taken the picture? Or was it just plain meanness?

Andrew turned around and put his finger against his lips, even though neither one of them had said anything for several minutes, and even though they had talked in whispers ever since they got off the bike. Andrew was walking slower and quieter now and peering off into the dark on the far side of the fence. Kite wondered if Boydy had a dog.

When Andrew came to a stop and crouched down, Kite crouched down beside him. Andrew reached between the strands of barbed wire and moved aside the leafy branches of a small bush.

"It's right through there. Can you see it?"

Kite could not see anything at all. He shook his head.

"Look where I'm pointing at," Andrew whispered. He pushed the leaves farther to one side.

"I see a light," Kite said. "Is that it?" The light looked far away.

"That's it. That light means he must be home. Or else somebody else lives there now too."

"He might have left a light on."

"I don't think so. I don't think he has electricity down here. That's either a kerosene lamp or a lantern."

As soon as they had stopped moving, the mosquitoes had begun to swarm. Kite imagined rings of barbed wire spinning around his head and settling down around his neck like nooses.

"Why are the skeeters so bad down here?"

" 'Cause it gets real swampy back down this way." Andrew motioned with one hand. "And there's a big garbage dump in the edge of the swamp."

"Let's get closer," Kite said.

Andrew put his foot on the bottom strand of wire and pulled up on the top one, and Kite ducked through; he did the same thing for Andrew; then they moved cautiously downhill toward the light. It was much closer than Kite had thought; it was just that the light was very dim. They had come to the edge of a small clearing, and the shanty was on the far side of it. Kite had thought it would be like a cabin, but it didn't even look big enough to call a cabin. And it wasn't made out of logs—just unpainted boards of different sizes, and running in different directions, without any plan or pattern. It had a rusted tin roof that glimmered piebald in the moonlight. The roof overhung the side they were facing—Kite didn't know whether it was front or back or what—so that that wall was deep in shadow. There was a narrow door, shut tight in spite of the heat—or because of the mosquitoes—and two small high windows. A big bush grew up in front of one of the windows.

The clearing—packed dirt dotted with tree stumps—lay between them and the shanty, but around to their left the trees came much closer to the corner of the house.

"Let's move around this way," Kite whispered, and took the lead.

He stayed in the edge of the trees and kept his eyes on the cabin, but as he moved toward it he became aware of a large dark shadow standing on the far side of the house, near the far edge of the clearing. It looked like the huge trunk of a tree that might have been topped out at about the height of a tall man. It was hard not to feel that there might be somebody standing behind it. He stopped moving.

"What's that?" Pointing.

"His outhouse," Andrew said.

Kite moved on.

They could see now that there was a broad stone chimney on the lower side of the house; the top of it seemed to be broken off just above the apex of the roof. On the other side of the chimney was another window, the only one on that side. They were not much more than twenty yards from the house now, but Kite kept creeping forward until he was on a line with the window. And from there he could see Boydy sitting at a table. The light was behind him, but he had his baseball cap on, and his silhouetted profile was unmistakable.

"That's him."

"I know it." Andrew was right beside him. "What're you gonna do now?"

"I don't know."

Kite was confused because he had imagined all along that they would get to the cabin before Boydy got back. In his mind he had seen them waiting for him, had seen him coming home with the picture in his hand; they would have caught him red-handed. How had Boydy gotten back here so quick? And what would he do or say if Kite went right up to the door and told him he knew he had the picture and he wanted it back? At best, he would just play dumb, would pretend he couldn't even understand what they were saying. At worst, he would come to the door with a loaded shotgun in the crook of his arm. Kite saw Boydy dragging his and Andrew's bodies through the woods to the swamp. Saw them being sucked up by the quicksand, never to be seen or heard of again.

"Come on," Andrew whispered, "these skeeters are eatin' me alive."

And just at that moment the lighted window went black.

Andrew turned and scrambled back through the trees, and Kite was at his heels. He was grateful that Andrew had not been willing to wait around for him to do something, because he still did not know what that something might have been. He kept wondering why he had felt so much sadder at the sight of Andrew's limp and blasted body than at the sight of his own.

When they got back to the road, Kite said, "I still don't know how he got back down there so quick."

"How long do you think you were locked in the store-room?"

"I don't know ... maybe ten, fifteen minutes. It seemed longer than that but I don't guess it was."

"And we waited around for about that long."

"I guess we should have headed down here right straight, but I thought he might come back."

"Then it took us about ten minutes to walk back over to my house and sneak my bike down to the highway."

"That's not much more than thirty minutes, tops. I don't think that old man can move that fast. I never have seen him, if he can."

"Maybe you were locked up longer than you think. Or maybe it wasn't ol' Boydy. Maybe it was somebody else."

"Maybe. But I don't think so."

"What're you gonna tell your uncle and aunt?"

"Nothin' yet. Not till I have to."

"Be funny if we get back to where we left the bike and the bike's gone," Andrew said.

"Funny, shit," Kite said.

But the bike was there.

Just after daybreak the light came on again in Boydy's house.

Kite had slept fitfully because of bad dreams and mosquito bites. At five o'clock he was wide awake, writing a note to leave on the kitchen table: *Me and Andrew are going fishing but will be back in plenny of time to go to work. Love, Kite.* He had ridden his bike as far as the place where the fence barred the road and had left it there and slipped into the woods again. Even though it was still dark, the woods felt different from last night. The air was moist and sweet, and the birds were raising so much Cain he could not even hear his own footsteps; he had smeared some of Hampton's foot ointment on the back of his neck to keep the mosquitoes off, and it seemed to be working; and in his jacket pocket he had a fried peach pie left over from supper last night, but he would save that awhile longer, even though his stomach felt empty and quivery.

When he got to the clearing he made a slow cautious circle of Boydy's house and then settled down in a spot that gave him a good safe view of the only door. He sat with his legs drawn up and his arms folded across his knees. When he yawned and looked up at the sky, it was still black, but a softer duller black than it was last night, or when he left the house. The black would be slowly leached way and the sky would fade to no color at all before it turned blue.

He had not quite finished his peach pie when the two windows on either side of the door began to glow. And a few minutes later that same orange light spread across the doorway, and Boydy came out into the yard. He had on a white shirt and overalls, but no baseball cap. He bent over slowly and put something down on the ground, and shadows began to swim all around it. When the shadows got still they were cats, three or four of them. Kite had not been able to tell whether they came out of the house or from somewhere else. Boydy stood looking down at them for a minute or more. Then he hobbled very slowly and stiffly toward the lower side of the house and disappeared around the corner. Then his white shirt reappeared, making its way toward the outhouse as if being jerked along on a frozen clothesline. Once he had gone inside the outhouse, Kite began to toy with the notion of locking him in, but he was not sure how he could accomplish that—especially since the stall looked so dilapidated that even old Boydy could probably have kicked his way out or just toppled the whole thing over from inside.

He stayed inside so long that Kite began to wonder if there might be a door on the other side. Boydy might have gone out that door long since, might have circled around, and might even now be sneaking up behind him. He could not resist turning around. But there was nothing there but the woods, and they were still so deep in shadow that a white shirt would have stood out like a flag.

When he looked back toward the outhouse, Boydy was standing in front of it. And it was light enough now to see his face and his overalls, not just his shirt; and by the time he got back to his doorstep Kite could tell that the bush in front of the window was a fig bush and that there were three cats, two tabbies and a calico. When Boydy went back inside, the cats followed him.

Kite was growing impatient now. It was important to get back to Andrew's house before he left for the shed—to make him aware of their fishing trip. But of course it was still very early; he was sure he had time to spare. He mustn't lose his nerve now, he was too close. All he had to do was wait. And so he waited. . . .

This time, when Boydy came out, followed by the cats, he

closed the door behind him. And this time he had his baseball
cap on. He stood in his yard just the way he had done that
day when Kite was mowing the lawn—like a bird dog on
point—and Kite wondered what he would do if the blind old
bird dog headed right in his direction. But he didn't. He
struck out across the clearing at an angle, moving somewhat
easier now, and entered the woods perhaps fifty feet from
where Kite was sitting. After a moment, Kite stood up. And
after another moment, he moved in the same direction. Staying at a prudent distance, satisfied to catch only an occasional
glimpse of white, he followed that bright shirt for perhaps
half a mile. Then, confident that Boydy was gone for the day,
he turned and jogged back through the woods, feeling light-
footed and clever and courageous. The picture of his mama
and daddy had long since grown less important to him than
the act of getting it back . . . of knowing for sure that Boydy
was the one who had stolen it . . . and of knowing he had not
gotten away with it.

He paused at the edge of the clearing and scanned the circle
of trees before he moved out into the open. He paused again
at the doorstep and turned and looked behind him, as if somebody might be spying on him the same way he had spied on
Boydy. The cats were not around. The door had a wooden
latch. He lifted it and went inside and closed the door behind
him. Although the sun was up now, it had not yet climbed
above the trees, so that the clearing and the shanty were still
in the shadow of the woods; the inside of the shanty was dim
and dusky. The first thing that Kite noticed was the smell—it
was Boydy's smell, but stronger, concentrated—and there
were other odors too: stale grease, ashes, the cats, and a sour
starchy mustiness that made Kite think of Mrs. Massingale
down at Baptist. From inside, the house did not seem quite as
small as it had from outside, even though it was just one
room, but it seemed crowded and confusing, though there
wasn't much furniture. A wooden table and chair, both of
which looked rickety; another smaller table with a small tin
washtub on top of it; next to that a tall and shallow metal cabinet, painted white but badly rusted; and in the corner near
the chimney a narrow bed (the metal bedstead and the sag-

ging mattress made Kite think of Baptist again); two cardboard boxes under the bed. As his eyes grew more accustomed to the dimness and as the day grew brighter, he
realized that it was the walls more than anything else that
made the room seem flimsy and crazy. The walls were plas-
tered with pieces of newspaper and pages from magazines.
They covered almost every inch and seemed in places to be
several layers thick. Most of them looked very old—yellowed
and ragged and crumbly. Some sheets had begun to curl away
from the wall, and others had peeled in strips, giving the walls
a weird, fluttery, three-dimensional effect.

Kite went to the metal cabinet and opened it. On the lower
shelves were several pieces of worn and faded clothing, folded
neatly. On the upper shelves, two plates, a cup, a butcher
knife, and a saucepan; a can of coffee, a jar of molasses, half a
loaf of bread, and a shoebox containing three sweet potatoes
and two turnips; on another shelf, two paper sacks, one half
full of dried beans, the other half full of cornmeal. It was not
until he found himself opening those sacks that Kite began to
feel guilty. He closed the cabinet and went to the window on
the far side of the door and looked out. The clearing seemed
to be waiting for something. The sun was just touching the
tops of the tress, and the ring of woods looked clean and
sparkly. What would it be like to live alone like this? Off in
the woods. With nobody but cats to talk to. With just barely
enough to eat. But with nobody to answer to. Nobody to
worry him. Or worry *about* him. He knew that it was wrong
to be here. What if Ruth or Hampton went into his room and
rummaged through his things and found the pictures he kept
hidden under his underwear? How would he feel? "Do unto
others as you would have them do unto you." But he was sure
that Boydy had locked him in the storeroom and stolen his
mama and daddy's picture. But he wasn't as sure as he had
been last night. Or even when he set out from the house this
morning. It seemed to him now that he was here for some
reason other than the picture . . . but what could that reason
be? He knew that he had had, in the back of his mind, the notion of doing some mischief here. If he found the picture,
something to let Boydy know that he had been here and

had reclaimed his possession. And if he didn't find the picture, something more destructive, something that would carry a threat, a warning.

Now, all that seemed pointless. Maybe the picture was here and maybe it wasn't. Maybe Boydy had burned it. Or buried it. Or maybe he never had it at all. What difference did it make? It was just a picture.

When he turned away from the window, he saw that the wall at the far end of the room, the fireplace wall, was not covered with newspapers the way the other three walls were. It was covered with *some*thing, but at first he wasn't sure what. It looked both more solid and, at the same time, less solid than the other walls. He moved closer. The fireplace itself was about a yard across and a yard deep, and there was a good-sized hearth that looked like slate; the mantel was low and there was nothing on it but the kerosene lamp and a small bowl. Starting, it seemed, at the back of the mantel, a dense and elaborate and splendid design made out of small pieces of broken glass flowed up toward the ceiling, out toward the corners of the wall, taking in the single window, and down toward the floor. There were a few bare patches where wooden planks showed through, especially near the lower corners, but all the rest of the wall was completely covered. And in some spots the glass, like the newspaper, seemed layers thick. The whole wall was encrusted. Thousands ... millions of bits of glass, the largest of them not much bigger than a thumbnail, and some of them as tiny as an okra seed. And a hundred different colors. It must have taken years and years, Kite thought, to make this design. Was it Boydy's work? Or had someone else lived there before him? He saw that there were pieces of glass on the mantel. Had they fallen out of the pattern, or were they soon to be part of it? He could not see any pieces on the floor. He moved closer still and stretched out both arms and touched the design with his fingertips, very gently, as if he expected the glass to fall away ... but the pieces were stuck fast; they were fitted together so closely and carefully that even though the overall surface was rough it felt smooth beneath his fingertips. And cool.

He let his arms fall to his sides and took several steps backward, so that he could tell more easily—now that the room was getting lighter—if the design made a picture. Or if it was just a design. It *was* just a design; and it stayed a design. But the parts of it shifted and shaded and flowed together, in and out, in such a natural and changeable way that it was possible to see all sorts of different pictures at the same time, all of them parts of each other and parts of the whole magic pattern. Ocean waves and spray . . . the scales of a fish or a snake . . . fronds of fern . . . clouds and stars . . . trees sheathed in ice. The wall seemed to be pulsing, roiling. It was like deep clear water, rain-spattered water. And it seemed to be making the sounds that moving water makes. Kite sat down on the edge of Boydy's bed.

And now the sun was clearing the trees and shining through the windows at the other end of the room, picking out the brighter colors in the glass wall, making them glitter and flicker, and casting reflections, freckles and blurs and bars of color, onto the other walls, onto the faded newspapers. The room was getting brighter and brighter. Alive with light and color. He could see the air. His eyes began to water. He felt the way he sometimes felt singing hymns in church—but different, too, because he was alone here and quiet, and because he had discovered this place, this . . . whatever it was . . . by himself. It didn't have anything to do with God or being good or bad or doing wrong or right. He felt the way he felt when he heard Andrew's voice outside the storeroom. He felt the way he felt that first morning in his new room at the Laceys', when he looked out the back windows and saw the mountains—the mountains he never had dreamed were there—waiting there, blue and bright and shining, changing from hour to hour all day long. He felt that he was in the mountains now, floating above the mountains, in and out among the hills, floating in the sunlight, cool and free, looking down at the mountains, looking down at all the colors . . . floating . . . floating. . . .

Some of the older people at the church still referred to the mountain trips as hayrides, but there was no longer any hay involved. Hampton provided his two flatbed trucks that the pickers used, and several layers of quilts and spreads and blankets were put down in place of hay. Mr. Dundean drove one of the trucks and saw to it that Shirley sat up front with him. Kite and Lynette, Andrew and a girl named Susan, and half a dozen others were on the other truck, which Dr. Estelle drove, with Mrs. Estelle riding shotgun. They pulled out of the churchyard a little after three. The sun was still bright and hot, but there were mounds of huge white clouds, like sailing ships, anchored low in the sky just south of town.

"I never have been up in the mountains before," Kite said. "I been looking forward to it."

"You really never been to the mountains before?" Susan said.

"I never had even seen any mountains till I got up here.

Ruth and Hampton been saying we would go up some time and have a picnic, but I think they used to do that with Little Hampton, so it makes 'em feel sad to be reminded of it."

"You ever been to the beach?" Susan said.

"No, not the beach either. I never have seen the ocean even."

"Gee," Lynette said, almost sighing. Then: "Mama and Daddy and me and Kip go down to Edisto Island for the first two weeks in August most summers. Maybe you could come with us this summer. Will packing be over by then?"

"Prob'ly," Andrew said.

"I don't know. Do you think your mama and daddy would let me?"

"Sure. They'd love for you to."

Susan said, "They're gonna think you're such an improvement over Pruitt, they'll go along with anything."

"I sure would like to."

They were sitting with their backs against the cab, watching the countryside roll away from them. Already there were fewer houses, and the land itself was getting hillier. They were riding through pinewoods striped with sunlight, bright green cornfields, vineyards, and orchards where the peaches had just now started turning.

"When we get up in the mountains," Kite said, "will there be peach orchards in blossom?"

"There won't be any peach orchards at all," Andrew told him. "It's not warm enough. Just apple orchards."

"If you come up here in the fall," Lynette said, "along in October, when the leaves are turning, you see these little stands all along the roadside selling mountain apples and mountain cider."

"It's just sweet cider at the stands," Andrew said, "but my daddy says you can get hard cider too, if you know who to go to. Bootleg, too, up in these mountains, if you know who to go to."

They were passing a fenced-in meadow where three fine-looking horses stood in the shade of an unpainted barn. Lynette's eyes lit up.

"Is Ty-rone as pretty as those?" Kite said.

"Prettier," she said.

"I think you oughta ride him to work some day."

"Maybe I will," she said.

The trucks made a sharp turn to the left, and then right there beside them—several miles away but looking much closer, close enough to be more green than blue—was a ridge of small mountains.

"Hogback," Andrew said, pointing.

"Can we see it from our house?" Kite said.

Andrew shook his head. "Too little."

Less than half an hour later they passed through a small town called Hogback, where the stores and houses on one side of the street were backed up against the mountain, and on the other side the valley dropped off so suddenly that the buildings were up on pilings and didn't even have back doors; or if they did, they opened onto air and a ladder. On the outskirts of town Kite noticed a series of hillside vineyards.

"Are we gonna see any tobacco fields?" he said.

"Not where we're going. That's on up farther north."

Kite turned back to Lynette. "Have you ever smoked grapevines?"

"Grapevines?"

"I never had either till Andrew showed me. If you ever smoked rabbit tobacco, grapevines—muscadine vines, anyway—are a whole lot better than that. Good and sweet. Maybe I can find some when we get up to the lake."

They were climbing now—Hampton's old trucks groaning and straining—and the countryside was not just rolling away but slowly sinking right out from under them. Fewer farms and open fields, now, and more woods, deeper and thicker and starred with mountain azalea and laurel. The air clean and light, laced with honeysuckle.

Then the road began winding, and the woods were mainly just on one side, on the other side the rough wall of reddish-gray rock that the road had been cut through. Sometimes there were small waterfalls coming off the rocks and splashing into the road. Every half mile or so the woods fell away, or had been cut away, and they had a quick view of the rolling countryside they had left behind and below, spread out for miles and miles, the houses and barns and cars just tiny specks.

The road kept getting steeper and the curves sharper—one curve right after another, like a corkscrew. The sun seemed to be swimming in circles just above their heads, and the way the shadows flicked across the truck and the road made Kite dizzy and queasy. His ears were popping. He wished the trucks would stop for a few minutes. He suddenly realized that the air had turned cooler; he put his arm around Lynette's shoulders.

"I don't think it's much farther now," she said.

"If your ears are popping," Andrew said, "it helps to swallow."

After they had climbed for another quarter of an hour, the breaks in the trees showed not the piedmont down below but the ranges of mountains to the north and west, layer after layer, moving from green to gray to blue to violet and finally blending with the sky at the horizon. Kite did not think that he had ever seen so far before. It took his breath away.

"Is that the way the ocean looks?"

"A little bit," Lynette said.

"It's beautiful."

A few minutes later, Andrew said, "Look down there," and nodded toward the left-hand side of the truck bed. Kite got up on his knees so that he could see. Through the tops of the trees he glimpsed bright scraps of blue-green water, and then, as they rounded yet another curve and started the downgrade, he had a fine quick view of the whole lake, shaped like a fat hourglass, sparkling and shimmering. It looked as if you could climb to the top of one of these tall pines and dive into it from here. But it was several more minutes before the trucks pulled up in front of a low and windowless log building. They could not see the lake at all from here; it lay beyond a narrow stand of pines and cedars. Most of the boys had their trunks on under their other pants, and the rest had not worn anything except their trunks and had their other pants rolled up with their towels. The girls, on the other hand, went into the log bathhouse to change. Kite and Andrew walked far enough into the woods to be able to see the lake and waited there for

Lynette and Susan. It felt good, Kite thought, just to be standing still; just to have his feet on solid ground.

"Do you all come up here a lot?"

"Oh, three or four times every summer. It's just cleaner and prettier than most of the pools and ponds around home."

"It sure is pretty, all right."

They watched some of the others dashing into the water, splashing, squealing. Dashing back out again.

"It's real cold, too," Andrew said. "Fed by streams right off the top of the mountain."

"How deep is it?" Kite said.

"It's nice and shallow around the edges—you can walk out waist-deep and still see the bottom—but out in the middle it's twenty–thirty feet."

Lynette was coming down the path from the bathhouse, wearing a pale yellow bathing suit, one-piece, and with a big blue-and-white striped towel draped around her shoulders, hiding her breasts. Her legs were very tan and smooth. Susan had a better figure, Kite supposed, but she looked a little pale and dull beside Lynette. And Susan sort of slumped forward when she walked, while Lynette held her back as straight as a ramrod, the way she had been taught to do as a rider, and even barefooted she walked with a definite springiness, as if she were striding up to the judges' stand to pick up a blue ribbon. When she got closer and saw that he was watching her, she folded back the corners of the towel with a big dramatic gesture, like an unveiling.

"Dah-DAH!"

Kite gave a quick little whistle, and both of them laughed. She really wasn't all that flat, Kite thought, and the fact that she didn't seem to care that she was still small, the way she kidded about it, that made up for whatever wasn't there yet, made it seem unimportant.

He noticed her glance down at the bruises on his thighs and knees, but then she lookd back up at his bare chest, which was hard and brown and unblemished. Sometimes he wished he would begin to get some hair on his chest, but most of the time he was happy it was still so smooth and clean: the muscles, such as they were, showed up better, he thought.

"Ready?" Andrew said. "We all gotta go in together."

The four of them joined hands and moved out of the woods and across the shore of smooth gray pebbles toward the water. The sun felt very warm and there was no breeze at all—but the water was even colder than Kite had imagined. They automatically tightened their hold on one another's hands and gritted their teeth, and before they were in even ankle-deep Susan was squealing and pulling back.

"Come on," Andrew said, "come on, come on." It was every bit as cold, Kite thought, as the water tunnel had been, but here, at least, he had some choice and control. When the water got just above their knees—they were still holding hands—Andrew fell forward and pulled the others with him. After the slow torture of wading in, that final fall felt delicious. Kite and Lynette and Andrew went all the way under, but Susan must have almost bounced off the surface; when they looked around she was already scrambling for the shore.

"You didn't even get wet," Andrew yelled.

Beyond Susan, standing farther back on the shore, were Dr. and Mrs. Estelle, both with bathing suits on; Mr. Dundean, still wearing his overalls and shirt and hat; and next to him, in a two-piece suit with red flowers all over it—Shirley Dundean. The background color of the suit was so close to the ivory color of her skin that it almost looked as if she just had flowers on. The sunlight haloed her blond hair and the swell of her hips, and when she turned toward her daddy it lit up the curves of her breasts and stomach and made Kite catch his breath.

"Jesus."

He turned quickly and looked behind him. Lynette was already ten yards away, swimming strong, headed out toward the middle. He glanced once more toward the shore and then plunged in and took off after her. Once he caught up with her, they swam side by side until they had gotten far away from the others. Then they joined hands again and floated on their backs.

"You're a pretty good swimmer," Kite said.

"Yeah?"

"Better than Susan."

She shoved water at him with the heel of her left hand. Her dark hair looked even darker and shinier now, and her whole face seemed to be sparkling. He caught her free hand in his and pulled her closer to him, both of them treading water. Their knees bumped together. Kissing.

Then they turned onto their backs again. Out in the middle of the lake.

The lake, Kite thought, was like blue soup at the bottom of a deep green bowl. The mountains rose on every side, low and gentle and sunstruck on the side they had come from; higher, craggier, deeply shadowed on the far side. It was very quiet and peaceful. The voices of the others, on the shore and in the shallow water, sounded muffled and faded. The cold water . . . the warm sun . . . Lynette . . . this seemed to be exactly what the view of the mountains had promised all along, from that very first morning when he looked out the upstairs windows.

When they got back to the shore, they stretched out on their towels in the sun, beside Andrew and Susan. Kite fell asleep within minutes and dreamed that he and Shirley Dundean were castaways on a tropical island. But he was wearing the pants and coat he wore on Sundays, and a shirt and tie, and socks and shoes. Shirley came wading up out of the water completely naked, and shivering, and asked him to dry her off with the big red flowers that were growing all around. She wouldn't let him touch her with his hands, just with the flowers. "Why not?" he said. "My hands are clean." But she wouldn't tell him.

When Andrew woke him up he had a hard-on, and the sun had sunk close to the top of the mountain.

"I'll race you across to the other side," Andrew said.

Kite hated not to oblige, since Andrew had been stuck there with Susan and had hardly gotten to swim at all so far. He got slowly to his feet and stumbled into the lake, still half asleep and more than half hard—but the freezing water quickly woke him and withered him.

"Be careful," Susan shouted.

The lake was less than a mile across at that point. They swam steadily and easily, not really racing at all. Even so, Kite began to feel tired before they got very close; and once they had come within thirty feet or so, Andrew put out a burst of speed and got there first by several lengths. They climbed up onto the bank to rest for a while before swimming back.

The other side looked farther away than Kite had expected—partly because they were sitting in the dark shadow of the mountain, while the other shore was still in bright sunlight. That made it seem as if they were not only a good distance away but also several hours older. There was a mild breeze at their backs now, and no sounds at all reached them across the water. They could barely tell which figures were Lynette and Susan, but they could see that they were waving, and waved back. Farther up the shore, nearer the woods, a fire was burning, flickering palely in the sunshine. They would roast weenies and marshmallows later on. Kite felt hungry already. He tried to spot Shirley Dundean, but most of the crowd near the fire tended to blur together. And it was impossible to recognize anybody in the water.

"Do you think they noticed I had a hard-on?" Kite said.

"I don't think so." Andrew was lying back against the pine straw, his hands behind his head.

"I hope not." Kite was examining the bruises on his legs, so numbed now by the cold water that he couldn't even feel anything when he pressed his fingers against the darkest places. "Something I wanted to ask you, Andrew. .About old Coble. Is it true what Pruitt said?"

"What?"

"About him being queer."

Andrew shrugged. "I don't know about him being queer. I think he just sucks cock sometimes. When he can't get cunt. Which is not very often, I guess, an old geezer like him. Either one."

"Lynette didn't seem very shocked or embarrassed by all that, did she?"

"Not very, I guess. Why?"

"I just wondered how much she knows. About stuff like that. It's hard to tell."

"Why don't you ask her?"

"That's not very romantic, is it, just to come right out and ask her?"

"Romantic?"

"You know what I mean. She's not like Shirley Dundean. Girls like that. I wanta be nice to her. I hadn't even felt like I wanted to do anything like that with her—I guess that's partly because I started feeling sick on the way up here—but then I saw Shirley Dundean and I began to wish I could take Lynette off somewhere for a little while, just by ourselves. You know."

"I don't much think you oughta try that up here," Andrew said.

"Seems to me it's a better time and place up here than I'll get back home." He gazed out across the water. "What if when we get back over there, we just sort of wander off, the four of us; and if anybody says anything, we'll just tell 'em we're going to look for grapevines. Then when we get off a ways, we can split up."

"You really think Lynette's in the mood, huh?"

"I sure do think she is," Kite said. "I may be bad mistaken. But I sure do think she is. So. Will you and Susan go along? Just so it won't look too suspicious. And maybe wait back at the trucks or somewhere till we get back."

"Just don't say I didn't warn you if somebody gets wind of it. Fuckin' at a church picnic. I don't know, Kite."

"I really need to, Andrew. I really want to bad. I keep having these dreams about it all the time."

"It would be nice, I guess, to have some grapevines to smoke on the way back."

When they got back to the other side, the girls had gone to the bathhouse to put their clothes on. Kite and Andrew dried off with the towels they had left behind, slipped their T-shirts on, and walked up through the woods to wait for them.

When they came out, Andrew said, "Let's go see if we can't find some grapevines."

"Yeah," Kite said. "Come on."

"Well, I'll go along," Susan said, "but I'm not saying I'll smoke any."

They took the path that led up the mountain to the lookout site. They could hear the voices of some of the others farther up the path.

"Why don't me and Lynette circle around and come up from the other side?" Kite said. "It looks like it's clear enough. Want to?"

"Okay," Lynette said.

"I guess we better stay on the path," Andrew said, "since Susan's got shorts on."

"If we come across any vines," Kite said, "we'll holler."

"We'll be listening," Andrew said.

As soon as they had moved a few yards off the path and into the woods, Lynette put her hand on his arm.

"Maybe you should go back down and get one of the quilts off the truck," she said.

She was looking at him so soberly that at first he wasn't sure if she was joking or not.

"Okay," he said, still watching her face. It occurred to him that she looked a little scared. "You really want me to?"

"Don't you want to?" she said.

He kissed her lightly on the cheek and turned and ran back down toward the trucks, grabbing hold of a sapling and snagging himself to a stop before he got to the edge of the woods. Dr. Estelle, Mr. Dundean, and a boy named Marvin were taking a large straw basket, two cardboard boxes and a Styrofoam cooler out of the cab of the second truck. He watched them until they had gone out of sight around the corner of the bathhouse. Then he walked nonchalantly into the open. Nobody else was around. He could hear the voices of the others on the far side of the narrow woods and could see the fire through the trees. He strolled alongside the first truck and was just getting ready to reach in for one of the quilts when the cab door swung open, and there, near enough to touch, curtained by one of her daddy's Sunday shirts, was Shirley's rear end, like a flowered balloon. She was backing out and bending over at the same time, looking under the seat.

"Hey, Shirley."

She jumped slightly and twisted around, and for just a second, as the shirt gaped open, it looked to Kite as if she had already taken off the top of her bathing suit and had nothing at all on underneath the shirt.

"God A'mighty, Kite," she said, "don't scare me like that. Where'd you come from anyway?"

"I'm sorry," he said. "I didn't mean to scare you. Did you lose something?"

"I'm tryin' to find the coat hangers; we're gettin' ready to roas' some marshmallows. What're you doin' up here? Did you follow me?"

"I didn' even know you were anywhere around. I'm looking for my socks."

She gazed at him knowingly and gave him a big happy smile. "What would they be doin' in here, Kite? You were in the other truck."

"Was I? Oh, yeah. Okay. That's right." He started edging backward toward the second truck.

"Wait a minute, Kite." She came much closer. She had tied the front ends of the shirt in a knot just above her navel, and now she was sort of picking at the knot with the fingers of both hands.

"You ever been up to the top of the mountain?" she said.

"No, this is my first time up here."

"There's a little path that goes right up to the top. It just takes about five minutes to walk up there, and it's a beautiful view. We could go up there and watch the sunset."

"I don't guess we better. We might get in trouble."

"I thought you liked to get in trouble."

"Sometimes."

"But not tonight?"

"No, not tonight, I guess. Thanks anyway."

"Where's Lynette at?"

"I . . . I don't know for sure. Back at the campfire, I think."

"Well. I don't wanta go up the mountain all by myself." She gave him a pouty look, and her voice was even slower and sulkier than usual. "So I guess I'll just go on back and roas' me some marshmallows with Lynette. I like 'em when they get all toasty brown and bubbly on the outside and all hot and gooey inside."

"Me too," Kite said. "I think I left my socks in the bath-house. I'll catch up with you." And before she could answer he had darted around the end of the truck. Instead of going inside the bathhouse, he circled the long building, trying to walk slowly and look inconspicuous. By the time he came around the front corner again, Shirley was sashaying back down toward the lake. No one else was in sight. He made a beeline for the first truck, pulled one of the quilts off the back, wadded it up in his arms, and ran back up the path.

Lynette had already ambled farther into the woods. When he failed to spot her quickly and stood peering into the layers of green, she gave a sweet little two-note whistle. It occurred to him that it was probably the same sound she used to call her horse. He moved toward the sound—and then she was right there in front of him. Smiling at him. Her eyes larger and darker than ever.

"See right through there?" she said, pointing uphill. "Where that big rock juts out?"

He nodded.

"There's a level place—almost level—just below it. I'll show you."

She was right. Over the top of a thicket of blueberry bushes he saw an open spot the size of a small room, shielded from above by the outcropping of rock, and, on the lower side, dropping away so sharply that it was not likely anybody would approach from below. He took her hand and led the way. And when they got there she took the quilt from him, shook it out, and spread it on the pine straw, close to the rock face. Standing on the far side, facing him but looking down at the quilt, she toed off the brown loafers she was wearing, stepped barefooted onto the faded colors, the stars and dia-monds, and sat down. Kite pulled his sneakers off, standing first on one foot and then the other, and moved across the soft quilt and sat down beside her. She was sitting with her knees drawn up to her chest, and he put his arm around her shoul-ders.

"Are you cold?"

"A little bit," she said. "Are you?"

"No, I feel pretty warm. Feel." And he took one of her hands and put it under his T-shirt against his stomach.

"You're so smooth," she said.

"You are too." He was briskly rubbing her upper arm, first with his palm, then with his knuckles. "Are you getting warmer?"

"A little bit."

"Maybe if we lay down we could fold the quilt over us."

"Okay." She seemed so quiet and shy all of a sudden.

She stretched her legs out and turned onto her side, facing him, and he reached across her and pulled the quilt up over her shoulder. She was almost trembling, he thought, and he reached farther down and gathered the quilt up around her feet and legs, and then scrubbed one hand up and down her thigh and hip; even through the quilt and her blue jeans he could feel how strong she was—and how tense.

When he lay back down beside her he saw that huge bright tears were sliding down her cheeks. She was clutching the edge of the quilt with one hand and held the other against her mouth.

"Lynette. What's wrong? What's the matter?"

"I don't . . . know what to do. I don't . . . know how." She was trying to smile, but she would not look at him.

"That's all right, Lynette. That's not anything to cry about. Don't cry." He put his hand on her shoulder again and gently stroked her side and rested his cheek against the top of her head.

"I'm afraid . . ."

"There's not anything to be afraid of." He drew back a bit and tried to look at her face, but she bowed her head even closer to the ground and seemed to be crying harder, though still without making a sound. "I just want to be with you," he told her. "I just wanted to be alone with you. We don't have to do anything."

"I'm afraid. Of what you'll think. I'm afraid. You'll think I'm teasing you. That I've just been teasing. All along."

"I don't think that. I know you really like me."

"I do. I like you so much. But I want you to like . . . me

too. I want to do ... whatever you want to. I thought I could." She glanced up at him for just an instant, smearing the tears away with her open hand. "I didn't know ... it would suddenly seem ... so different. I have never done *any*-thing with a boy before."

"I *know* you've kissed a boy, 'cause it was me."

"But just kissing. That's all." She was feeling at the pockets of her jeans. "I don't even have a Kleenex."

"I don't either." He skinned off his T-shirt and handed it to her, and she pressed her face into it. "I'm glad you haven't done anything but kiss, Lynette. You're the first girl I've been with who didn't know more than me. Who hadn't done more than me." And as he said this, he wasn't sure but what he felt as much relief as disappointment, and that surprised and baf-fled him as much as Lynette did.

"I know a boy as cute as you has done things with lots of different girls. Older girls. I wanted to be like them."

"No, I haven't either. Just one. I swear to God." He was sitting up cross-legged now, one hand cupping and patting her head, the other stroking her shoulder. "But I'll tell you the truth," he said. "That one knew enough for ten." She looked up again and tried to smile back at him. "It's because of her I know how to do a lot of things that feel good. Sexy. But you don't have to do any of those things—or let me do 'em—to make me like you. I already like you. I thought you could tell that."

"I can," she said. "I know you do. I just don't want you to stop liking me. I want you to like me more."

"I like you more all the time." It occurred to Kite that in a way he was like Jarlene now, and Lynette was like one of the puppies or kittens Jarlene was so gentle with. It occurred to him as well that he might feel more noble still if he didn't keep thinking about Shirley Dundean: wondering if she found somebody to hike up the mountain with; wondering when he might have another chance like that; wondering if *she* was wondering where he and Lynette were.

As if she were reading his thoughts, Lynette said, "I feel so ashamed of myself. I feel like such a baby." And the tears began to flow again.

"Please don't cry, Lynette. Listen. Listen, we'll just lie here and talk. Okay? There's something I wanta tell you about. Something I wanta show you sometime soon. It's something I discovered just by accident. And it's beautiful. I'm sure you've never seen anything like it."

"What is it? You're making this up."

"No, I'm not. I swear to God. But I don't even *know* exactly what it is. And I don't know how to describe it either. It's something you have to see."

"Where is it?"

"It's not too far from the shed. But we can't go there just any time, we have to pick the right time. Early in the morning is the best. Before sunrise. Would your mama and daddy believe you if you told 'em you had to go to work before sunrise?"

"I don't think so."

"Do you ever spend the night at one of your girlfriends' houses?"

"Sometimes. Not very often." She was frowning slightly now, but she had stopped crying. "I still think you're making all this up."

"No, I'm not, you'll see. It's beautiful."

"Who else knows about it?"

"Nobody else. I'm the only one. Well, one other person."

"Who?"

"Not anybody you know."

"A girl?"

"No." He couldn't help laughing. "Not a girl."

"Is it somebody—what was that?"

"What?"

"I thought I heard somebody calling."

They lay still, hardly breathing, and listened. The wind made a smooth whirring sound in the tops of the trees, and the voices they could hear sounded as far away as they had from out in the middle of the lake. But then they heard a much closer voice. On the path. Calling their names.

"Uh-oh," Kite said, getting quickly to his knees and scrambling toward his shoes while Lynette was still kicking her way free of the quilt.

"Where are mine?" she said. "Where are mine?" Half whispering and half crying again.

"Right behind you."

"What're we gonna say?"

"We'll go up a little farther, then cut over to the path and say we went up to the top. Okay?"

They heard their names again, closer still.

"What about the quilt?"

"We'll have to leave it. For now, anyway. Where's my T-shirt?"

"I gave it to you."

"No, you didn't."

They stood on either side of the quilt again, looking down at it in much the same way, it flashed through Kite's mind, that he and Aunt Ruth had looked down at the filled-in well that first Sunday morning. Then he moved to the other side, flipped back one corner, and snatched up his shirt.

"I'm sorry," Lynette said.

"It's okay." He grabbed her hand and they circled away from the path and up through the trees. They kept climbing until they had gained some distance on the voice and then moved quickly back onto the path and stood there panting and gasping, eyes wide, throats aching; hanging onto each other and shifting from one trembling leg to the other, as if in the final stage of a dance marathon. The next time the voice called, Kite answered and they started down.

"Where you two been anyway?" It was Dr. Estelle—angry, red-faced, and sweating, still wearing his swimming trunks. "Didn't you hear me yellin' my head off?"

"No, sir," Kite said. "We just went off looking for some grapevines and then decided to go on up to the top. It's still bright up there; we didn't realize it had got so late down here."

"What's wrong, Lynette? You look like you been crying."

"No, sir, it's just from swimming. I'm fine. We didn't mean to get you worried about us."

Dr. Estelle gave them both a funny look but didn't say another word, just turned around and went back down the path. And they followed right behind him.

On the way back home, lying on his back beside Lynette, with the cool mountain air surging over them, full of the smells of honeysuckle and dew and woods and cornfields, Kite fell asleep and dreamed that they were floating on their backs out in the middle of the lake late at night. Then they heard somebody screaming. . . . It was the truck braking. He sat straight up, uncertain for a moment just where he was but with the definite sensation that he was falling. Lynette put her hand against the small of his back. He could see the glimmering lights of houses far below them in a valley. When he lay back down, she put her hand in his. Lying there watching the stars stream through the sky, Kite kept thinking about the quilt spread out up there on the mountainside; small animals pausing and sniffing at its edges, snakes slithering across it. In the fall, red and yellow leaves would drift down on top of it and imprint their patterns on the stars and diamonds. And then the snow would cover it. But it would still be there in the spring when the snows melted. It would surely be there for many years before it rotted into the ground.

When they got back to the church, the Estelles, who lived in town, offered to give Lynette a ride home, so she got in the car with Mrs. Estelle, and Kite got into the cab of the truck with the doctor.

Once they were out on the highway, Dr. Estelle said, "Now, Kite, I'm not gonna say anything to Lynette's daddy or to your Uncle Hampton about you all going off the way you did. I hate to think what they would have to say if I did. But I hope you know now you shouldn't have done such a thing as that, and I better not hear tell of it again."

"No, sir," Kite said. "I'm sorry. I should of known better. We didn't mean to upset you all." It sure would be dumb, he thought, to get in bad trouble when they hadn't even done anything.

"All right."

"And I sure wish you wouldn't say anything more about it to Lynette. She already feels bad about it. And it really was my fault, not hers."

When they got to the shed the other flatbed was already there, and Mr. Dundean's truck was gone. Kite stood out at the road and waved good-by to Lynette and the Estelles and watched their red taillights float away into the dark. He felt too strange and wide-awake to go inside and go to bed. It was almost as if tiny bright lights were floating free all through his limbs and body. Why was it, he wondered, that something that hadn't happened could make him feel so different? More different, he was almost sure, than if it *had* happened—even though it was something he realized he had been looking forward to and hoping for since that first day he saw Lynette in the Clock. Maybe it was because now he still had it to look forward to. Maybe, sometimes, the looking forward was almost as good as the fucking. He certainly felt, right now anyway, that he would be content to go on looking forward to it for a long time. The only thing that was really important was to keep on seeing Lynette and to be alone with her again sometime soon. When he had said that to her up at the lake, it had just come out; it was just a way to try to get her to stop crying. But now it seemed true, and he believed it himself.

He wandered around to the back of the shed and then down the narrow dirt road that led into the orchards. Trees lined both sides of the road and seemed very close and still at night, and the air was still here too—warm compared to the air in the mountains, but not uncomfortable—and heavy with the sweet, cottony odor of peaches. There had been times during the past few weeks when he had thought he never again wanted to see or smell or taste a peach; but now their fragrance, already as much a part of summer as the heat of the sun, made him feel that he was home, and that the rest of the summer was going to be good. He thought of the peaches lining the windowsills in Ruth's kitchen, where the smell was as strong as it was in the orchard. He had had peaches and cream for breakfast three mornings that week; and on Monday and Wednesday they had eaten peach cobbler twice a day, hot for dinner and cold for supper. Tomorrow afternoon, after church, Hampton had said that they would churn peach ice cream; and Ruth would soon begin putting up preserves.

The smell of peaches grew so strong, so full-bodied, there in the dark, that he could almost see them glowing among the deep shadows of the trees—large and elegant ornaments, seamed and peaked; fleshy; florid. He jumped the ditch at the side of the road, moved into the edge of the orchard, and stuck his hand into the clusters of slender curved leaves. The limb creaked under the weight of the fruit. This was one of the orchards where some trees beside the road were left for people in town who wanted to pick their own tree-ripened fruit. Overripe peaches came off in his hands; others thudded into the grass. When he came on one that was not too soft, he picked it and wiped the fuzz off with the tail of his shirt. The juice and the flesh were warm and mellow.

"Don't move. Hold it right there."

The voice came from behind him, and at the same instant something hard prodded into the small of his back.

Then Pruitt's voice came out of the darkness somewhere in front of him—close by, but he couldn't see him.

"That's a shotgun Sammy's holdin', and he'd just as soon blow you right in half if I tell him to."

Kite held his breath. He wondered if it really was a shotgun. It might just be a stick. And even if it was a gun it might not be loaded.

"You don't know about my brother Sammy, do ya?"

Kite didn't answer. He was trying to decide if he should act even scareder than he was. That was mainly what they wanted, he thought—just to scare him.

"He's five years older than me," Pruitt said. "In years. But in the head he's about ten years younger. And stuck. He went to school for a few years, but then we decided it wasn't no point in it. Tell Lover Boy here what they called you at school."

A choked-off giggle, and the pressure on his back eased a bit. "You."

"*Tell* him."

"Simple Sammy."

"Simple Sammy," Pruitt said. "He'll do what I tell him. And if he was to get sent away we'd be better off."

Was he lying? Were they making all this up? Kite could not remember ever hearing that Pruitt had a brother. But he no longer felt so sure that all they wanted to do was scare him.

Something glimmered in the corner of his eye, and Pruitt was standing right there beside him, pressing something cold and smooth against his cheek.

"Have a good time up at the lake, Lover Boy?"

Kite felt that if he opened his mouth to speak the knife would slice right through.

"I ask you a question, asshole." He lifted the knife a fraction of an inch.

"Yeah."

"Yeah what?"

"I had a *great* time up at the lake."

"Yeah? Yeah, that's good. I wanta hear all about it. I bet Lynette wore her little yellow bathing suit, didn't she? I've seen her in that little yellow bathing suit. I've seen her in her birthday suit too. So has Sammy. You don't think you're the only one that's fucked little Lynette, do you?"

"I never have."

"You never have what?"

"Fucked her. I never have."

"You expeck me to believe that? I keep an eye out on you two."

"I want my mama and daddy's picture back."

Pruitt snorted. "You do, huh? Well, you can just keep wantin'."

"You old enough . . . your wants not to hurt you," Sammy said.

"I took your mama and daddy's picture home, and me and Sammy pissed on it."

Sammy giggled and Kite felt the end of the shotgun barrel jog against his backbone.

"How'd you like to piss on Lover Boy here, Sammy?"

Sammy giggled again.

"Lay down," Pruitt said, his voice harder, pointing the butcher knife at the ground.

Kite felt his knees sink into the soft ground and then felt the cool grass under his palms. He stretched out on his stomach, his eyes on Pruitt's work boots.

"Fold your arms acrost your back."

Kite suddenly remembered that when he was a small child somebody (who could it have been?) taught him how to take a bow with one forearm across his back and the other across his stomach.

"Now turn over," Pruitt ordered.

Kite turned over, and now his arms were pinned underneath him. "Gimme the gun," Pruitt said, and Kite saw now that it was a real gun, a double-barrel. He still hoped it might not be loaded, but there was no way to find out.

And then Sammy was looming over him. He had on a white T-shirt and light-colored baggy wash pants held up by suspenders. He was much bigger than Pruitt. Shaped like a potato, Kite thought, and his chin looked like a potato. His nostrils were huge and black. As he slowly unbuttoned his fly he gazed off into the darkness, and it looked to Kite as if he was smiling in a sort of shy embarrassed way.

Then all of a sudden Sammy seemed to light up from inside, like a jack o'lantern. His T-shirt got brighter and one of his ears was glowing. When he turned his head his whole face got pale and shiny, and his mouth dropped open like a big doll's. Kite thought for a minute that he wasn't even real.

"Shit fire," Pruitt said, "somebody's up at the shed. Come on, Bubba." Kite saw Pruitt reach out and grab Sammy's arm. Then the end of the shotgun was swinging back and forth just above his face. Kite longed to turn his head aside, but he forced himself to keep his eyes on those two black holes, like Sammy's nostrils.

"You stay right where you are, asshole—and keep quiet," Pruitt said, "or you'll get your head blowed off."

Then the gun swung away, and Kite heard the two of them move off into the orchard. He lay still and looked up into the leaves of the trees. The lights from the shed picked out patches of green and brown and red in a way that made the blackness behind those patches seem even blacker. Kite eased his arms out from under his back and braced his heels against the ground, ready to make a dash for it if the lights went out. He stayed that way for what seemed a long time, listening, straining, for any sound that would let him know how far away Pruitt and Sammy had gone. There was no sound that he could be sure of—not in the orchard and not up at the shed. Just crickets. The lights stayed on; he wondered what Hampton was doing up there this time of night. Was he staying awake waiting for him to come home? Worried because he was late?

He rolled very gently onto his stomach and lay still again, keeping his head low. He waited. Listening. Then he rolled over several more times and dropped like a log into the shallow ditch. He had no sooner hit than he was on his hands and knees, and then up on all fours and scrambling toward the shed, expecting any instant to hear the shotgun blast.

There was an open space of half a hundred feet between the end of the orchard, where the ditches started, and the shed itself. He paused there in the edge of the trees long enough to take a deep breath and then, still bent almost double, his shoulders hunched, sprinted for the truck. Flattening himself across the hood, he looked back through the windshield. The trees, so still and vivid in the lights from the shed, looked almost unreal. He told himself that Pruitt and Sammy were probably halfway home by now. Even so, he eased in a crouch back into the shadows of the shed and then did half a cartwheel up onto the loading platform and then fell back against the wall just inside the doorway. Sammy was standing in the shadows not more than ten yards away, gazing right at him. But it wasn't Sammy. It was Boydy. And Kite could tell that the old man was even more surprised and scared than he was.

"It's okay, Boydy, it's just me—it's Kite. I didn't mean to scare you."

The old man turned his head sideways, as if he could see better out of one eye than the other. Or maybe just out of the corner of one eye.

"Mistah Kite?"

"Yessir. You know me now. I know you do. Where's Mister Hampton?"

"He tol' me keep an eye open."

"He's not up here?"

"Not up here? Nosah." He turned his head toward the front of the shed and Kite followed his gaze, but there was no one there.

"You were the one turned the lights on?"

"I bes' turn 'em off now." He looked somewhat shame-faced, as if he thought he was being reprimanded, and began to move toward the switch on the back wall.

"Ahn-uh," Kite said, "that's okay. Leave 'em on a little while. Some boys might be out there in the orchard. Up to mischief."

Boydy had come closer, but stopped now and looked at him more directly. "You all been out in the orchert?"

"I was in trouble out there. That's why I'm glad you turned the lights on." Kite wasn't sure whether what he felt was mostly gratitude or mostly guilt. But he knew now that it wasn't Boydy who took the picture. And so it didn't seem possible either that he had had anything to do with Little Hampton's death.

Boydy moved a couple of slow steps closer and Kite saw that he still looked scared and trembly, and that made him look even older than usual.

"Did you see my boy out there?" he said.

"Who?"

"My boy. Kilt in combad. Was he one of 'em out yonder in the orchert?"

Kite wasn't at all sure he was understanding him right, but he shook his head. "No. No, it was Pruitt and Sammy."

"He come back sometimes. Summer nights. Lookin' for his girlfrien'. But he's not a bad boy. I was mis-took. I needs to make it up to him. But he won't have nought to do with me."

"I reckon he understands," Kite said. He didn't know what to make of all this, but he could tell that the old man was troubled. Crazy. He wanted so badly to tell him how much he liked the glass wall; he wanted to ask him if he could come down sometime and help him work on it, add some pieces to it, maybe finish out the empty spots. But he didn't know how Boydy would feel if he knew that he had been down there, practically spying on him, and had been inside his house when he wasn't at home.

"I reckon it's time for me *and* you to be headin' home to bed, don't you?"

"I reckon you right," Boydy said. But he stood very still, gazing in Kite's direction for several seconds. Then he turned and wandered back toward the front of the shed. He eased sideways down the three wooden steps, holding onto the single railing with both hands.

Kite felt sure that Pruitt and Sammy were home in their beds by now. He thought of them lying in the dark, side by side, laughing about how funny he had looked stretched out on the ground, his Adam's apple twitching, waiting to get pissed on by Sammy. He hoped that would keep them happy for a while.

He went to the light switch and pulled down the handle. Then he jumped off the platform and ambled down the path toward the house. He knew it must be close to midnight, but he felt wide awake. He felt light-headed. So much had happened in just one day. Good and bad surprises. Narrow escapes. New feelings. And the thing of it was, he hadn't done anything wrong. He had stayed out of trouble. And it hadn't been so hard to do. It seemed to him now that if he took things as they came, if he didn't get lazy or too easy on himself, if he minded his manners . . . then every day, even every hour, would be another piece of glass fitted into the pattern. And sooner or later his new life would become as good as he wanted it to be. As good as he knew it was supposed to be. Then it would not just be his *new* life anymore—it would be his life.

On the way home from church, Hampton had gone past the turnoff, headed on toward town, before Kite realized it.

"Hey, where're we goin'?"

Hampton glanced up at him in the rearview mirror.

"Your Aunt Ruth felt like you deserved a little re-ward, since you been workin' so hard." His aunt nodded.

"What kind of a reward?"

"You'll see. Just hold your horses."

Kite thought maybe they were going to have Sunday dinner at a restaurant in town. That wouldn't be too great of a reward as far as he was concerned. All it would mean was that he wouldn't have to wash the dishes. Then it came into his mind that they might be going to a restaurant where Lynette and her mama and daddy and Kip would be having dinner too. The thought of seeing her again began to get him excited. Especially the thought of seeing her with both their families around, so they wouldn't really be able to say much of anything to each other, but they would both be thinking about what happened yesterday, and they would smile at each other in a way that would show that that was what they were thinking about. Maybe the Bakers would even ask him to go back home with them for a while after dinner. He leaned away from the seat, so the air could get to his back.

When they got to Lenfield, Hampton drove down the main street and then turned left across the railroad tracks. When he began to slow up, all that Kite could see was a Dari-Queen. He didn't think the Bakers were very likely to have Sunday dinner at a Dari-Queen. Then Hampton pulled off on the other side of the road, in front of a long grimy brick bulding with a wooden porch. A sign painted on the back wall of the porch said SNYDERS COAL & ICE. A man in overalls and a dirty T-shirt was stretched out on a thin gray mattress at one end of the porch.

Hampton handed a dollar bill back to Kite.

"Tell that fella you want a real good cold 'un," Aunt Ruth said.

By the time Kite was halfway up the porch steps the man was ambling toward a heavy-looking wood door with a big metal handle that he pushed down on with both hands. Kite was right behind him and saw that there were three big ice picks stuck in the door. On the floor to the right of the door lay several pairs of worn and blackened work gloves and a huge pair of tongs, like the gaping jawbones of some ferocious animal. And the animal's breath, smears of white steam, quickened and shifted when the man swung the door partway open. Kite followed him, somewhat hesitantly, into a cold cave of a room, where both the light and the smell seemed wrong; the wrong side of a mirror. The floor was wooden slats, like the floor of a bathhouse, and the walls were tin, the color of a gun barrel. Blocks of ice sat all around like pieces of furniture, some as long as a couch, some as tall as the wardrobe in his bedroom, some not much bigger than footstools. And against the wall on the left were two rows of watermelons, cannonballs.

"Take your pick," the man told him.

"Are they all of 'em good and cold?" He was already shivering.

"I 'magine so, they been in here all night."

"How 'bout this one here then?" Kite touched a medium-sized one with the toe of his shoe and saw himself, come fall, kicking a field goal in the high-school stadium while everybody cheered.

"Looks good to me."

Kite handed the man the dollar bill and picked up the cold, slippery, wet melon, holding it carefully away from his Sunday clothes. The man shut the thick door behind them, followed Kite back down to the car, and gave Hampton some change.

"If it ain't a good 'un come on back and I'll let you have another'n."

Hampton said, "We thank you, Bobby."

Kite had put the melon on the floor in the back, and on the way home he slipped his shoes and socks off and put his bare feet on it and tried to feel the cold flow up his leg, to his crotch and then to his stomach and then to his face. He wished he never had thought about the possibility of seeing Lynette, because now he felt disappointed and frustrated. As if they had just missed each other. The way he felt sometimes when he woke up too soon from a good dream.

When they got back home they left the melon in the car until after dinner. Then, while Kite went out to get it, his aunt spread newspapers on the cleared table and his uncle rinsed off the butcher knife that he had carved the cold baked chicken with. The melon was dry now but still cold, and Kite held it against his T-shirted stomach as he carried it across the yard. And onto the porch. He set it down in the center of the table. Dah-DAH. This would be the first watermelon he had had since last summer. It made him think about Jarlene. And since he was already thinking about Lynette, the two of them sort of blended together in his mind.

"You want to be the cutter?" Hampton said.

"You," Kite said.

Hampton sited the knife blade across the middle of the smooth dark-green surface, the same color and sheen as an oak leaf; then he sawed very carefully against the far curve of it until the blade was almost out of sight; then he pulled the knife back toward him, as if he was shifting gears, and bore down. Kite held his breath. At first there was just a black slit; then, like the first hint of dawn, a red glow that made you feel like you wanted to blow on it; and then, as the split got wider and the red got brighter, a single mouth-watering crack, like the sound of ice beginning to thaw on a river. And then the two halves fell apart. Two bright red targets. Two stoplights. Jarlene and Lynette.

"Oooo-ooo, looka there," Ruth said.

And it did look just about perfect. Full ripe but not too ripe. Crisp but frothy. Like frozen crepe myrtle blossoms. Hampton cut one of the halves in two.

"Is that gonna be too much for you?" He touched the knife point against the glittery flat of tender red flesh, as if he was going to flick out a seed. He was talking to Aunt Ruth.

"Oh, sakes yes. Why don't you and me divide that piece?"

So Hampton sliced that section into two even wedges, one for Ruth and one for himself, and then he set the other full quarter piece in front of Kite. Ruth handed him an iced-tea spoon, and he reached across the table for the salt shaker. The first bite he put in his mouth seemed as sweet as anything he ever had tasted. And the second bite was even sweeter and juicer than the first one.

"Boy oh boy," he said. "I think I've died and gone to heaven."

"I don't reckon they grow melons this good down yonder in the sand flats," Hampton said.

"No, sir," Kite said.

He leaned over to spit out a seed and saw something in the newspaper that made him swallow. It was an ad for a movie at a drive-in, and he couldn't help but stare at it. The movie's name was *Tawny*, and the ad showed a drawing of a tall full-breasted woman standing with her legs spread wide apart and with her hands on her hips. She had thick wild-looking black hair, and all she had on was a sort of loincloth that looked like it was supposed to be made out of fur, and around her tits a narrow strip of something that Kite imagined to be soft and supple leather. She was barefooted. Kite had to reach down and tug at the crotch of his cut-offs. He didn't think he had ever gotten so hard so fast.

"I guess we need us some napkins, don't we?" Ruth said.

Kite thought she probably expected him to fetch them from the kitchen, but he couldn't stand up. He pretended he hadn't heard her and very carefully scooped out another egg of melon. Hampton got up and went to get the napkins.

Kite looked back down at the ad again. The word TAWNY was spelled out in letters that turned into flames at the tops; and beside the picture of the woman it said, *She ruled strong men with her body.* Those words made Kite feel strong. And unruly. Near the bottom of the ad, in smaller print, were the words *Adults Only.* Then came the name of the drive-in: King Cotton. The o's made to look like fluffy cotton bolls and a little crown on top of the capital C. Kite knew he had seen the King Cotton, knew they had driven past it some time or other, but he couldn't remember where it was. And the ad didn't tell.

Hampton was poking a paper towel at him.

"I never knowed you to like to read better'n eat," he said.

Kite put his arm down on top of the picture. "I just wanta make it last," he said. He saw that they had almost finished their smaller pieces. He took another bite. But the thought of seeing the woman in the picture, seeing her up on a big screen, in color and alive, moving, took most of the taste away. He could have eaten the whole melon and not known what he had eaten and still felt like he was starving. He had never wanted anything as bad as he wanted to see that movie. It was all he could do to keep from begging God to let him see it. Instead, he prayed to be delivered from temptation. The next bite of watermelon stuck in his throat.

Hampton and Ruth were getting up from the table now.

"When you get finish," Hampton said, "just take the rinds out back and throw 'em on the compost pile."

"Yes, sir," Kite said.

Hampton took the half of the melon that was left into the kitchen, where Ruth was clearing space in the refrigerator. Kite leaned back in his chair and stuck his spoon upright in the edge of red meat he hadn't eaten yet. He waited until he was sure that Hampton and Ruth were in their rooms, undressed for their afternoon naps. Then he carefully tore off the part of the page that the ad for *Tawny* was on. He folded it neatly, taking care not to crease the picture. He stood up and slid it gently into the back pocket of his cut-offs. He put the two smaller rinds on top of his own, folded the paper around them, put those on top of the other sheets of paper, and folded those. Then he carried the whole package across the back yard. Tawny was standing on top of the well house, legs wide apart, her hands on her hips. She was standing just inside the barn door, so that most of her body was shadowed, but the hot sunlight coated her thick thighs, her legs and feet. She was standing on the far side of the garden, where the path came out of the woods, and she tossed her mane of blue-black hair like a wild mare. Kite dumped the melon rinds behind the barn and put the newspapers in the trash burner.

Upstairs in his room, he took the picture out of his pocket and looked at it again. He would have liked to jack off then and there, holding the picture in one hand and his cock in the other. But he decided to wait. Not to give in. He slid the picture under the tissue paper under his underwear in the second drawer. Then he put on his tennis shoes and went back downstairs. Back across the yard. Around the upper edge of the garden. And into the woods.

When he got to the Crowleys' nobody was home. Sometimes they went over to Andrew's grandma's house for Sunday dinner. He sat down on the back steps. He wondered if he could have called Lynette while Ruth and Hampton were asleep without waking them up. But what would have been the point in that? He knew Lynette's daddy didn't like for boys to call her, and there was probably no way they could have gotten together on a Sunday afternoon. Maybe they could sneak off together at the lunch break tomorrow.

It suddenly dawned on him that the newspapers Ruth had spread out for the melon would have been old ones. But how old? It was usually the same movie on Friday and Saturday—

but how about Sunday? He didn't know. He didn't even know if they showed movies on Sunday. He didn't even know if the papers were this week's.

He got up off the steps and headed back home. It was the hottest time of day. Every leaf, every fencepost, Andrew's bike, Chap's wagon, everything in sight—Kite's own face and hands—seemed made out of wax and on the verge of melting into shapelessness and flowing like lava. There was no sound. Nothing was moving. The air had the same sort of dead no-smell the icehouse had had.

Inside the woods it was as close and breathless and steamy as it was inside the shed on afternoons like this.

The trash burner sat in a sandy spot separated from the barn by several small pines all tied together by honeysuckle vines. Kite went around to the front corner of the barn so that he could see the whole back yard and the back door; he wanted to be sure nobody was in sight. Then he went back and pawed through the soggy, sticky, sweet-smelling papers until he found the piece he had torn the ad out of. It was Friday's. Two days ago. He felt tantalized.

Back inside the house, on the card table in the den, he found parts of the morning paper, the *Sunday Sentinel.* He turned the pages as quickly and quietly as he could. He became a spy trying to photograph secret documents before the Gestapo broke down the door. When he found the amusement page there was the same ad exactly: the same picture, the same words. It seemed like a promise. Like if the dove had come back the second time, with another olive twig. He felt himself starting to get hard again.

"You sure have got in-ter-ested in the news all of a sudden." Hampton was standing in the doorway right behind him.

"Yes sir." He put the paper back down. "It sure is hot, idn't it?"

"Too hot even to sleep."

Kite moved toward the door, his hands in his pockets. "I'm gonna go over and see if Andrew's at home. We might go down to the river to cool off some."

"Maybe Andrew and Chap would like to come over this evenin' and help you finish up the watermelon."

"Yes sir, I'll ask 'em."

The Crowleys were not back home yet. Kite went around to the side of Mr. Crowley's tractor shed, where there was a spigot, two feet high, at a wooden trough. When he first turned it on, the water was almost hot enough to scald. While he waited for it to get cool he peeled off his T-shirt. Then he got down on his knees and stuck his head under the faucet and held it there for a minute or more. The gush of cold water, gently massaging his scalp, felt as good as the melon had tasted and made him think of the time Jarlene had washed his hair in the river. He held his T-shirt under the faucet and got it soaking wet and then put it back on. He lay down on the grass in the shadow of the shed and gazed up into the bright shiny leaves of a chinaberrry tree.

Too hot to sleep.

Jarlene.

Crying like a baby when Loper got run over.

He had carried him back to the barn and got blood all over his new shirt.

Lynette.

Her yellow bathing suit.

He was lying on the flatbed truck again, weaving down the mountain.

Too hot to sleep.

He saw himself dressed out in a brand-new red-and-white football uniform. But without a helmet. And barefooted. He was getting set to make a place kick. The grass was bright and shiny under the white lights. The lights were like full moons in sets of three. He had half-moons of blacking under his eyes. The crowd was holding its breath. He shifted from one foot to the other, rubbed his hands together, let one knee bend a bit, then the other; eyed the ball. He had never felt more confident. More famous.

A split second before his toe touched it, the football turned into a watermelon and his foot sank into it up to his ankle. He couldn't get it off. He was trying to run with the melon still

stuck on his foot. The crowd was roaring like thunder. Now
he had melons on both feet. The football field had turned into
a melon patch full of ready melons that seemed to be swelling
like black balloons. He was scared to death. Somebody was
right behind him, but he didn't know who. He glanced to one
side and saw Jarlene. She was running too. She was naked as a
jaybird. The melons began to explode all around them. The
gobbets of flesh were warm and sticky, and the seeds stung
his face and arms and legs. He thought about poor Jarlene. He
could hear her crying.

"Kite."

The crowd got quiet.

"Kite."

"Yeah."

Andrew was looking down at him.

"You okay?"

"Sure."

"You were frownin' like ol' man Baker was coming after
you with a shotgun."

Kite sat up. His T-shirt was dry in front but still wet in the
back. And itching. He tugged it off. "Where you been?"

"We had dinner at Grandma Green's and Chap got stung
by a yellow jacket and we had to take him to the doctor, his
face swelled up so bad."

"Is he okay?"

"Yeah, he's okay. He don't feel too good. Or look too swift.
He has to stay in bed the rest of the day, but he'll be okay by
tomorrow."

"Maybe I should go in and say somethin' to him."

"He's already asleep. He's out even colder than you were.
Dr. Alben gave him a shot, he was dead to the world before
we got halfway home."

"Hampton bought us a watermelon after church today at
the icehouse in town. He said maybe you and Chap would
like to come over later on and have a piece of it. Maybe you
could bring back a piece for Chap to have tomorrow."

"Okay, sure. Thanks."

"Somethin' else I need to ask you about. Where is the King
Cotton Drive-In at? You ever go there?"

ιothing but adult movies, but I know where it is. You
Mac Tinsley's fillin' station, where Terry Penninton
ν s some? It's about half a mile on out that way."
"How far is that from here?"
"If you go out to Mill Road and then turn onto Highway
Twelve, it's maybe three–four miles."
"You wanta go?"
"To the King Cotton? Are you kiddin'? First, you gotta
have a car. Then you gotta have a I.D. Then you gotta have
the price of a ticket. I'm naught for three."
"I figured we could climb the fence. Or maybe even see
good enough from outside. Climb a tree or somethin'."
"What's got into you?"
"I saw a picture in the paper about the movie that's on now.
It looked so damn sexy I've had a hard-on all afternoon."
"So? You forgotten how to jack off?"
Kite balled up his damp T-shirt and threw it at Andrew's
face. "What direction is it from here? What's the shortest way
if I don't wanta go by the road?"
"You really goin'?"
"Just tell me."
"Lemme think a minute." Andrew sat down on the grass
and spread the T-shirt out between them, as if he might be
going to draw a map on it. "Okay, you know how you can see
the water tower from the top of that rise across from your
uncle's shed."
"I can't see no water tank at night."
"But you know what direction it's in, right? You'll be able
to see some lights over toward Lenfield. If you head straight
in that direction, you'll be in the orchard a good part of the
way, then in Sam Gault's pasture. Okay?"
"So far."
"Yonder side of Sam's pasture you cross Brushy Creek
Road, but keep straight on in that same direction. You'll have
to go between some houses, but in back of those houses it's
mostly pinewoods and open fields. Then you come out on
Bridge Road. Half a mile up Bridge Road is the innersection
where Tinsley's Esso is. That's Number Twelve. If you don't
aim to go down the highway, then a coupla blocks before the

innersection there's a little street that prob'ly comes out right behind the drive-in."

"Prob'ly?"

"I mean, unless it's a dead end or somethin'. But now most of that's a nigger section, that's why I'm not too sure. But at least there wouldn't be nobody down in there likely to reco'nize you. And maybe you're tan enough not to look too noticeable at night."

"You sure you don't wanta come with me?"

"Are you crazy? My daddy'd nail my ass to the side of this shed if he caught me sneakin' out at night to go see a sex picture."

Kite thought that might be mild compared to what Hampton would do to him.

Soon after supper, while Hampton had the TV on, Kite had unlatched the window screen in his bathroom and pushed it loose. Now he carefully lifted it free of the hinges at the top and laid it down very gently on the slope of the roof. He went back to the door at the stairway, eased it open, and listened again. No sound. And no sign of light. He knew that Ruth and Hampton had gone to bed but he wasn't sure if he had given them time enough to get to sleep. From out on the roof he would be able to see if the light was still on in their bedroom. Not that that would make much difference. He couldn't wait any longer. It already seemed like he'd been waiting for days.

He had spent most of the afternoon at the Crowleys, talking and playing Chinese checkers and peggoty with Andrew and Connie. Around five thirty Andrew had come back home with him for some of the watermelon. Even if Andrew wouldn't go along, at least he had helped him pass the time. But the three hours since supper had dragged by as slow as cold molasses. More than once he had changed his mind and told the devil to get behind him. Then he had opened his drawer and looked at the picture again, testing himself, telling himself he was going to tear it up and flush it down the toilet; failing the test. Just before dark he had begun to feel so drowsy (it had cooled off a little but not enough to make much difference) that he had stretched out on his bed, half-way hoping that he might fall asleep and not wake up until morning. Just as he was drifting off he made the mistake of turning onto his stomach, and the next thing he knew he was hard again. And wide awake.

He closed the stairway door, then the bathroom door. With one foot on the rim of the toilet bowl, he put his other knee on the windowsill and ducked his head and shoulders through, then brought his other knee up. Straightening a bit in order to shift his left foot out onto the roof itself, he scraped his back painfully against the bottom of the window and cursed under his breath. Then he stood up. He had had the lights off in his room for half an hour, so that his eyes would get used to the dark. And now, outside, it seemed lighter than he had expected. There was a half-moon, bright enough to cast shadows. No clouds.

Crouching slightly, he moved at an easy angle down across the dark grainy shingles toward the lowest part of the gable above the flat roof that sloped out over the kitchen. It would have been an easy jump, but he was afraid that might make too much noise, so he sat down, twisted onto his stomach, and slid off feet first. Being on the roof made him think of the evening he had spent on the roof of the shed waiting for Shirley Dundean to come along. And then he thought of Boydy. He stopped at the edge of the roof and looked out blindly across the back yard toward the woods. Then he reached up and out and caught hold of one of the magnolia limbs. Keeping one foot on the roof, he slid the other along a lower limb, testing it, feeling it give. But he could not see any other possibility. He caught hold of the limb above with his other hand and shoved off from the roof. The limb he was standing on cracked like a gunshot and he scrambled monkeylike toward the trunk and fell against it, scraping the side of his face. He stayed still, hugging the trunk, holding his breath; listening for a sound from inside the house, waiting for a light to come on. After almost a minute he climbed on down. As soon as his feet touched ground he took off running, loping easily across the front lawn toward the path that led to the packing shed, feeling like an Indian feeling like a deer.

He could have followed the path blindfolded.

A dim apricot-colored light was burning near the back of
the shed, and the tin roof had a grayish luster in the moonlight. He stopped at the road, listened, then dashed across and
into the orchard. Even though the ground was rough in the
orchard, it would have been easy running if the pattern the
trees were planted in had conformed to the direction he had to
take; but it didn't. So it was like running an obstacle course:
he was constantly zigzagging, bobbing, ducking to keep from
getting slapped in the face, and trying at the same time to
keep his mind and his eyes on the compass in his head and on
the lay of the land. Fallen fruit was soft and slippery under
his sneakers, its smell as warm and sour-sweet as if somebody
had been baking peach pies and pickling all afternoon.

He came out of the orchard and up against a woods thick
with underbrush. He pulled up short. He should have seen
the woods sooner and veered ... which way? He wanted to
keep the moon just behind his right shoulder. That meant
veer to his left. He moved along the edge of the orchard,
walking now, and came almost immediately to pastureland. A
small herd of cows made still, heavy shadows, flower-shaped
blotches of white. Beyond the cows, several hundred yards
away, a farmhouse in some trees. No lights. It would be safer,
he knew, to stay in the edge of the woods, but the dense undergrowth would slow him down too much. He stepped
through the strands of barbed wire. The ground was smooth
as carpet now; he wished he could run, but he would have to
wait until he got past the cows. As he got nearer, they began
to shift uneasily; the big dumb heads swung slowly round and
stared; some that were lying down got clumsily to their feet
and moved off. What if he caused a stampede? He wondered
if that ever happened with milk cows. He was moving in
among them, now, and laid his hands gently on the warm
flanks. "Easy. Easy." Instead of rotten peaches, he was step-
ping in cow flop. The smells were not so different.

At the farmhouse a dog started barking. Then another, farther away. Kite was moving parallel to the wall of woods; he
was glad he had thought to put on a dark shirt.

Once he was well past the cows, he started jogging. Except

for occasional outcroppings of rock, the ground was level and springy. He was sweating freely, but he was hardly aware of the heat. He felt free and exhilarated. He was not thinking about the movie either. It felt good just to be running, in the dark, by himself; he felt that he could have kept on running for a long time and that it didn't much matter where he ended up. Ahead of him he saw some lights, some of them moving, but it took longer than he expected to get to the road. The lights that weren't moving came from a row of small white houses that faced the pasture. They were flanked at one end by woods and at the other by a cluster of stores and the brighter colored lights of a used-car lot. Kite jumped the ditch, crossed the road, and walked in the direction of the woods. Most of the houses were close together, but between the last house and the one before it there was a deep field of broomstraw. He turned and strolled casually into the field. He had gone perhaps fifty yards from the road, just beyond the backs of the houses, when two dogs came bounding across the field from the house on the right, barking as if they were starved for blood. He bent down and felt along the ground for rocks. The dogs circled behind him. He turned and raised his empty hand and they drew back a bit. A porch light came on at the house. Kite crouched down in the waist-high broom and searched for rocks with both hands. A woman's voice began calling the dogs. "Rusty! Rowdy! Come on back here! What is it, Rusty? Rowdy!" Kite tried crawling on his hands and knees, and his knees found the rocks his hands had not been able to find. The dogs were still barking, but he could tell that they were moving back toward the house. When he looked over his shoulder and saw the porch light go off, he got to his feet and ran all-out toward the line of woods, black and saw-toothed, at the far end of the field. That, too, proved a greater distance than he thought, and the woods were on the far side of a gully some six feet deep, which he did not see in time; he fell headlong down the soft clay bank—but he kept the momentum of his fall going and scrambled up the opposite bank and into the woods. Then rolled onto his back and lay still, breathing hard. The bright stars were twirling right in front of his eyes; he felt he could have reached up and grabbed handfuls of them. And for the first time that night he was aware of the throb of crickets, though he was sure it had been there all along. He sat up and looked back across the field toward the houses. The dogs were still barking. Rusty and Rowdy. He suddenly felt sad and lonely. As if he was lost. Like a little kid.

He got up and started walking. He was in a young stand of loblolly pines, clean and open: easy walking except that the needles were slippery underfoot. As long as he was running he had felt terrific, but now that he had slowed down he felt different, uneasy. The floor of the woods was striped and glittery in the moonlight. He thought about turning around and going back home. But he kept on walking. He thought about walking all the way into Lenfield and finding Lynette's house, throwing pebbles up at her window, and then climbing the drainpipe or a rose trellis or sheets she had tied together up to her bedroom. That was something he had seen in a movie. But he had never seen anything like Tawny in a movie. Or anywhere else. He saw Lynette every day. But not Tawny.... He imagined himself crouching down between those widespread legs, gazing up at the thrust of her tits, smoothing one of his hands along each of her thighs, and taking hold of the furry loincloth with his teeth....

He was headed downhill now and the pine straw was more slippery still. He could hear the sound of water, louder than in the woods at home—though that might just be because it was dark. The way things seemed closer than they turned out to be. But the stream he came to *was* a stream, not a branch. It was much too wide to jump, but he didn't want to waste time looking for a narrower spot, so he waded across. Even at the deepest part the water hardly came to his calves. When he had almost reached the far side, he bent over and scooped handfuls of cold water against his face and into his mouth. Then he started climbing uphill, his sneakers making squishing sounds and sliding, sliding. Halfway up the hill the woods thinned out. And when he reached the crest of the hill he was looking down on Bridge Road. He stood there amazed. And thankful.

And full of admiration for Andrew, who had been able to give him such accurate directions. He looked forward to the day when he would know this whole countryside that well.

Off to his right, perhaps half a mile away, he could see the intersection and the red ESSO sign. He could see the traffic moving on a stretch of Number 12, and farther along a tall black slab against the grayness, blocking out a thin wedge of lights. Directly below him were windowless buildings with junk cars and piles of scrap metal and rubbish out back. He waited until a car turned off Bridge onto a street this side of the intersection. He could follow the taillights for no more than a block, but then they reappeared briefly farther on, moving in the direction of the screen.

He stood in the shadows at the corner of one of the buildings until no cars were in sight along Bridge and then darted across and kept on running, fast but light, until he got to the side street. He slowed down to a canter then because the street was so dark, the darkest place he had been all night, narrow and lined with trees and small houses, some of them not much more than shacks. Instead of a sidewalk, there was only a packed-dirt path, and when he stumbled over the roots of a tree he slowed down to a walk. Most of the houses were dark as caves, and even when there were lights the lights were dim and reddish, like the light from a fire. Very few cars were parked along the street, and there were no driveways between the houses. The smells were different here, too: the smells of food cooking, the smell of dust and woodsmoke. And even from the houses that looked pitch black and lifeless came sounds: voices, a baby crying, music and laughter . . . all muffled by the darkness and the closeness. Kite slowly became aware, too, that at some of the houses people were sitting, still and quiet, in the deep shadows of the cramped porches and the tiny yards. He saw the glow of a cigarette and a palm fan swaying slowly back and forth like a large white leaf.

After several blocks the street curved sharply to the right. There were houses on only one side now, and on the other side the trees were thicker. Ahead of him, where the trees came to an end, he could see a wall, high and thick, like the wall around a prison. He looked above the tops of the trees and there was the back of the screen, looming above him like a huge cut-out section of starless sky . . . imitation sky. He was almost directly under it; it couldn't have been more than thirty yards away. The height and the blankness of it, the silence and the suddenness, the closeness, surprised and unnerved him. It seemed unreal. And the thought of what was on the other side made it seem even more unreal. As if the sky itself was the inside of a bowl, black and solid, and the outside beautiful colors, bright designs.

Where the trees got sparser he moved close to the wall and saw that it was made out of concrete block and had barbed wire strung along the top. It was too high and smooth to try to climb. He moved back along the wall, between the wall and the trees, hoping there might be a tree close enough to jump from; but most of the limbs on that side had been hacked off. The alleyway between the wall and the trees was littered with broken bottles, tin cans, and waste paper—and what looked like scraps of clothing, underwear, old shoes, comic books. Discarded rubbers too, Kite thought. He kept glancing up at the screen, like the sheer square face of a mountain of coal waiting to be climbed. And he imagined himself rappelling down the other side: down through the jungle of Tawny's coal-black hair, down her sturdy neck, down between her boobs, down her smooth belly. . . .

When he got to the corner of the wall he found that a cornfield had been planted on that side. This corn was farther along than Hampton's and came right up against the wall; he wondered how it could even have been plowed that close. Toward the far side of the field, like dark clouds bringing rain to the corn, were two large hardwood trees. If he could get up into one of those it would probably give him a good view of the screen. He set off in that direction, moving diagonally across the field, lifting the paper-sharp blades away with his forearms to keep from getting cut any more than he could help. Or any itchier. The ground was soft and the corn had a thick sweet smell. Each time he glanced back over his shoulder at the screen he could see a little more of the front of it, the picture, like a door opening slowly into a lighted room. At first it was only a sliver of light, then color and movement, then recognizable shapes: thin people with flat faces. When he got close to the trees and turned to look back he saw off to one side a small dilapidated shed, and he felt sure it would offer an even better angle and greater comfort. It was obvious, when he got there, that somebody else had had the same idea. Two shallow wooden crates were leaning up against the back wall, and two boards in the wall had been kicked loose to make a sort of ladder. Kite put one foot on top of the taller crate and hoisted himself up till he had his elbows on the edge of the roof. Two colored men and a small boy were sitting at the front of the shed, their legs dangling. All three of them turned around and looked back at him. The one in the middle was Boydy; he had his baseball cap on.

The other man said, "Come on up, son; it's jes' gettin' good."

Kite looked beyond them at the screen. It was unbelievably bright and beautiful. He felt like he had been blind and was seeing again for the first time. Hundreds of rose-colored fla-mingos stood in a silvery lake, each reflection as clear and still as the birds themselves. Beyond the lake a wall of jungle, brilliant green and black, and above the jungle a snow-crowned mountain soaring in front of a cloudless blue sky.

Just at that moment there was a sort of quiet rumbling from inside the shed. Then it seemed to be coming from some-where under the shed. Kite felt the board that he was stand-ing on move under his feet, and the board that he was leaning on pushed against his chest, as if it was trying to push him off.

"Whoa, here! Whoa, now! Oh, sweet Jesus!" That was the man who had spoken to him. "Come on, boy." And he saw the three of them topple out of sight. On the screen two men in bush jackets and helmets were talking to each other very earnestly, stupidly oblivious of what was happening. And Kite could not decide whether it was the screen or the shed that was swaying. Or both. Then one corner of the screen cracked and fell away, so that it looked like an unfinished jig-saw puzzle. The shed was trying to take life and walk away, and Kite jumped backward and landed on his ass in the corn-field. Car horns had been blowing for several seconds and now more and more joined in. Kite thought the end of the world had come, just as Rev. Fairforest had said it would. Except that he hadn't seen any fire or heard any bombs. And now, with all the horns blaring, he might not hear a bomb if one fell. He got to his feet and moved around the side of the shed. The men and the boy were nowhere in sight. When he looked toward the screen the picture was gone too; all he saw was a huge piece of paper with one corner torn off.

When he got close to Brushy Creek Road again he decided to avoid Rusty and Rowdy by staying at the edge of the pinewoods and circling around. That brought him out in front of more houses, and he walked half a mile before he found another spot that seemed to offer a safe shortcut. This was a long field of peanuts that narrowed into a valley at the far end. The upper side of the valley was a good-sized hill, and he reasoned that he might be able, from the top of that hill, to get his bearings. It was a hard climb in sneakers, and before he got to the top he stopped to catch his breath and looked back down the field. On the far side of the road, beyond a bend, he could see another orchard—not one of Hampton's, he was sure. A clean young orchard was always a pretty sight but this one was even prettier than usual, partly because he was looking down on it from a distance and partly because the irrigation pipes were on. Three tremendous rainbows of white water arced over the trees and rained down on them, so that every leaf seemed to be trembling and shimmering, wet with moonlight. For a moment or two the sight took his mind off everything else. Then he realized that there was no reason to be watering; there had been plenty of rain lately. He wondered if the earthquake had triggered the system.

From the top of the hill he could see, in the opposite direction, an orchard he was positive was Hampton's, and all he had to do to get there was cut through the woods at the bottom of the hill and then move along the lower edge of another cornfield. He glanced back at the rainbows of water, then started down.

He had been praying all the way that the earthquake had not waked Ruth and Hampton, that they had not discovered he was gone, but he knew that was too much to hope for. What were they going to say to him? Maybe they would be more fearful than angry. More disappointed than hurt. He told himself that he should have the strength to tell them the truth, but he also told himself that that would cause them needless pain. And yet, what kind of lie would not cause them pain? Especially if they discovered it was a lie. He felt certain that Ruth was already crying. Perhaps, in the long run, the kindest thing he could do would be to tell them the truth and accept the consequences—even if that meant going back to Baptist. Maybe, after all, he really didn't deserve to live with people who were good and faithful Christians. Even if he got by this time, there might well be another time when he wouldn't get by, when he would cause them even greater shame and sorrow, in return for the kindness and love they had lavished on him so generously. But he knew that they would be sorry to see him go back to Baptist—regardless of what he had done. Perhaps ... if he tried harder—if he prayed every day for help, for forgiveness, for strength—perhaps he could learn, in time, to be good. Perhaps the earthquake had been a warning; perhaps it had been God's way of keeping him from sinning—and he *had*n't sinned, after all; not the way he had expected to. He hadn't really done *any*thing so terrible, had he? Maybe he could just tell Ruth and Hampton that he had not been able to sleep and had decided to go out and run for a while. What was wrong with that?

The first thing he would do when he got back home would be to take the picture he had torn out of the paper, set fire to it, and hold his hand in the flame.

He came out of Hampton's orchard in sight of the shed and jogged loosely down the road. As he turned into the driveway, a figure came out of the shadows between the shed porch and the truck. At first he thought it was Pruitt again. But it was Boydy. How had he gotten back here so quick? Somebody must have driven him. Or maybe it wasn't Boydy he thought he saw at the drive-in. He raised his hand. But Boydy moved away. Kite would have liked to ask him about the earthquake, but he didn't know how to do that without giving himself away. Instead, he headed down the path.

When he got to the edge of the lawn he stopped. The house was dark. Quiet. Then he heard a footstep on the path behind him. He moved quickly and silently across the front yard and sat down on the kitchen steps, under the magnolia. In a moment Boydy came into view. He stopped exactly where Kite himself had stopped. Kite could see the bill of his baseball cap swing slowly from side to side as he scanned the yard. Whether or not Boydy saw him he couldn't tell.

Staying close to the edge of the trees, Boydy moved slowly toward the driveway. Then he stopped again and looked all around, lifting his head as if searching the air for a scent. He took a few more steps, then turned and began to wander across the yard toward the house.

What the hell did he want? Maybe he was going to tell Hampton that he had seen Kite at the drive-in. Maybe he was actually going to wake Hampton up. Why else would he be coming to the house? If he had wanted to talk to *him*, why hadn't he said so up at the shed?

Kite glanced up into the magnolia tree. Maybe he could get back inside, change clothes, and come back down before Boydy even knocked on the door. And even if Hampton got waked up, he could say that Boydy had waked *him* and could deny whatever Boydy said. Which of them would Hampton believe, after all? Boydy couldn't prove anything.

He stood up, wearily. But when he looked back across the yard, Boydy had vanished. He blinked his eyes and looked again. He felt the sweat on his back and shoulders turn cold; he felt, for the first time, that he might be in danger, felt that Boydy might be very near. But that wasn't possible. He had not taken his eyes off him for more than a few seconds. The only explanation was that he had turned around and gone back into the trees. Then Boydy touched him on the leg. He gasped and twisted away, swinging his arm back blindly into space. But it was only Clown. He stooped down and hugged the dog around the neck and scratched the top of his head—all the time keeping one eye on the yard. He expected to see Boydy reappear any minute. He walked around to the front of the house, taking care not to go too close to Ruth and Hampton's window. Then back around by the kitchen and out across the back yard as far as the well house. Boydy was nowhere in sight. "That old fool," he said to Clown, under his breath. He waited a few more minutes, moving back and forth under the magnolia, peering into the shadows. Then he patted Clown on the head, climbed into the tree, onto the roof, and back into his room.

When he turned on the light and looked around, he saw that the picture of Daniel in the lions' den had fallen off the wall. Everything else seemed just the same.

When he woke up the next morning he heard Ruth's and Hampton's voices, but they were not coming from the kitchen or the porch, where they usually came from in the morning; they were coming from outside. He got up and looked out the window. The two of them were standing in the front yard, gazing down at the ground. They were standing exactly where he and Ruth had stood the first morning he was here.

He pulled on his pants and went outside. The well had sunk again. Ruth and Hampton were looking down at the hole the same way they looked at Clown when he had been bothering the neighbors' chickens. Kite came up beside them and leaned over the ragged edge. The only bottom was blackness, about the size of a jar lid.

"Don't get too close," Ruth said.

"Radio says we had us a little earthquake last night," Hampton told him. "Did you feel anything?"

"No, sir," Kite said. "What time was it?"

" 'Bout quarter after 'leven," Ruth said. "Me and Hampton didn't feel it either."

"Shows how sound you sleep when you got a easy conscience," Hampton said.

"Yes sir."

"Me and Ruth are goin' into town and find somebody that can come fill this in for us. You tell 'em up at the shed I'll be there tereckly."

Kite went back inside to finish dressing. He heard the car doors slam and heard the car pull out of the driveway. He opened the second drawer of his chest, tugged the piece of tissue paper out from under his underwear and socks, and laid it on the bed. He put the ad for *Tawny* in the center of the paper, face down. He took all the pictures out of the spiral notebook and laid them on top of the ad. Then he crumpled the tissue paper into a ball. When he got outside he held a match to the paper, and once it was blazing good he dropped the ball of fire down the well. Then he turned away and walked slowly up the path.

When he got in sight of the shed, Tawny was standing on the roof, her legs spread apart and her hands on her hips.

At the lunch break that day he did not try to talk Lynette into sneaking off somewhere. Instead, the two of them and Andrew and Susan went down to the house and watched the trucks dumping rocks and cinders into the well. By midafternoon it was full again. More than full. There was a heap of woods' earth on top, rounded off like a little burial mound. Ruth said that as soon as it settled she was going to plant flowers there again.

Two days later, at the supper table, Hampton said, "I ain't seen old Boydy around lately. I hope he didn't get hurt in the earthquake."

"May have just got so scared he's afraid to venture out," Ruth said.

And the day after that, Kite was sitting on the back steps at dusk, scratching Clown's head and talking to him, when Hampton drove in.

"I been down to Boydy's cabin just now. Looks like it must have collapsed in the earthquake. Ben Pollert and his boy already got it split up for firewood. They said they ain't seen hide nor hair of Boydy since the quake hit neither."

"His *cab*in?" Kite said. "His *cab*in's gone?" He felt sick inside. He had never even had a chance to show it to Lynette.

Hampton gave him a funny look. Kite was already on his feet. It was all he could do to keep from taking off like a shot, running like a crazy man across the back yard and down through the woods—but he couldn't even tell if he would have been headed toward Boydy's clearing or just running, just running to get away from something. Something bad that he never had known was there before.

"What's the matter with you, boy?"

Kite sat back down on the steps.

"Nothing," he said. He could not meet Hampton's stare and looked out across the side yard toward the mound of new earth. Then he remembered sitting there the night of the earthquake, the night Boydy had followed him back from the drive-in. He could almost see the old man again, standing in the shadows on the far side of the yard. And he knew then that Boydy had fallen down the well. That was how he had vanished. That explained it. And he had been down there, down in that well, when Kite set fire to his pictures. He might even have still been conscious and might have seen that ball of fire floating down toward him like a meteor. Would it have gone out, burned up, before it hit him? He might even have still been conscious when the trucks started dumping the rocks in on him. While he and Lynette and Andrew and Susan stood around watching.

"You look a little green around the gills, boy. You musta been eatin' too many peaches."

"I guess so," Kite said.

"You ain't seen old Boydy around lately, have you?"

"No, sir. I can't even remember the last time I saw him."

Part Three

The harvest is past, the summer is ended,
and we are not saved.

Jeremiah 8:20

On Wednesday morning, the week after the trip to the mountains, when Kite stepped up on the platform at the culler, a girl named Judy was in Lynette's place. "Where's Lynette?" he said, but she didn't know. At lunchtime Hampton told him that Lynette's daddy had called to say she had a bad stomachache. When he got off work that afternoon, Kite called her house, and the maid told him that she had had to have her appendix taken out; she was in the hospital at Willisburg.

The next day Ruth offered him a get-well card that she had bought more than a year before for a friend who had died before she could send it. He did not much like the idea of sending Lynette a card that had been intended for somebody who was dead now, and he thought the card looked too flowery and mushy—he would have preferred one with a horse on it—but he sent it anyway. He wanted to write something inside, but he was not sure what to say, or who else would see it. So at the bottom—under the verse that told her God would make her whole "in Body, Mind, and Soul"—he drew a wavy line like a range of mountains and above that a little picture of a kite with the initials K.C. on it.

The Wednesday after that, when he got home from work, Ruth said, "There's a letter for you. It's on the table in the hall." He was sure it must be from Lynette, and if she felt well enough to write so soon, maybe she would even come back to work. Or maybe he could go to see her before long. He took the letter upstairs and opened it in his room. It was not from Lynette. It was from Jarlene.

> Dear Kite,
>
> I have something I have to tell you even tho I hate to worse than anything. I dont know what else to do. I am going to have a baby. I knew something was wrong since a while back and I was afraid it might be that and day before yesterday I went to see Dr. Gulledge and he says it is true. He called up Mrs. Massingale and told her. I will have to move out of the girls house and live with Nurse Mabry and Mr. Mabry in the infirmery until the baby comes. I wont be able to go to school next year. I will have to have the baby but I will have to give it up to be sent to a orphanage soon as its born. They will not tell me where it will be sent to, but that I will never be able to see it again. I have not told *any body* that you are its daddy and I wont, even tho they ask and ask. Miss Terrell even said is it Kite Cummings? I said no. They act like I have commited a crime. I know what we did was wrong and that it was me as much as you that wanted to do it and I am willing to take my punishment, but it makes me feel so sad to think about a little new born baby being put in a orphanage all by itself and never even getting a chance to know that me and you are its mama and daddy, and alive—and not dead or in jail or in a insane hospital. I know it is not right for me to ask you but the only thing I can think of that would make things different is if your

aunt and uncle would let me come up there to
live—and us get married. If you do not want to get
married I dont blame you. I know you have a nice
home and life up there and this would only spoil it.
I hate it that I have to ask you but I feel so terrible
and I dont know what else to do. If I dont hear back
from you I will understand. I miss you.

Love,
Jarlene

At first he could not even remember exactly what Jarlene
looked like, and that made him feel ashamed. He closed his
eyes, but what he saw was Lynette lying in a white hospital
bed and holding a little baby. The way he remembered what
Jarlene looked like was by thinking about Miss Hefner's class-
room, where Jarlene sat diagonally across from him, three
rows closer to the front, and turned around to look at him
every time he got called on, and smiled or laughed every time
he said something funny.

It did not seem real that Jarlene was going to have a baby; it
seemed like something in a movie or on a TV show. He read
the letter again, and it made him feel even sadder than the
first time, though he still could not believe what it said. It
made him sad to think how scared and lonely Jarlene must
feel. The only times he had ever known her to be sad and
quiet was when Loper got killed and when he was leaving.
But she must have gotten over him pretty quick, he reckoned;
she had written him only that one other letter before this one.
Maybe she would get over the baby easier than she thought,
too. But of course it wasn't really the same at all. She had
known that *he* was coming to a real home. She would know
that the baby was going to an orphanange. It might get
adopted—it probably would—but she would not have any
way of knowing that. It might be living in a good home with
nice parents, but since she would not know that—would not
know anything—it would be almost as if the baby was dead.
It could even *be* dead, and she would not know it.

He looked down at the letter again. There was one word in
it that seemed more unreal to him than any other, and it was

the same word that made him feel sadder and stranger than any other, that made him feel that he was not himself, not who he thought he was: *daddy.* "I have not told anybody that you are its daddy." He thought of the picture of his own mama and daddy. Lost for good now.

He got up off the bed and went into the bathroom and looked at himself in the mirror. He did not look like anybody's daddy. But he was. Even though the baby wasn't born yet, even though it was just getting started, he was still its daddy. And Jarlene was its mother. It was their baby. How could somebody else—anybody else—take it away from them? It was their baby.

At the supper table that night, halfway through the meal, Hampton said, "I hear you got a letter today." His eyes were twinkling.

"Yessir," Kite said. "From Jarlene. Down at Baptist."

Both of them looked surprised and disappointed. They had thought it was from Lynette too. He knew that they were glad that he and Lynette had taken a liking to each other—as long as they didn't know how much of a liking. Mr. Baker was a very successful businessman and they were a good Christian family (even though they were Methodists).

"How is everything down there?" Hampton said.

"Just fine."

"I thought we might have had another visit from Reverend Sills by now."

Kite just kept on eating.

"Have you heard anything from Lynette?" Ruth said.

"No ma'am. Just what we heard at church yesterday. That she was getting along all right."

"I have to go into town tomorrow morning," Hampton said. "I'll stop in at the store and ask about her."

"I sure would like to hear," Kite said. He began to wonder how he could ever tell Lynette about Jarlene, and he was very quiet for the rest of the meal. No second helpings.

While they were clearing the table, Ruth said, "You don't still miss being down at Baptist, do you, Kite?"

"No, ma'am. I don't miss it a bit. I never did realize how bad it *was* down there til I got up here."

"You just seem a little broody this evening. I thought maybe you were thinking about your friends down at Baptist. But you've made some good new friends up here, haven't you?"

"Yes ma'am."

After they had cleared the table, he fed Clown and sat down on the back steps, just as he did most nights, and watched the dog eat. But that night he thought about the other nights—the first night, when everything here was so new to him, and the others since then, all the ones that he had taken for granted. When Clown had finished scouring the dish with his tongue and had sniffed at the patch of grass all around the dish, he came to the steps and began to nuzzle Kite in the ribs. Kite put his arm around the dog, patted his side, and scratched the top of his head. Then, in response to Clown's urging, he got up and walked slowly across the back lawn and around the upper side of the barn, the dog at his heels.

How could everything have changed so much so quickly? Not even the garden or the mountains looked quite real to him. They just made him feel sadder. For a long time he watched Clown nosing in circles through the field of broomstraw, hoping to scare up a rabbit. When it began to get dark, he went back to the house.

That night, up in his room, he knelt beside the bed, as he did every night.

"I don't know what to do. Or what to say. I don't know how to tell Aunt Ruth and Uncle Hampton what's happened. But I know I have to tell them. I want to try to help Jarlene the best way I can. And I don't know any way to do that except for us to get married. And that's what I *want* to do, because I want to be the baby's daddy. I don't think it's right for us to have to give the baby away to an orphanage or to anybody else. I know that what we did was sinful—what I did with Jarlene and what I think about doing with Lynette, and even with Shirley Dundean. I know that even what I do by myself is wrong. And I know that I should not expect not to be punished for what I do that's wrong. But why should the baby who hasn't even been born yet be punished by being sent to an orphanage to grow up in when me and Jarlene could be a good mama and daddy to it if you would let us. And help us. I guess it is wrong and selfish for me to ask for help after I have sinned so bad. But I still don't understand why what we did was so wicked, not like killing or stealing. That's why I am asking for help—to understand. And help to be stronger to resist the temptations of the devil, if that is what it is. And I am asking for help and courage to know how to tell Aunt Ruth and Uncle Hampton about Jarlene. And help to be able to marry Jarlene and to have the baby and keep it.

"You have given me so much to be thankful for here with Ruth and Hampton. And I *am* thankful. I guess it is wrong—but since I don't understand yet, I am even thankful for Lynette and Shirley. And for a good friend like Andrew. For everything I have here. The good food, the mountains, my own room, the peaches, the river, the church, the chance to go to school in September, and maybe on to college after that. I guess I haven't been as thankful as I should have been all along or I wouldn't be having to ask for so much now. So much forgiveness and help. I thought that maybe since I had spent all my life up to now in an orphanage, that maybe now I could make up for all those years just by having a good time and getting enjoyment out of everything. I guess that's not the way it works.

"Please bless Jarlene. And the baby. And Ruth and Hampton. And Andrew and his family. And Lynette and her mama and daddy and Kip. And Shirley Dundean. And Jimmy. . . .

"Amen."

The peaches they were packing now would be shipped out of state, and for that reason each basket had to be stamped. That was Kite's job that week. It was much easier than loading but not as easy as culling. It demanded slightly more attention and effort—especially the first day—mainly because there were four different stamps: the name of the peach (most of Hampton's were Rosy Dawns), the grade, the orchard mark, and a three-digit shipping code. After each basket came out of the water tunnel and after a man named Karlett had snapped the lid of wooden slats into place, the basket glided on down the conveyor belt toward the loading ramp. Kite was stationed midway between the tunnel and the ramp, sitting (most of the time) on the end of one upturned crate and with the stamps and the ink pad laid out on the end of another one. He had tried to make his job more efficient by fastening pairs of stamps together with rubber bands, but because each stamp was a different size and shape, that had not worked very well: one side was invariably blurred or faint. So it was a matter of using the first two, one in each hand, then tossing those down and snatching up the other two before the basket got past him. Occasionally, when they began to come down the belt at a faster than average clip, he felt like Charlie Chaplin in a scene from a silent movie he had seen once on television.

But the main disadvantage was that he was working by himself again. Neither Karlett nor the loaders were close enough to talk to very easily above the racket the machinery made. And by Thursday, the day after the letter came, the routine had grown so familiar and he had become so dextrous at it that there was nothing, and nobody, to keep his mind off Jarlene.

When he had first waked up that morning, he felt as if he had had bad dreams all night, but he did not, for a second or two, remember the letter at all. Then it came back to him— and though the whole thing seemed even more unreal than it had the night before, it came back with such sharpness and force that he felt stunned, the way he had when he was crawling on his belly through the tunnel and the ice-cold water had suddenly pounded him senseless.

If only he *had* been dreaming. . . . But there was the letter, on top of the chest. Then he thought: maybe Jarlene was mistaken. She was so young. She didn't even have any hair down there yet. How could she be old enough to have a baby? He was not even sure how long it took after fucking before a girl would know—but he was sure that Jarlene had had long enough to know for sure; she was bound to be pretty far along. It couldn't be a mistake. He couldn't get off that easy. Then it occurred to him that something might happen, something might go wrong. But he felt ashamed that he had even let himself think such a thing. He didn't want anything to go wrong. That would be even worse punishment. Especially for Jarlene.

He heard Ruth and Hampton downstairs in the kitchen. He had to tell them. But how? What were they going to say to him? And think of him? And how could he tell Lynette? How could he stand for everything to be over with Lynette?

At work that morning the same questions kept going

through his mind, over and over again, until they seemed to be stamped on his brain as indelibly as the words and numbers that he had stamped on hundreds and hundreds of baskets. But no answers ever came. Just the questions.

At lunchtime, after they had finished eating, Susan moved a little distance away to talk with three girls who (once Pruitt and his pals were no longer around) had started eating lunch on the green and shady hillside. Kite and Andrew were left by themselves, and Kite reached into his back pocket and pulled out the letter from Jarlene and handed it to Andrew.

"What is it?" Andrew said.

"Just read it," Kite said. "I don't know how to tell you."

Andrew read the letter slowly and carefully, without ever looking up. Even after he got to the end, he just kept holding it and staring at it. When he finally raised his eyes and met Kite's, he looked so worried and bewildered that Kite wished he had not shown the letter to him at all, wished he had found some better way to tell him.

"Is it true?" Andrew said. "You're the daddy?"

"Yeah."

"How do you know? How can you be sure?"

"I just know," Kite said. "I know Jarlene wouldn't say so if I wasn't."

Andrew looked down at the grass, where his hand, as if it were not connected to him, had been breaking off bits of clover.

"I don't know what to say, Kite. I just didn't think anything like this could happen to you. I know it happens. I've known about other people it happened to. But I didn't think it could happen to you."

"Me neither," Kite said. "But it has. So now I got to decide what to do."

"I don't think you should tell Mr and Miz Lacey," Andrew said.

"How can I not? I have to.'

"It's gonna change everything. They won't understand at all. They won't even try. I know they won't. They won't ever feel the same about you again if they know about this."

Andrew's eyes looked so troubled and his voice sounded so

urgent that Kite felt scared. Not just worried or confused or ashamed—but scared.

"What d'ya think they'll do?" he said.

"I don't know," Andrew said. "I just know I wouldn't tell 'em if it was me. I'm afraid if you do, you'll wish you hadn't of."

"But I want for me and Jarlene to be able to keep the baby. How else can we do that unless she can come up here and we can get married?"

"You really think your aunt and uncle are gonna let you get married?"

"When they know how things are. They'll have to. Won't they?"

"I sure wouldn't count on it. Wouldn't they have to adopt Jarlene—and the baby too? That's never gonna happen, Kite. It's never gonna work out the way you want it to. I may not know Mr. and Miz Lacey any better than you do, but I know other folks just like 'em. Good as gold—up to a point. Then they snap shut tight as a tick."

"But what else can I do?" Kite said. "What do you think I should do?"

Andrew studied the grass and the back of his hand for a long time. Then he looked at Kite straight and hard, and kept looking at him, and his voice got louder and more ragged as he talked.

"I'll tell you what I think you should do, Kite. I think you just oughta try to forget you ever got that letter. I think you oughta make up your mind it's somebody else's baby. I think you oughta try as hard as you can to make yourself believe you never even knew anybody named Jarlene—much less fucked her and got her pregnant. Just *forget* about all of it."

Andrew seemed so different now, even more like a brother in a way, but like somebody's father too. And like a stranger.

"I can't," Kite said. "I can't do that. I *want* to be the baby's daddy."

That afternoon seemed long and hollow. And even more humid than usual. There were swarms of flies and gnats in-

side the shed, and one of the girls at the culler got stung by a
wasp. Kite felt dazed and weighted and wished, more than
anything, that he could go to sleep for a while and not have to
think and wonder. Around four o'clock the sultriness and
boredom were broken briefly by a thunderstorm. From where
he was working Kite had not seen the slate-blue clouds building up over the mountains and had not heard the thunder
above the din of the machinery. Then it got very dark outside
and a few minutes later the rain came down hard—big elon-
gated drops, falling straight down, like lead, bright against the
darkness. Kite stood up and looked toward the other side of
the shed, where the trucks were unloaded. The rain was so
dense that the wide doorway seemed to frame a dark discol-
ored mirror, streaming wet, reflecting the winks of lightning.
Still no sound of thunder. Then—even more suddenly—it
was dark inside and bright outside. The power had gone off.
The machines stuttered to a standstill, and as their roar faded
the drumfire of rain on the tin roof and on the ground took its
place—a much better sound, hard and cool and clean.

Everybody was happy to get an unexpected break and
began talking and laughing as if they were at a party. Kite felt
left out and wished Lynette was there. He could hear the
thunder now, as if the mountains themselves were tumbling
toward them. He moved up the belt and stamped the baskets
that had not yet reached him when the power failed. Then he
and Karlett carried them back to the loaders. Through the
other large doorway Kite saw the trucks coming up out of the
orchards, their lights on, loaded with peaches and pickers,
some of them sitting on the fenders, others standing on the
running boards, all of them soaked to the skin, their faces
black and shining. Whooping, cackling, they crowded under
the edge of the roof, but none of them came up the steps. The
smell of sweat was strong. Kite stood for a moment longer
watching the rain, then turned and went back through the
shed.

Andrew was talking to the driver of the truck that was
being loaded. They were standing at the end of the water
tunnel. Andrew had crawled up inside it to pull out the bas-

kets that were near the end, and the driver was now taking the best-looking peaches off the top of each basket, before Karlett put the lids on.

"Looks like you're getting the cream of the crop," Kite said.

"Yeah, man," the driver said. He had a light, breathy voice. "These are gonna get me in a cat house up the road. These and reputation."

He seemed all prepared to tell them in great detail how he had gained his reputation, but he had no sooner started than the lights came back on and the machines ground away again. Kite walked back to his place, but by the time he got there the lights were flickering, and a moment later they went off again. He sat down on the crate and waited, glad that he had had an excuse not to listen to the driver's tales. The rain was still drumming against the roof, and a cool wet breeze blew through the shed; it made him think of the trip to the mountains. Less than five minutes later, as if prompted by his memories or by the truck driver's plans and hopes, Shirley Dundean came strolling toward him. Her dress, made of a coarse and flimsy pinkish material, had gotten heavily splattered with rain and clung to her breasts and hips even more disturbingly than it ordinarily did.

"I was on my way back home from town when this storm came up," she said, "and it's coming down so hard I couldn't scarcely see the road in front of me, so I decided just to pull in here and maybe buy some peaches and see how you were gettin' along."

"I'm okay," Kite said.

"So they got you stampin' this week, huh?"

"That's right."

"Well, that's not too bad of a job." Then: "I guess your Uncle Hampton'll have you in charge of this place before too long."

"I don't know about that. It'll be a while."

"He sure does think the world of you. Him and your Aunt Ruth."

"I think a lot of them too."

She had picked up one of the stamps and was trying to read the reversed image.

"I hear Lynette's been in the hospital," she said.

"That's right. She's s'posed to come home tomorrow."

"I guess it'll be a while, though, before she's . . . you know, out and around."

"I guess so."

"That's why I was wonderin' how you been gettin' along." She had continued to puzzle over the face of the stamp, and before he could answer she said, "What does this thing say anyway?" and playfully pressed it (upside down) against his white T-shirt, just above his heart, studied the result intently for a moment, then flipped her wrist and stamped the other side of his chest. "Ah! Rosy Dawns."

"Rosy Dawns," he said, glancing down at the faint smears of red.

"So how?" she said.

"What? Oh. I told you: I'm getting along just fine."

"You sure?" she said, and lifted the hem of his shirt and pressed the stamp against his bare stomach. Smiling sweetly.

"I'm sure," he said, not looking down.

"Well then"—and she tossed the stamp back down on the top of the crate—"in that case I don't guess you'd be interested in coming over to my house for supper tonight. Since my daddy's go'n' be gone off."

"I guess I better not," he said. "Thanks anyway, but Aunt Ruth'll be expecting me at home."

"Well, she could do without you one night, couldn't she?"

"I guess I'm just not in the mood, Shirley."

"For what? For supper?"

"You know. For anything."

"I declare, Kite, sometimes I think you just don't like me very much. I don't know what's wrong with you."

"It's just that something's happened that I'm worried about. I don't think I'm gonna be in the mood any time real soon."

"Well, as a matter of fact, I'm not all that much in the mood myself," she said, getting huffy now. "I just heard about Lynette, and so I thought you might be lonesome. I felt sorry for you."

"Yeah. Thanks."

"And unless your uncle pays you a lot more than I think he does, you prob'ly couldn't afford anything but supper anyway."

"Prob'ly not."

"Well, I'll see you in church sometime," she said.

"Okay."

On her way toward the front of the shed, she stopped to talk with the truck driver. Kite sat back down on the crate, and a few minutes later the power came back on and he went back to work.

That night he wrote to Jarlene.

Dear Jarlene,

I feel so bad that you have had to go through such a bad time all by yourself, and I think the sooner we can be together the better it will be for both of us. When I first got your letter I felt like I had been hit by a truck, but now that I have had time to think about everything I think the main thing is for us to get married so that we can keep the baby, which is ours. I have not told my aunt and uncle yet because I was trying to think if there was some other way, but I don't think there is, and I am going to tell them on Sunday after church. I will write to you Sunday night and tell you what they say. They do not have a lot of money to spare and it may not suit them for us to live with them, if it doesn't we will have to find some other way to be together, because that is the important thing. So don't worry. I want to be the baby's daddy. And I am praying to God so that He will understand and help us, and I hope that you are too.

Love,
Kite

Before he got the letter from Jarlene, it had seemed to Kite that he spent a good part of every day thinking back about the trip to the mountains. And that had been especially true on the two Sundays. Even while he was in church. The way Rev. Fairforest's voice swooped from soft to loud and loud to soft and the way he swayed from side to side and back and forth made Kite feel that he was on the back of the truck again, winding around those corkscrew curves. And then he thought of the lake. And then Lynette.

On the Sunday after he got the letter he made a special effort to listen carefully to the sermon, and not only to the sermon but to the prayers and to the words of the hymns as well.

The title of the sermon that Sunday was, "Do Good People Go to Heaven?"

After the congregation had sung the second hymn, "Bought with His Blood," they sat back down, and Rev. Fairforest sat back down too, the way he always did, with his right elbow on the broad arm of the high-backed golden-brown oak chair that Kite thought of as a throne, and with his right hand cupped above his closed eyes, his head slightly bowed, his left hand holding the Bible. After more than a minute of silence, the silence growing more and more intense, he stood up very slowly and walked slowly to the pulpit, laying the Bible down on top of it and gripping both sides of it with his small hands, as if he were going to try to lift it off the floor. He gazed out lovingly over the congregation, his big brown eyes slowly sweeping the sanctuary from side to side, from front to back, from back to front, as if he was counting heads or checking to see if there was anybody there he didn't know. Then, still looking right at them—at *all* of them somehow, though speaking as if he was talking to just one other person, only slightly louder—he said, "Do good people go to heaven?"

Again, his eyes swept across their faces, and he repeated the question in exactly the same matter-of-fact tone: "Do good people go to heaven?" He leaned his chest against the edge of the pulpit and laid his forearms, one behind the other, across the top of it. It seemed to Kite that he was waiting for an answer. The silence got very tense again, only to be broken by the Reverend an instant (Kite felt) before one of his flock (perhaps he himself) would have broken it.

"Now you say to yourself, 'Now, Reverend, what kind of a question is that? Of course good people go to heaven. Of course they do.' "

He pursed his lips and cocked his head.

"And I say to you, 'Good people *would* go to heaven. Certainly. They *would. If. If* there *were* any good people.' " And then he looked down at the Bible and his voice got very quiet and sad. " 'If there *were.* Any good people.'

"But the Scriptures tell us very *plainly* that there is not even so much as *one* good person—*truly good* person—on the *face* of the *earth.*" He was gripping the sides of the pulpit again, and each time his voice rose he rose up on his toes until his arms were straight and he seemed to be holding on to the pulpit to keep from blasting himself right through the roof with the power of his own voice.

"*David!* A man after God's own *heart.* Declared, 'I was *sha*pen in in*i*quity; and in *sin* did my mother conceive me.'

"Paul tells us, 'Wherefore, as by *one* man sin entered into the world, and death *by* sin; and so death passed upon *all* men, for that *all* ... *have* ... *sinned.*

" 'There is *none* righteous, *no,* ... *not* ... *one.*'

"I repeat: 'not one.

" 'There is *none* that seeketh after God.

" '*All* we like sheep have gone astray. ...' "

Kite thought of himself and Lynette straying off into the woods in the mountains. Before he realized it, the risings and fallings, the swoopings and swayings, the twistings and turnings of Rev. Fairforest's voice and text had become a kind of musical accompaniment for his own thoughts. Was it true, he wondered, that there really were no good people? Were Ruth and Hampton—and Mrs. Massingale and Rev. Sills and the other people down at Baptist and even Rev. Fairforest himself—were all of them just as sinful as he was? Had Rev. Sills ever jacked off five times in one day, two of them outdoors? Had Mrs. Massingale ever taken all her clothes off and licked somebody's cock and let him fuck her? It did not seem at all likely—or even, in those terms, at all pleasant—but it was, in a more general way, a comforting thought. Especially comforting if he could believe that Ruth and Hampton—when he told them about Jarlene—would keep in mind that he was really no worse than anybody else. Unfortunately, he could not quite convince himself of that.

When one of Rev. Fairforest's outbursts brought his attention back to the sermon, he tried for a while to concentrate on what the preacher was saying, but he had lost the thread and could not get past the gestures and the sounds to the sense of it. He decided that the time would be better spent praying fervently to God to give him the courage to tell Ruth and Hampton what he had to tell them, and to tell them in a way that would make it possible for them to understand and forgive and help him.

He did not tune the sermon in again until near the end, when he heard Rev. Fairforest changing gears: from his preaching voice to his storytelling voice:

"Now I know that almost all of you are aware that me and the Reverend Mr. Turley take turn-about going over to Willisburg on Saturday afternoons and preaching downtown there outside the old depot on Poinsett Street. Many of you all have come by to join us in our worship over there from time to time, and we're always grateful and happy to see you. Well, it was my turn to witness over there yesterday, and I spent a right good part of the afternoon preaching on the burden of sin. In fact, I used that very phrase, 'the burden of sin,' any number of times in the course of my remarks. As is always the case, there were folks coming and going, going and coming, but I noticed for about the last half of an hour before I finished up, a young man—a teenage boy, I guess he was— standing very close to the front of the crowd and listening, so far as I could tell, very intently to what I had to say. He had on very tight light-colored britches and black boots and no shirt at all, and on each side of the upper part of his chest was a small tattoo of a bird in flight—like the silhouette of a swaller, maybe. And he was carrying in his hand a motorcycle helmet with what looked to be his shirt stuffed down inside of it.

"Well, after I had finished up and had prayed with those that were still there at the end, this young man came up to me and said, very earnestly, 'Preacher, I been listening to you talk about the burden of sin and about how it's a burden all of us share, but the fact is I don't feel no burden. How much does sin weigh anyhow? Ten pounds? Fifty pounds?'

"I said to him, 'Now, friend, before I answer your question, let me ask you one. If you laid a four-hundred-pound weight on the chest of a dead man, would he feel it?'

" 'Of course not,' the boy said. 'Because he's dead.'

" 'And in just the same way,' I told him, 'the person who doesn't feel his load of sin is dead spiritually.'

"Well, he looked at me very troubled, but I saw a light in his eyes that I hadn't seen there even a few seconds before, and he said, 'You know, Preacher, I never had thought of it that way before. I guess I been spending most of my life trying not to feel that pain, trying to drown it or deaden it one way or another. Is it too late for me to shoulder my share of that burden?'

"I said to him, 'My friend, that's the *glo*ry of Jesus Christ. It's never too late.'

"And I say to you today, *all*. *All* of us are sinners. But it's never too late.

"Pray with me now."

"Please help me," Kite prayed. "Please help me. Please help me."

On the way home from church—in fact, soon after they pulled out of the parking lot—Kite said, "I have to tell you something."

"What's that?" Hampton said, and Ruth turned her left ear toward the back seat.

"Something I have to talk to you about. Something bad."

Ruth turned in the seat so that she could see him, already looking badly worried.

"What is it?"

He stared out the window. Nothing looked quite real.

"You remember last week I got a letter from Jarlene Wilson down at Baptist? Me and her were good friends?"

"Yes?"

When he had first got in the car his stomach had felt very queasy, then it had turned cold, and now there was just a deep hole there.

"She wrote to tell me ... that she was going to have a baby." He suddenly knew that Andrew was right; it was a terrible mistake to tell them. "And I'm the daddy."

Neither of them said anything at all. Nothing. He could not see Hampton's face, he was sitting directly behind him, but Ruth looked at him as if he had suddenly become a complete stranger to her, as if she had never seen him before and was trying to figure out what he was doing in the back seat of the car.

Then she said his name, in a way that made it seem that it had suddenly occurred to her that he might be somebody she had known a long time before.

"Kite? Kite? . . . You don't mean . . .?"

"Wait. Wait, Ruth. Just wait." Hampton stuck his hand out toward her and patted the air. Then he turned his head so that Kite could see his profile. "I don't think we ought to talk about something like this in front of your Aunt Ruth." His voice was quiet but he sounded very angry. "We'll talk about it when we get home. Just me and you."

"But Hampton," Ruth said, "I want to know. . . . Please. I don't understand. . . ."

"We'll talk about it later," Hampton said. "There's no use to get upset. I don't think Kite realizes.   ."

It seemed to Kite that this was one of those times when his aunt and uncle made a kind of exchange, so that each of them suddenly began to act and talk the way the other one ordinarily did. It made everything more confusing. Ruth had opened her pocketbook and was holding a Kleenex against her mouth. Hampton was staring straight ahead, driving, perhaps, a little faster than usual. The silence in the car was like the silence in church after Rev. Fairforest had said, "Do good people go to heaven?"

When they got home, Hampton said, "You go on ahead and get lunch ready, sweetheart. Me and Kite'll be out on the front porch."

Kite followed him up the hall, but before they got to the front door Hampton turned and said, "I want to see that letter."

Kite went upstairs, praying over and over to himself, "Please, God. Please, God." The letter was in the chest of drawers, under his socks and underwear. He almost wished he still had the pictures of the naked women, so that he could take those back downstairs, so that they would know once and for all what he was really like. He wished Boydy was still around to tell what he had seen. Or maybe he should call up Dr. Estelle.

When he came onto the porch, Hampton was sitting in the swing. Kite handed him the letter and pulled up one of the heavy high-backed rockers. They seldom sat on the front porch except at night, after supper. In the mornings it was too hot and bright, even though there were trees and shrubs on all sides. And now the noonday sun against those layers of leaves gave a watery greenish cast to the white walls, and even to the air. It seemed the wrong place—much too pretty and pleasant—to talk about what they had to talk about. Kite felt they should have been in a small dark room somewhere, or up at the shed, or out in the barn.

As Hampton read the letter he squinted his eyes and drummed his fingers nervously against the seat of the swing, and his head twitched from side to side. He seemed much older than he really was, like an old man.

He laid the letter down beside him on the swing and peered out through the leaves.

"This just makes me sick to my stomach, Kite. I never would have imagined such a thing could come to be." He sounded more tired than angry now. "And why you had to go and mention it in front of your Aunt Ruth I can't understand to save my life. Don't you know what this is gonna do to her?"

"I'm sorry," Kite said. "For everything. I wish I hadn't had to tell either one of you. And I see now I should've talked to you first. But she was bound to find out about it sooner or later."

"Well, I don't know why. I don't know why she would ever have had to know about it."

"Because me and Jarlene want to get married. We want to be able to keep the baby."

"How in thunderation do you think you can do such a thing as that, Kite? How on earth do you think you could support a wife and baby? Why, you can't even support your own self yet; you're still just in high school, boy. Why, here I am been working like a nigger for twenty years and it's all I can do to support me and Ruth—and you now. How in the world do you think I could take on two more mouths to feed?"

"I could work after school. I could get some kind of a job and help out."

"How could you hold down a job and keep up with your schoolwork too? You wanta make good grades, boy, so you can go on to college and make something of yourself."

"I could work and make good grades too, I know I could. And when the baby got big enough Jarlene could go to work too. She'd want to, she's a hard worker, just like me. She'd be a big help to Aunt Ruth around the house too."

"Kite, don't you see what this little girl's up to? Don't you see she's just using you to get herself into a nice home? Why that could be anybody's baby. A girl like that."

"But it's not anybody's. It's mine. I know Jarlene wouldn't have said it was mine if it wasn't."

"You may want it to be yours, Kite, but that don't mean it is. You just think about it. If she had relations with you, why she must have done the same thing with other boys too."

"No, she didn't. She didn't like any other boys but me. I was the only real cute boy down there. Besides—"

"There's gonna be other girls, Kite. Nice girls. Lots of 'em. You got plenty of time. You don't wanta let this one little mistake ruin your whole life for you. And think about Aunt Ruth. Think about our lives. Think about how much you mean to us. How proud we are of you. How's it gonna look if you suddenly turn up with a wife and a baby, out of nowhere, a young boy like you? What're people gonna think? Why, your Aunt Ruth couldn't hold her head up. She couldn't look folks in the eye, she'd be so ashamed."

"I don't know how I can hold my head up if I let a little baby that I'm the daddy of be sent off to an orphanage soon as it's born. I don't know how I can think about that the rest of my life and feel right about it."

"But it'll be taken good care of, Kite. Prob'ly better than we could. You know what it's like to grow up in an orphanage. You know it's not as bad as people think. Why, if orphanages were such terrible places, how did you turn out to be such a good boy?"

"I don't think I am such a good boy. I don't think I'm nearly as good a boy as you all think I am. And if I don't do right by Jarlene and the baby, I won't think much of myself at all."

"I know it seems now like you may not. I know it seems hard right now. But you'll get over it. Time's a wonderful healer. You'll forget about it."

"I don't see how I can. Just like you and Aunt Ruth can't forget about Little Hampton."

A strange whimpering sound, like a hurt animal, made Hampton look toward the door, and Kite turned around in his chair and saw Ruth standing there behind the screen, tears rolling down her face.

"Lunch is ready," she said, but her voice sounded pitiful. Then she moved out of sight.

Kite stood up. He still had on his coat and tie. His shirt felt soaked with sweat and his face was gleaming wet.

"I don't feel like any lunch right now," he told his uncle and turned toward the door.

"Please try to understand our feelings too," Hampton said. "You know that we just want to do what's best for you."

"I understand."

He went up to his room, took off his clothes, and washed his face. Then he lay down across the bed and wrote a short letter to Jarlene. He got up, put on blue jeans, a T-shirt, and his tennis shoes, and went downstairs and telephoned Andrew.

The Bakers' house was in a section of town that he had never been in before. Most of the houses were large and seemed, in a way, almost new, though it was clear from the size of the trees and the shrubs and from the settled look of things that they had been there quite a while. The lawns were deep and the grass, thick and green, had just been cut the day before. In some of the yards sprinklers were twirling. There were shiny new cars in the paved driveways.

Lynette's house was built of brick and the brick had been painted white. There were dark blue shutters at the windows and a white fence around the front yard.

Andrew parked his motorcycle at the curb. When its sputter died away, the shady street seemed strangely quiet and still and empty; nobody was in sight in either direction. Kite opened the gate and walked up the long brick walkway, lined with boxwoods, and rang the doorbell. Mr. Baker came to the door wearing bright green shorts that came down almost to his knees and a tan shirt.

"Yes?"

"Is Lynette home, Mr. Baker?"

"No, she's not."

Kite waited, awkwardly, for him to say something else, but he didn't.

"Will she be back later?"

"Lynette and her mother have gone to Greensboro to visit relatives for a couple of weeks."

"Is she getting along all right?"

"She's recovering nicely, thank you. Yes." He seemed to be about to close the door, but then he said, "Are you the Laceys' boy?"

"Yessir."

"I thought so." Kite felt that Mr. Baker was staring at him as if he was trying to memorize what he looked like. "As long as you're here, I may as well tell you that Lynette's mother and I would prefer that you not see Lynette again. Do you understand?"

"Yessir." He did not know what else to say, and turned away quickly before Mr. Baker could see the tears that came to his eyes and that made everything a green blur as he headed back down the walkway.

When they got to the Clock, it was almost empty. Andrew sat down at the counter and Kite, after he had gotten a handful of change from the cashier, went to the telephone booth at the back. He laid the money out on the shelf under the phone, found out the number and the charge from the operator, and placed the call. He had tried to plan what he was going to say, but now it seemed to have gone out of his head. He kept imagining Mr. Baker picking up the phone at the other end. When Rev. Sills's slow and sleepy voice came over the wire, it not only blocked out that picture but sounded more reassuring and comforting than Kite would ever have imagined it could.

"Reverend Sills, this is Kite Cummings. You remember me, don't you?"

"Well, of course I do. My memory's not that far gone, I hope."

"No, sir. Well, I'm calling long distance from Lenfield because there's something I have to ask you about. It's important."

"Yes, Kite."

"You know about Jarlene Wilson, don't you, sir?"

"I don't know if I do or not. What is it I'm supposed to know, Kite?"

"I mean about why she had to move out of the girls' house. You know."

"I know she's living with the Mabrys in the infirmary now. But how is it you know about that, Kite?"

"I know about it because Jarlene wrote me a letter. Because I'm the baby's daddy." He paused, expecting some sort of response, but there was only silence. "And so what I'm calling to ask you is if there's any way it would be possible for me to come back down to Baptist to live and for me and Jarlene to get married and keep the baby?"

Again there was silence.

"Reverend Sills?"

The voice that broke the silence was like somebody else's voice, a stranger's voice.

"How can you even ask me such a thing as that, Kite? You and Jarlene are children! Both of you! You're children! You talk like this is just playing house. How can you even think we could do such a thing as you're asking?"

He wanted to hang up. He wanted not to hear what he was hearing. It was another mistake; he shouldn't have called. His own voice sounded strange to him now: quavery, like a child's.

"We know we've done wrong. Me and Jarlene both know it. And we know we have to pay for what we've done wrong. But we just don't think the baby ought to be punished."

"The baby won't be punished. The baby will be brought up in a fine wholesome Christian environment."

"But why couldn't it be brought up down there at Baptist, so that we could at least see it and be with it?"

"Listen to me now. Think what you're asking, son. The very fact that you're in the predicament you're in, you and Jarlene, means you've proved yourselves unworthy of being with that baby, of raising that baby. Don't you see that if we let you come back down here under these conditions—if we let Jarlene keep that baby—we'd only be con*don*ing what you've done? We can't do that. We can't do it."

"But it's our baby. It's ours."

"It's God's baby first, son, and as His servants it's our obligation to protect that soul from the very wickedness that brought it into this world in the first place. Now you have to try to understand that, you and Jarlene. You have to learn to accept the judgment of those of us who have lived longer and seen the ways of the world. You ought to give thanks and glory to God that you're as well off as you are, Kite, up there with Mr. and Mrs. Lacey. Jarlene's the one I feel sorry for. Do you think for a minute your aunt and uncle would ever have taken you into their nice home if they had known this is the kind of boy you are? Now, please don't burden them with this sadness, Kite."

"No, sir." He felt the tears like a big piece of ice stuck in his throat.

"Let me ask you just one special favor, Kite. Let me just ask you, wherever you are, to just close your eyes and pray with me. That's all I ask. Just join with me and ask God—"

Kite put the phone back in its cradle.

He sat there in the phone booth for several minutes and tried hard not to think of anything at all, tried to make his mind as blank and smooth as the caramel-colored wall he was looking at. Then he went into the restroom and splashed cold water against his face. He looked at himself in the mirror and thought about the time he had cut himself on the catsup bottle.

When he came out of the restroom he saw that Andrew had moved to a table and was talking to an older boy with curly black hair that looked like it hadn't been washed lately. He had a dark tan, darker than either of theirs, and his yellow T-shirt said, DAYTONA, FLA. and showed an orange rising, like the sun, out of the ocean. Or setting.

"This is J.K.," Andrew said. "Kite Cummings." They shook hands. "That's J.K.'s bike out there." Through the window Kite could see a bright blue Harley and whistled admiringly.

"You from Lenfield?"

"Jesus no," the boy said. "I didn't even know that was the name of this place. I'm from Arkansas a long time ago. But like I was tellin' your buddy here, I been on the move since I was fifteen. Since my daddy took an ax handle to me one day. Best thing he ever done for me. I been free as a bird ever since."

"Where you headed?" Kite said.

"I'm headed for some high country. Up the Appalachee Trail. Prob'ly far as Maine by August—but I'll be makin' lotsa stops. Pussy stops, in partic'lar." He winked at them and grinned in a way that made Kite think of Pruitt Gibson. "I just take it from one day to the next."

"That sounds like a sweet life," Kite said.

"I wouldn't have no other. You oughter try it sometime."

"I'd like to, sure 'nough. How you make it, though? Whatcha live off of?"

"Oh, now and again I have to take on a job for a week or so. I picked citrus down in Florida for a spell back in early spring. But most of the time I can find somethin' easier than a reg'lar job. Not all of 'em favored in the eyes of the law, seems like—but I ain't spent but five days in jail in the past year and a half, and two of them was partly by choice. Why, they's ways to pick up a easy buck I bet you boys never even heard tell of." He lowered his voice and bent his head closer to theirs. "Just yesterdy I made me thirty-five dollars just fer lettin' this country preacher boy put his little pecker up my ass. Didn't take but five minutes or so—and thirty-five smackeroos! 'Course my asshole's a little bit sore today, but I got a full belly, and I ain't gonna be lookin' for no job right away."

Kite and Andrew had exchanged a wide-eyed glance.

"Was this over in Willisburg?" Andrew said.

"Is that where the picture show's called the Peach Blossom?"

"That's right."

"You all know that sidewalk shouter over there?"

"We heard about him," Andrew said.

"Preacher boys is always a easy mark."

A few minutes later J.K. asked them how to get to Highway 26. They followed him outside and admired his bike at
closer range and then watched him crank it up and roar off
down the street.

"Do you think he was telling the truth?" Kite said.

"He wouldn't have no reason to make up a story like that
that I know of."

"Lord."

"What d'ya think your aunt and uncle and my mama and
daddy would say if they heard about that?"

"They wouldn't even believe it. They don't know *any*body
does such things as that, let alone Bobby Fairforest."

"What did the preacher down at the orphanage say?"

"What I should've known he would say all along. Said it
was God's baby. Said I couldn't come back. There's no way
that I can see now. I just wish I could get it off my mind for a
while."

"Where you wanta go to now?"

"I don't seem to have much place *to* go but back home. Not
for now anyway."

"You wanta come over to my house for a while?"

"I sure would."

Dear Kite,
  I am so sorry that I have not been able to get a
letter mailed to you before now. I hope you will
understand that I wanted to more than anything,
and must have written a hundred in my head, but
my daddy laid down the law and told me not to
write to any boy whatsoever. Besides, I wasn't even
able to get out of bed for a long time. When I first
got sick with my appindix it hurt so terrible that I
got scared I was going to die. My mama says that
when I was deeleerious with fever I said your name
over and over again and some other things that she
won't tell me. When I was feeling okay again my
daddy started asking me a lot of questions about
you, but my mama made him stop. I didn't tell him
anything except that you're a nice boy and I like
you a lot.
  Once I began to get better my mama made up

her mind to take me up here to this place where I don't know a living soul and all I see is old people all day long. I don't know how long it will be before we come back to Lenfield. Not long I hope because I will go crazy if it is. I will call you the minute I get back home, but we will have to get together on the sly, until my mama and daddy get over being so terrified for me to be around boys at all. But I know we can find some way to.

Kite, you are the cutest and sweetest boy I have ever known. I think about being with you up in the mountains all the time, and I wish more than anything that we had done what you wanted to. I feel so bad and childish because I acted the way I did, I don't know what got in to me. I want to be alone with you again as soon as I can. I hope that you are thinking about me too, and that you don't hold it against me, and will want to be with me again as soon as we can. I love you and I will see you soon. Love and kisses XXXXXXXXXXX and X for Andrew.

Love,
Lynette

P.S. I still am curious to know what that secret surprise is you told me about.

Dear Kite,

I knew all along that it would not be likely to suit your aunt and uncle for me to come up there to live, so I had not gotten my heart set on it and was not to bad disappointed when I got your letter. I know that you have tried as hard as you know how to find a way for things to work out, and I have been trying hard to. I hope you wont be upset or unfavored about what has happen now and what I have done. This is what it is. After I got your letter and I didn't know what else to do I wrote to my uncle Jacky down in Predlow, Ga. He called me up after he got my letter and talk to me on the phone and said that him and Louise (his wife) would like to adopt me and for me t̶o̶ and you to come live with them down there so that we could get married and have the baby. He said that he could get you a job in the big textile mill that he works at and that we could live in the mobile home with them until we are able to afford a place of our own and pay them back later on. I know that I have told you some bad things about him but I know that when me and you are married nothing like that kind of thing will go on. I think that the both of them are real sorry for our problem and want to help us out. You know how spinickity Mrs. Massingale and Rev. Sills and Mr. James are about who they let adopt the babies but they are so glad to get shut of me that I think they would let me go off with the Devil hisself. I guess I will go down to live with uncle Jacky and her even if you dont want to or cant. But I hope more than anything that you will want to. That you still want to be the babys daddy. And my husband. I just dont know how else we can manage it. I have rack my brain. And I want to be with you again so bad. Please write and say that its ok and that you want to go. I love you.

Write soon,
Jarlene

Two weeks later, late one afternoon, Jarlene called from Lenfield to tell him they were on their way to pick him up, and he gave her directions for how to get there. He had been upstairs when the phone rang and had heard Aunt Ruth go into the bedroom and close the door even before Hampton hollered up to him and told him the call was for him. Kite did not think he had heard his aunt say more than a dozen words since that Sunday when he had told them about Jarlene. They both seemed so sad and so cold to him that he had started spending as much time as he could at the Crowleys'—though he still slept at the Laceys' and still ate breakfast there. By himself more often than not. He had continued to work in the shed all along, right up until yesterday.

After he hung up the phone he went back upstairs and brought down his suitcase and the two cardboard boxes and set them out on the front porch. Then he sat down in the swing to wait. The heat had been broken just after noon by a hard shower, and the air was clean and fresh, the trees and grass still sparkling. Kite had heard Hampton moving around in the kitchen, and he wondered if he should go back and say good-by to him or if his uncle would come out onto the porch before he left. He did not expect to see Aunt Ruth again. He had said good-by to the Crowleys the night before and had not been able to keep from crying. Andrew and Chap were the ones he would miss most. Maybe even more than Lynette, in a way.

Hampton must have been listening for the car, because almost as soon as it turned into the driveway he came out onto the porch and offered to help Kite carry the boxes. Jarlene's Uncle Jacky was driving a big cinnamon-colored Buick, older even than Hampton's Chevrolet and very battered and dirty. As soon as it came to a stop, Jarlene jumped out of the back seat and came running across the side yard, barefooted and wearing orange shorts and a sleeveless white smock. Kite had never seen her with lipstick on before and that was one of the first things he noticed; it made her look different. He kissed her on the cheek and put his arms around her. Her stomach felt hard and swollen. Kite knew that the only way he could get through all this was to keep thinking about the baby, and about how good it would feel to be the baby's daddy.

Hampton walked on past them to the car and shook hands with a tall thin man whose cheeks and chin were gray with stubble. "I guess you all have had a hot drive," he said. Kite had thought perhaps he would ask them to come in, at least for a drink of water, but he didn't.

"Hot as blazes," Uncle Jacky said.

His wife had now come around from the other side of the car. She was almost as tall as he and considerably heavier, bigger-boned, and with bright blond hair. Both of them had on shorts, T-shirts, white socks, and sandals. They looked younger than Kite had expected.

"You all sure got pretty country up here," she said. "Down where we are it's flat as a pancake."

"Yes ma'am," Hampton said, "we think it's mighty pretty."

Kite introduced himself and shook hands with both of them. Then Uncle Jacky opened up the trunk and they put his suitcase and the boxes in. Jarlene was leaning against the front fender, petting Clown and talking baby talk to him. Her aunt came up beside Kite at the back of the car and whispered in his ear, "Jarlene's been feelin' a little bit carsick, so we're gonna let her sit up front for a while and me and you'll hop in the back."

"All right," Kite said.

He looked around for Hampton, who had moved away from the car, back onto the lawn, and was standing still and gazing at them as if they were already far away. Kite went over and held out his hand and Hampton took it, but neither of them said anything. When he turned back to the car, the other three had already gotten in.

The air inside the car was stale and steamy, and the plastic seat covers, even through his jeans and shirt, felt like they were melting. The floor in the back was littered with paper cups, candy wrappers, Coke bottles, and comic books. When Uncle Jacky started the car and began backing down the driveway, a black rubber spider hanging from the rearview mirror started to jiggle and dance. Kite figured that alone was enough to make Jarlene sick.

Once they were on the highway and picking up speed, Jarlene turned the radio on and rock and roll music poured through the car, blurred and broken by the wind rushing in at all four windows. It would have been hard to talk even if they had wanted to. Jarlene's aunt reached down into a big straw pocketbook and pulled out a pack of Camel cigarettes and offered one to Kite.

"No thanks."

She had to bend over and put her face down between her knees to get hers lit. A moment later she leaned over against Kite and said,

"Don't look so sad, honey, we're gonna have us a good ol' time." And she put her hand on his leg.

"Yes ma'am."

He glanced up at the rearview mirror again to see if he

looked as sad as he felt. His face was browner than he had realized, his eyes dark and shiny. Then he thought that he might be blocking Uncle Jacky's vision, and shifted a little toward the door. Just as he did, the mirror gave him a quick and final view of the mountains.